Stella Maris

by

Nan O'Dell

This edition published electronically by Fledgling Press Limited 2001

ISBN 0 9521579 1 8

Note: The characters in this book are purely imaginary. Any resemblance to real people, living or dead, is coincidental. Some places are real, others in the imagination of the author. Any errors are those of the author.

Printed by TJ International Limited

i

Stella Maris   by   Nan O'Dell

Foreword

About the author

Nan O'Dell was born in 1925 in Edinburgh, Scotland. In 1948 she moved to Chicago, where we met and married. In 1979 we moved to Edinburgh, her beloved home. Nan had successful careers as wife, mother, grandmother, Antique dealer, instructor and lecturer, but her first love was writing. She started as a child writing poems & plays. Through the years she wrote many short stories, and finally the novel, Stella Maris. She was teaching creative writing classes in Edinburgh when she became blind in 1995.

In 1983 Nan won the Martha Hamilton Award for a short story, "Auntie Con" in the Extra-Mural department of Edinburgh University. This gave her the impetus to start writing the novel, "Stella Maris", of which "Auntie Con" became the last chapter.

Nan submitted the partially written novel to the Scottish Association for Writers, and for it was awarded the Constable trophy in 1986. The book was never really finished until after her death in 1999, when I gathered all of the rough drafts and manuscripts, and edited them into the finished novel. This book is her memorial.

Glenn O'Dell

From the publisher

My Fledgling Press publishing is international, but based in the centre of Edinburgh City (which is, of course, the centre of the world). I was born here in the 1930s, and moved back here about 15 years ago.

So it was a pure delight to be offered a novel about growing up in Edinburgh before the Second World War. Edinburgh is a beautiful and ancient city, with a history of culture and civilization going back a long way. It also has a dark side, and what is called the "Old Town", the medieval densely packed buildings running the Royal Mile from Edinburgh Castle to Holyrood Palace, were in my aware youth, full of poor people living in tough and often primitive conditions. This gripping novel tells the tale of a child growing up there.

Leith, the port of Edinburgh and proudly independent of it in culture and spirit, has a different dark side. Sea-ports are gateways to the world, down the motorways of the sea. Their trade thrives with a population of hard-working, and often roughly mannered people. Religion is also a strong theme in the novel, and in Edinburgh, and indeed in Scotland generally. Religion in Edinburgh is mostly refined, liberal and sophisticated, but narrow, harsh and unforgiving varieties also exist.

Times have changed. The poor have been shipped out to housing schemes (described by my ex-student, Irvine Welsh), and the Old Town has been gentrified, and exploited as a magnetic tourist attraction. Lives like that of Stella Maris, the star of the sea, are vividly remembered by senior citizens. But I have never read a book like this, and am thrilled to be publishing it as my first printed book this millenium.

Zander Wedderburn

Contents

Stella Maris   by   Nan O'Dell

Chapter 1 : Edinburgh, 1935

It was a main thoroughfare where traffic thundered day and night, but that didn't stop the tenement children from playing on the pavement. In the long daylight hours of summertime they played all day and well into the evening. When dusk softened the light and peaver beds became indistinct, games would move to the front of the lighted shops and became "I spy with my little eye".

When someone passed holding a lighted cigarette there would be a rush towards him. (Him because in the world of the thirties it was rare to see a woman smoking in the streets.) "Any cigarette cards, mister?" The boys collected the cards with pictures of film stars, the girls chose flowers.

One by one the children would be called for bed or pieces and jam. In that neighbourhood it was never for a bath. Indeed, there were no baths in the tenements. On every stair landing there was a common toilet shared by the occupants of that floor, sometimes 20 people, sometimes more. Yet the tenement children survived, and even flourished, without the baths and balanced meals and dental care that seemed so necessary to children born in gentler circumstances.

They fought and blasphemed, and as fourteen was the age when they got jobs or got out, they looked on that age as full maturity and then they'd also fornicate as casually as did their parents, and with as little thought or concern for the children they might produce. The craving for sex was as natural as the craving for food, and often easier to satisfy.

In time they would take over the tenement flats vacated when parents died or ran away. Then it would be the turn of the boys to go to the

1

buroo[1] every week to collect their welfare money and of the girls to hang out the windows and call their children in at bedtime.

---

[1] Labour Exchange, now the Unemployment Benefit Office

Chapter 2 : Stella Maris Malcolm, 1925

She was called Stella Maris because her mother once read that it meant Star of the Sea, and since the child's father was a merchant seaman, the name seemed appropriate. That it was also one of the titles given the Virgin Mary, Rachel Malcolm didn't discover till her mother stormed into the room above the chip shop and demanded that the papish[2] name be changed.

"Don't you care that they burned Protestants at the stake?" Alice Morrison had to pause in her tirade while a tramcar clattered by outside. She didn't once glance into the wicker clothesbasket that held her two-day-old granddaughter.

Rachel, dull eyed with depression, roused herself to say, "Why should I care? Protestants burned Catholics too."

Alice pointed a shaking finger at her daughter. "The Lord will spew you out of his mouth."

That snapped Rachel out of her lethargy. "Like you spewed me out of yours?" She said it bitterly for her mother had refused to see or speak to her after she learned that Rachel was pregnant. That was months ago, and when Dennis Malcolm's ship next put into Leith it wasn't a minute too soon. Rachel was, by then, nearly five months gone and only a few days

---

[2] Roman Catholic

before had been dismissed in disgrace from the house where she worked as a live-in maid.

Her mistress delivered a lecture with her final pay. "You've been a silly girl and now you must pay the penalty of your wrongdoing."

Rachel, in retaliation, took the corset that had bound her so cruelly and ineffectually, and stuffed it into the innards of the grand piano. Then, head held higher than her hopes, she marched out to find lodging and a place to wait for her baby and its father.

The joining of Rachel Morrison and Dennis Malcolm in Holy Matrimony was witnessed only by Constance, her older sister, and Stanley, his best friend. No photograph recorded the event, so Rachel, in a nearly-new dress handed down from her former employer, didn't know she looked pretty that day. Dennis didn't tell her and Con was too embarrassed by Rachel's tell-tale bulge to see beyond it. Certainly, when Rachel started flirting with Stanley during the wedding repast, Stanley flirted right back, but then he was half drunk. Dennis, who had drunk twice as much as Stanley, remained sober and withdrawn. Con, in a bulky maroon suit that added years and inches to her, looked on uncomfortably.

"Cheer up sobersides," Rachel urged her, "it's a wedding, not a wake." She glanced across at her reluctant bridegroom and started to cry. "You could try to look happy."

Con placed an arm about her sister's shoulders. "Don't get upset, or drink any more either. You have to think of the baby."

Rachel turned on her. "Damn the baby. I wish I could get rid of it."

4

That broke up the party and the only comment Stella was ever to hear about her parents' nuptials was, "He struck me on our wedding night."

But now Rachel was outraged that after so long a silence, her mother should break it with demands. She determined to leave the baby's name as it was, though in fact she feared her mother.

Rachel wished Stella could be ignored but she was always there, a constant reminder of her parents' furtive coupling and therefore responsible for the miserable existence they lived thereafter.

Though Alice Morrison was secretly grateful to Dennis for taking a difficult daughter off her hands, it took her a long time to recover from the disgrace of her daughter's forced marriage. She didn't show face in the Kirk[3] for several weeks and when the minister called to enquire after her, she had Con tell him that she was away through to Glasgow for a holiday. When finally she brought herself to look in the clothesbasket, she came to love Stella as much as she could love anyone. It was her unyielding nature that made the showing of it difficult.

Stella's grandfather Joseph Morrison, away in Salt Lake City, Utah, didn't learn of the marriage and birth till much later but when he returned to Edinburgh, nine years later, he and Stella had one glorious summer together.

Stella's other grandmother, Agnes Malcolm, never forgave Rachel and was convinced to her dying day that Dennis would have amounted to something if Rachel hadn't trapped him into marriage. Though this Granny came into Stella's life but briefly, the love that sprang up between them made a whole summer sing... except for the times when she saw Rachel in the child. And those were the times when the conflict within Agnes Malcolm all but choked her.

So Dennis, with the unconditional love of his mother and the grudging gratitude of his mother-in-law, got off more lightly than Rachel, and both fared better than Stella who had earned the hatred of both her parents even before she was born.

---

[3] Church

Chapter 3 : Flittings [4]

The Malcolms moved many times in their early years. The single room above a chip shop became a slightly bigger single room above a pub. The pub sign, a parrot perched on a sailor's shoulder, hung just below their window. Its rhythmic creaking on windy nights was Stella's lullaby but when a gust would send it clattering against the wall, she'd waken with a start, and cry. Rachel said she'd go mad between the noise of her and the noise of the sign and took to going out on windy nights, giving Stella a few drops of whisky in her milk beforehand.

It was on a windy night that Dennis returned unexpectedly from the sea and found the baby lying in her own mess. He shouted that he'd kill the bitch when she came in, but she didn't come in and he had to go out and look for her. She hadn't gone far. Just to the establishment below. He dragged her up the stair and when he demanded that she clean up the bloody kid she screamed that Stella was as much his as hers so he'd better get on with cleaning her up himself. Dennis hurled Rachel to the wall and every dish in the house after her. He was threatening to do the same to Stella when the landlady rushed in and ordered them out. "They could stay till morning", she said "for the sake of the bairn[5]."

They had nowhere to go and Rachel was too proud to ask her mother for help, but news travelled fast in that neighbourhood, and on hearing of their plight an old bachelor in the next stair took them in.

---

[4] Moving House

[5] Child

Mr. Meldrum was rather simple minded so the arrangement was ideal. Rachel found him indispensable after Dennis went back to his ship. He was good for the odd shilling when funds were low and, doting on Stella, was always willing to watch her while Rachel went to the dancing. In exchange for his not telling Dennis of this, Rachel promised Mr. Meldrum that she would never take the child away from him.

He fed Stella, played with her, brought her frilly dresses and, "It's a wonder the old sweetie-wife doesn't knit for her as well," Rachel remarked to her current dance-hall friend.

Then one night she came home to find him parading in front of Stella, and the wardrobe mirror, in her bra and knickers. Even more shocking than the sight of Mr. Meldrum was Stella's reaction. She was laughing and clapping her hands.

"You filthy old swine," shrieked Rachel.

Mr. Meldrum stopped parading and looked stunned.

"...Filthy dirty old swine.

His face crumpled. "I was only trying to please her," he whimpered.

Stella, used to her mother's screaming, joined in the din only when she saw Mr. Meldrum crying. Had they been making less noise they might have heard the woman upstairs pounding on her floor. When Rachel yelled that she had a good mind to get the police to him, Mr. Meldrum panicked and tried to choke her into silence.

But someone in the stair had already run to the police box on the corner for help and Mr. Meldrum was taken away, still crying, in Rachel's bra and knickers. In the interests of mercy a blanket was flung over his head before he stepped out into the street.

The factor of the building, summoned the next morning, checked over the missive to the flat and found that Mr. Meldrum had been breaking the rental agreement by taking in lodgers. He was delighted to be able to put Rachel out. Her reputation had spread and no one there had any sympathy for her, and having Stella didn't help her this time. Mr. Meldrum had been well liked and considered harmless, and they all felt that Rachel must have egged the old boy on. Dennis, always ready to believe the worst of his wife, agreed with them when he heard the story.

It was back to a room even smaller than the first one had been. Dennis quit the sea to keep a suspicious eye on Rachel so the Malcolms were seldom more than six feet away from each other now. When he could find them, Dennis did labouring jobs around the docks; enough to keep them alive, enough to get him out of the house, for he missed his freedom as much as Rachel missed hers.

The thing that finally sent him back to the ship's pool to wait for a berth filled him with shame for it seemed a reflection on his manhood. It was the fear of Rachel that had grown in him. Fear of the violence in her that roused an answering violence in himself. He dreaded the sudden changes of mood, the pale blue eyes darkening, the soft voice shrieking obscenities. He didn't dare let her see his hate and resentment. It was safer to show it to Stella. Had he been wholly convinced that the child was his, he might have behaved differently, taken her to Dumfriesshire for his mother to raise, but he felt sure that he hadn't been the first in Rachel's life. Nor, he suspected, the last. Look at how the trollop had flirted with Stanley on the very day of their wedding and she sticking out a mile! No, this one, this Stella - who was to blame for his marrying Rachel - deserved the mother she got and he felt no pity for her. Nor had he any compunction about leaving her with a woman he feared. Every month, the shipping line would send Rachel a check to keep the two of them and it was more than they deserved.

Then one day he saw resemblance to his mother in Stella. The hair was Agnes Malcolm's, and the shape of the nose. But where his mother's expression was usually serene, this grave child's was already watchful. Something stirred in him that sent him seeking better accommodation in which to leave her.

He found a spacious, comfortably furnished room overlooking the Eastern Cemetery where she could look out and see grass and flowers. Dennis reasoned that it was almost as good as living in the country.

All that summer, and into autumn, Stella watched bigger girls sitting on the flat tombstones stringing hips and haws into necklaces and, her third birthday just past, she longed to sit with them and string necklaces too. But before she was old enough to qualify they were off again.

Dennis had left Rachel pregnant and when it started to show, the landlady told her they'd have to find somewhere else to live before the baby's birth.

Con, who visited her sister as often as home duties allowed, took this back to Granny Morrison who sent grudging word to Rachel that she and Stella could come to her on a temporary basis. This last was stressed and Rachel said she'd rather die in the snow. She nearly did, for winter had set in with a vengeance, and the birth was imminent, before she found a place to live.

Stella Maris   by   Nan O'Dell

It was going cheap because the previous tenant had been dead for two weeks before her body was found dangling from the pulley hook in the ceiling. Despite a thorough scrubbing of the rooms with disinfectant, something lingered. No one could say what it was and no one who viewed the flat tarried there, but Rachel, desperate, snapped it up. It was actually their best shelter yet. Two unfurnished rooms with a boxroom[6] that served as a bedroom for Stella, and a lavatory all to themselves. It was also the worst neighbourhood to date. Whores and drunks abounded in the street far below.

Once when Stella said that she wished they were back where she could play in the cemetery, Rachel laughed, "There's a lot more life here." It was true enough. All day long buses and trams crowded the road far below their top flat. It was so high up that Stella had to press her forehead hard against the window to see onto the pavement below where people jostled about, even into the night.

Rachel said it was too dangerous down there to let Stella out to play. "Too much traffic, too many drunk men, and those women... Here she always paused and tightened her lips as Alice did to show disapproval. When Stella asked who were the ladies who stood under the lights, Rachel snapped "They're not ladies!"

At this point Stella always said, "Please can't I go out to play Mam?" because she wanted to hear Rachel's stock answer, "No! I'd go crazy if anything happened to you."

Stella was happy then for that showed that her mother loved her.

---

[6] Room without windows

Even more alarming than the bad neighbourhood, from Granny Morrison's point of view, was the proximity of the Roman Catholic cathedral. She examined Stella carefully, every chance she got thereafter, to make sure she wasn't breaking out in papist tendencies. The child liked these visits to Granny's, for Sundays brought out the worst in her mother and she was glad to get away from her, and besides, her Auntie Con always fixed something special for her tea.

But now Rachel swallowed sufficient pride to accept some of the household furnishings Granny didn't need after she stopped taking in boarders. She also condescended to let Con help with the first quarter's rent. To show appreciation, she told her sister that should the baby be a girl she would be named Constance.

The baby was a boy, and to make peace with her mother, Rachel asked her to select a name. After racking her brains for one that wasn't likely to be a saint's, Granny came up with Archibald. Rachel was horrified but said nothing. Dennis fussed from afar and vowed he'd have the name changed to his own as soon as the ship touched home port.

Now Granny had always maintained that the name Dennis was Irish and therefore suspect, and Rachel, caught between her mother's bigotry and her husband's demands, was beside herself when she read Dennis's letter.

"If he doesn't get his way he'll make me suffer, and if he does get his way, she'll never forgive me. What in God's name am I going to do?" she cried in a wail that woke the baby.

Stella ran to the basket that was Archie's bed now. "Don't cry wee tottie, don't cry..."

Rachel pulled her away. "You've wakened him you bad little bitch..."

"I didn't waken him Mammy."

Rachel slapped her. "Don't you argue with me. God has a way of dealing with people who argue with their mothers. Just get to your room and don't let me see your face again today."

Stella was glad to go but she heard her mother's wails for a long time, even above the baby's crying, "What am I going to do, oh what am I going to do?"

The problem solved itself. Archie was dead and buried before Dennis came home.

Chapter 4 : Stella at Age Four

"...this wretched orb knows not the taste of rest; a maniac world, homeless and sobbing through the deep she goes."

(Alexander Smith)

My Mam says God punishes people who think bad things about their parents. "Honour thy father and thy mother." Mam knows a lot of things from the bible, nearly as many as Granny Morrison knows.

I don't like God very much. It seems to me that He makes life hard for some people. I wish He'd stop watching me and writing down all the bad things I do. Mam says on the Day of Judgement He'll read what He has written about me and if I have disobeyed her, or talked about her, or even thought bad things about her, I'll be cast into a pit where fires blaze and I'll burn forever.

Mam said a woman she knew was so bad that her soul went to Hell while she was still alive. The woman was in bed and anyone who went close to the bed nearly got burnt because of the heat. I hope I don't get that hot.

Mam says the mills of God grind slowly but they grind exceeding small. I'm more feart of God's punishment now than I used to be. When I was wee, I used to go outside and shake my fist at the sky. I wouldn't do that now but I still don't like Him. I think I might like Jesus. He seems to

14

like children. "There's a friend for little children above the bright blue sky." But does Jesus like people who think bad things about their parents?

I tried to tell Granny Morrison once about mother and me but she wouldn't listen. She pressed her lips tight and when she unpressed them all she said was, "She's your mother. You mustn't talk about your mother. Now hand me my bible and I'll find the bit that says you must like your mother."

I gave her the bible but I didn't listen. I thought about being old enough to go to the school. A big girl told me once that at the school, children get the strap when they're bad. I think the strap's better than the bible. I hope God doesn't punish me for thinking that. I hope His punishment won't hurt me too much.

Chapter 5 : Rachel's Story

They condemn, who don't know loneliness. They think I should be content to sit at the fireside every night with my knitting or a trashy novel for company. They think that's all any woman should need. Mother and Con ...those two old maids! Con says: "You're not alone, you have Stella." As if I need reminding...

And mother...she acts as though she didn't know how many beans make five. And it was five...five times at least. It's hard to imagine. Con, me, George, Jim, and Eddie. She hated every second of our begetting if her starched nightgowns, reeking of mothballs, are anything to go by. No wonder he ran away! Those gowns were worn as a repellent I'll swear. Not that I look on father as an insect. Old goat would be more like it. Sex! The bait, no doubt, that attracted him to Mormonism, and then to Salt Lake City where Brigham Young, its founder, is supposed to have said, "Bring 'em young." Young nubile women. Not old prunes like mother. I wish he hadn't gone - or if he had to, that he had taken me with him. I was young enough to qualify, God knows. Fourteen. The age of Juliet, maybe even the age of the Virgin Mary. I'd have run his house. I'd have been his hostess.

"This is my daughter"; he'd have told his friends proudly. "She shares my love of music and good books and the finer things of life." He'd never mention the others and in time he'd have forgotten them completely and serve them right. They never cared for him like I did; their hearts didn't break when it became apparent that he wasn't going to send for us.

It took a long time to come to that realisation myself. He and mother had quarrelled as far back as I could remember. We'd hear them shouting at night after we'd gone to bed. He'd call her a religious bigot and (after he joined the Mormons) she'd call him a religious fanatic. It was when they stopped shouting that I started worrying. They became too polite to each other. She never said a word when he came late from one of his meetings and he'd remain silent while she ripped some belief of his apart. She did it obliquely so he was probably never quite sure if she was digging at him.

"It's getting worse," I'd tell Con. "Something's going to happen."

"Just be glad they're not shouting about it then," Con would answer, but I'd still be uneasy.

"They've gone beyond the stage of shouting."

Con would just shrug and go on with what she was doing. The boys seemed oblivious but there was never much communication between them and us. I was frantic to know what was happening. I took to listening outside their door at night when Con was asleep and the light under the boys' door had gone out.

Then one night I heard him say what I had dreaded to hear. He was leaving us. Father was going away. To Salt Lake City. So far! I couldn't blame him but I minded very much. More than the others would. He couldn't mean as much to them as he did to me. It wasn't possible. My heart hammering in my ears nearly drowned out the rest of what he was saying. I stopped breathing to see if it would help.

"I'll send you money as soon as I get a job. Con's working and Rachel's coming on fourteen and can leave the school so you won't starve and I'll send for you as quickly as I can."

Relief! My father wasn't deserting us - he would send for us. I had to lean against the wall of the lobby till my trembling legs could carry me back to my bed, but I didn't sleep. I'd have to give up my schooling and I regretted that. The headmaster said I had promise and could go far. It would be worth it in the end though, for America was the land of opportunity, everyone knew that, and some even said the streets were paved with gold.

That was nonsense of course but it was true that there was no limit to the heights that one could attain there. That I could attain...

So when the time came for me to leave the school, I did it gladly. For someone with a limited education there wasn't much open, and it was either a shop or service. I chose the latter to prepare myself for the life that awaited me in that Promised Land across the sea.

It was a big house and the work was hard but I was young and strong and I was learning - that was the main thing. I studied the people I worked for. I soon found out that I was intellectually superior to the people I served and that all I needed to acquire were the social graces. Which fork to select from a bewildering array of silver, which wine to serve with which dish; how to walk and talk properly, and even how to flirt. I watched those ladies. There wasn't much that escaped me and I saw that in that rarefied society flirting was an art. There were none of the crudities one witnesses in closes or in the threepenny seats at the pictures. A long look, a sly smile, a slow crossing of one leg over the other. All charged with sexual significance. And later, none of your working class embarrassment at someone seeing the stained sheets. I changed them regularly. I looked at it as almost a sacred trust. The rest of the staff sniggered over them; the laundress, the skivvies. Slopping their tea, laughing with their mouths full of food. "Have you heard the one about...?" The way they reduced the act of love to the level of bathroom functions sickened me. Coarse, that's what they were, those menials with their fat feet and thick fingers. Sometimes they laughed at me too, for they knew I was different, better than they were. So I was lonely even then.

My job was live-in and I was glad of that for I couldn't have borne living at home with my father not there. As it was, when I went home on my half-days I'd try to pretend that he was just out at work, that even if I didn't see him this week, he'd be there the next. Sometimes I managed to convince myself for all of an hour, and then I'd have to ask, "Have you heard from father?"

Mother's reply was always the same, "Nothing."

The boys would get in from the school while I was there. Jim and Eddie would be out playing in the street within five minutes. George, never my favourite, would hang about, all ears, before he stuck his nose in a book and pretended to read. Sly, sleekit⁷ George. Con, in at six, always kicked off her shoes the minute she was through the door. Then it was tea before I caught the tram back to my place. I'd look at them all and think it was no wonder father left. Mother, her lips as tight as her corsets. The boys, comic papers propped up against sauce bottles, shovelling food into their mouths. Once I forgot myself and spoke my thoughts aloud. "My God, this is worse than the servants' hall." Five pairs of eyes looked up at me, startled. No one spoke. "Well goodness, there's no need to pig it, is there?"

Mother spoke first; "You'll mind your language in this house."

"What did I say?"

"You blasphemed - you took the Lord's name in vain.

"Well I'm sorry, but look at them, just look at them." I nodded towards the boys. "Reading at the table, and Con's shoes fly off the minute she comes in."

Con had the decency to flush. "If you were on your feet behind a counter all day, you'd get your shoes off in a hurry too."

"I work as well, you know." I said.

"Hark at her," said weaselly little George. "Emptying the gentry's' chamber pots has gone to her head."

It was all Jim and Eddie needed. Jim: "That's a fetching hat you're wearing Rachel."

Eddie: "Ta ever so. It's the latest in sha-pos."

When even sourfaced mother laughed the pair of them went mad. Eddie started mincing around in Con's discarded shoes and then he bowed to Jim. "May I hov this donce modom?"

"Oh dear me no," said Jim in a falsetto voice, "you're too fraightfully common."

"Shut up the lot of you," I shouted. "You're all jealous because I mix with a better class."

"Oh quite," said George, "they wouldn't sink so low as to use chamber pots."

---

[7] Cunning

I leapt at him and he ducked. "They don't even use bathrooms -they leave that to the commoners." I managed to hit him hard but still he went on, "In fact, I hear that they don't have to go at all."

"I'm never coming back here," I cried.

"Stop it the lot of you," mother shouted above the din.

"It's them," I said, "they started it."

"Never mind who started it. It's no way for Christians to behave."

I saw Con roll her eyes heavenward and a jet of tea shot out of Eddie's mouth as he tried not to laugh. Mother had turned to me and didn't see them. "And you, young lady, are too easy impressed by a lot of show and the Lord doesn't hold with it."

I muttered, "How do you know?" under my breath.

"What's that?" she said.

"Nothing."

"It's just as well." She paused. "While you're all here there's something I want to tell you."

Eddie's hand shot out to tickle Jim and mother gave them a dirty look. "ARE YOU TWO LISTENING TO ME?"

They stopped clowning and listened. I saw her breathe deeply.

"We're flitting[8]."

---

[8] Moving house

I jumped to my feet and clapped my hands. "Father's sent for us."

"Yippee, we're going to America." said Jim.

"I'm a sheriff, bang, bang." said Eddie.

Mother glared at them and they fell silent. "No, we're not going to America and your father hasn't sent for us." She clasped her hands and her cheeks grew quite pink. "I've got a job."

We all just looked. "Oh it's nothing as grand as Rachel's. It's caretaker to a doctor in George Square. We can live in the basement rent free."

"Is that all?" I said trying to cover up my disappointment.

She looked at me with angry eyes. "It's enough. It means the rent is paid and coal and light are found."

"But a basement! Fancy living in a basement."

"It's either that or living in the street but since you don't live with us anymore it doesn't matter what you think."

George gave me a malicious look. "Some go up in the world and some go down."

"Do we have to flit?" Con asked. "It will be an awful job."

"Yes we have to flit. It's either flit or sit here till we have to do a moonlight[9] and end up in a slum."

---

[9] Moonlight flitting: Moving by night to avoid paying debts

"We could do a moonlight anyway." Eddie was bouncing with excitement.

Jim started to stutter as he did now when he was very excited. "Ye-ye-ye-yes. And the milkman's cuddy[10] could pull the cart."

"No," said mother, "we'll be taking not much more than we can carry. The flat's furnished. We'll sell the stuff we have here. We can use the money."

"The piano," I cried, "you can't sell father's piano."

"Don't tell me what I can and can't do. The piano's going with the rest."

I started to cry. "Please," I pleaded, "don't sell it."

"Nobody plays it now and you don't even know how." Mother sounded defensive.

"I'll learn how."

"Don't be so daft. The piano's going."

"But he'll want it if he comes back...please..." Even in my distress I was aware of the picture I was presenting but I didn't care. Mother seemed to sag and she ran her tongue over her lips. I thought I had won. "Thank you, oh thank you, mither", I said, using the name I called her when I felt love for her. I didn't use it often.

"We're not taking it." She sounded very tired.

---

[10] Horse

23

"Please." The tears started again. They tasted salty.

"I-th-th-think w—w—w—we sh-sh-should take it." Jim said.

"See? He agrees."

Mother shook her head. "I don't want to hear another word about it."

"I'll pay - I've saved some money."

"No Rachel no."

"Why can't we take the money from the furniture and go to America then? Why can't we do that?"

"It would take an awful lot more than what this junk furniture would bring in to go to America," said George looking pleased about it.

"Who asked for your opinion?" I was so angry now that my tears had stopped. I looked at Con who had never stopped eating while all this went on. "Why don't you back me up," I said "you can play a little."

"Don't drag me into it - I don't have time to argue."

"Why? Why don't you have time?"

"Because I'm going out."

"That's the third time this week," said mother.

"Who with?" I demanded to know.

"John Semple." She pushed back her chair and got to her feet.

Eddie started making smacking noises. "I love you Constance dear from the tip of your pointed head to the soles of your flat feet and you must marry me and make me the unhappiest man on earth."

"You're not leaving me with the dishes," I said.

"I wasn't going to, but since you've mentioned it, you could take a turn."

"A turn for the worse," said George, winking at Eddie.

"Why should I? It's my afternoon off."

"Duty before pleasure," said mother. "You'll both do the dishes. And Rachel, you haven't given me your money yet."

My money. Was that all I meant to my mother? I came home one afternoon a week and was expected to do dishes as well as hand over my earnings. There were better ways to spend my time off. "I won't be down next week - in fact I don't know when I'll see you again; maybe not till you've moved. Let me have your new address so I'll know where to send my money," I muttered, "Since that's all you care about."

I had set a trap there. I wanted to see if mother would ask why I wouldn't be back; if she'd show regret at not seeing me so often. She did neither. Just a nod as she wrote the new address on a bit of scrap paper. Then, "Don't desert the sinking ship. You know we depend on your money."

That was it then. My few shillings was the sum total of my worth.

Chapter 6 : Trapped in Marriage

I took to spending my afternoons off at the pictures, treating myself to tea in a shop afterwards. When the family was away in August for the shooting the housekeeper and I were left in Edinburgh, she to see that the house was kept up and I to help her prepare the house for winter.

Without constant interruptions it was easy and we each had more free time than usual. One of us always had to be in the house to take messages and answer the telephone. Thus we always got warning if some member of the family was returning to Edinburgh for a dentist or hair appointment. We didn't mind that for it gave us time to flick a duster and get back into uniform in time for their arrival.

Sometimes Mrs. Adams would slip me half a crown and tell me to spend the day in town and "Don't hurry back." She wasn't always that lenient or generous so I knew fine that she was entertaining someone on the sly. She'd be too busy with her own affairs to see me slip out dressed in Lady Durham-Smith's Paris hats and couturier clothes.

I was taking an awful chance but I loved it. Loved sitting at her dressing table and pretending it was mine; that all the jars and atomisers and brushes were mine too. Loved sweeping into the expensive shops, asking questions, fingering the merchandise that the assistants spread before me. "You've nothing better?" I'd ask and when they assured "modom" that the quality was unequalled anywhere I'd murmur regretfully and pass on.

And I did look like "modom" in Lady Durham-Smith's hats and dresses.

Once I nearly got caught. It was the time I nearly knocked Mr. Jervis down in Jenners. I saw him from two aisles away and darted up an adjacent aisle, which I thought would lead us in different directions. But he had changed direction too and as I was keeping my head down, I went careening into him. He apologised as he steadied me. I looked up at him and seeing it was he, I mumbled that it was quite all right and would he let me past please? But he didn't move. "I know you from somewhere. Have we met somewhere?"

I shook my head. "Please let me past." He stepped aside and as I practically ran for the exit, I was aware that he was still watching me.

Con caught me at it once. I hadn't heard that she had changed jobs till I saw her at the lingerie counter. She had been staring at me while someone else served me. Her eyes were round as saucers. I moved away as soon as I could and I made sure I was waiting at the staff entrance when she came out. "Don't you breathe a word of this to anyone, especially not to mother."

"I hardly recognised you dressed like that. I was flabbergasted when I saw who it was." She looked like she might cry.

"You promise me you won't tell."

She seemed not to know what I was saying. "Where did you get them Rachel? Who bought you those clothes?"

It dawned on me what she thought and I shook her by the arm. "Listen dozey, it's not what you think. This hat and the rest belong to Lady Durham-Smith and I'd get the sack if anyone found out so you promise me that you'll keep your big mouth shut."

"Oh that's a relief. I thought you were being kept."

"Promise me. Promise me that you'll keep your mouth shut about this."

"I'll promise if you want me to but you're taking an awful chance. Suppose someone sees you who recognises the clothes. Suppose they think you're Lady Durham-Thingummy?"

"Suppose...suppose. Do you promise? You haven't said it."

"I promise."

"Look," I said, "I have to get back to Inverleith, so I don't have time to talk. But has mother had any word from father?"

Con shook her head.

"Can you get me his address?"

"I don't know how, if mother doesn't have it."

"She must have it. Ask her and let me know."

"Ask her yourself."

I shook her by the arm. "Try."

"Why don't you try? Someone at the Mormon meeting might know."

I let go of her arm. Why hadn't I thought of that? "I'm off then," I said.

The very next Sunday I dressed in her ladyship's clothes and went to the Mormon meeting. A few people turned to look as I slipped in the back seat and I saw one of them nudge another and whisper. Two girls in the front row were convulsed over something and I concluded it had to do with the three good-looking young men who were seated at a table facing the room. There was a large picture on the wall of a youngish man with a weak chin, wearing a high stock[11]. When the opening hymn was announced the room wasn't even a quarter full. I got to my feet with the rest, and the woman at the harmonium struck the first chord. Discord would describe it better.

A few thin voices piped up and then a large imposing woman, with a large imposing bird nested on her hat, let rip. The rest might as well have shut up for she carried the day. I shall never forget the hymn and the meaning it held for me. "Oh my Father, Thou that dwellest in a high and glorious place, When shall I renew thy presence and again behold thy face..." If it had not been for the sly glances in my direction I might have broken down.

The preaching followed the ritual ceremony of passing little bits of bread and shot glasses of water! I had hoped to hear more about Salt Lake City but there was a lot of talk about persecution in Missouri. The man with the weak chin was a martyr they said. All this talk about saints and martyrs! My father wasn't either one. Neither a pallid saint with a wan face nor a resigned martyr. He was fire and brimstone and charm. There was nothing wishy-washy about him. Nothing at all. Yet he had cast his lot with people like these who drank water from shot glasses and fancied themselves picked upon. And not a looker in the lot. Except perhaps for the young men at the table who spoke with American accents. I headed

---

[11] Collar

straight for them after the closing prayer. "How do sister, how do?" said one of them extending his hand for it to be shaken.

I asked them both, but they didn't have father's address.

I stayed away from mother's for weeks, but against my better judgement I did go back. I had to find out if there had been word from father. There hadn't, nor had mother changed her mind about selling his piano. It was a miserable visit and was, I believe, the first time I went into one of the slumps which have plagued me through the years since. It was no wonder - seeing my home disappear before my eyes. Feeling apart from my family. Con, busy at the shop, busy at home, the two younger boys. I felt so apart from them. Like they were busily swimming in a goldfish bowl and I watching from the outside. A barrier of glass between us. I could watch but I couldn't join. When I went home that evening, to the only home I had now, I still had the feeling that I was apart. Different. Unaccepted. I can only describe the feeling as trying to swim through treacle. It was with great effort that I moved or spoke and the housekeeper sent me to my bed early because she said I was a danger.

I was vaguely aware that the hour was early for going to my bed but I went without protest and to my surprise I must have fallen asleep immediately. I woke at four thirty with thoughts of father churning through my brain. "No". I said it aloud in a panic. It couldn't be happening again, I wouldn't let it. I'd fight whatever it was that took possession of me yesterday. I jumped out of bed and the cold linoleum under my feet made me wince but I realised with relief that I was feeling something this morning. I had escaped the nothingness of last night. In the other bed the parlour maid slept on, her face smeared with cold cream and her hair in metal curlers that must have cut into her head cruelly as she slept. No sensitivity. I envied her. When Mrs. Adams came down I had her tea ready and we chatted as we drank. "You gave me a turn last night. I thought I might have to get a doctor to you. "What happened? You were acting like you were in shock."

I saw my chance of an excuse and I seized it. "I was. Someone died." She was immediately all sympathy. I didn't tell her it was myself.

Mother, who had worked some time now as a caretaker for a doctor, suddenly announced that now the boys were grown up she'd risk her savings on a boarding house.

If she was so hard up, how did she get savings? Do you suppose she'd been sleeping with the Doctor?

The years were going on and I was nearly nineteen and still there was nothing said about joining father. In fact mother never mentioned him. If someone else did, she'd remain silent and no coaxing would get her to talk about him.

Then, at long last, Con got father's address for me. "I never see his letters. I think she burns them. I got the envelope out the rubbish bin."

I wrote to him and waited but there was no return letter. After many long weeks I wrote again and asked him when would we be coming out to him? Finally, he replied; "When your mother's ready." He went on to say he missed us all and me particularly. He didn't say he was coming back. I wrote back and suggested that I come on alone. I had some money saved and if he could help a little I'd be on my way. His answer to that one was that he was strapped for money.

Before I could add much to my savings, I was pregnant with Stella.

Dennis Malcolm was never my type either. I think the scullery maid picked him up at the pictures and when his ship was in Leith he took to calling around to see her. He'd sit at the scrubbed pine table and drink tea while she peeled vegetables at the sink. He talked to her but his eyes watched me. I hated it and dreaded someone else noticing and making my life even more uncomfortable than it already was.

Then one day Dennis came when the scullery maid was out. He looked handsome with his Cheese Cutter hat and golden buttons on his jacket.

"Oh, it's you – she's not here but you'd better come in anyway. You're soaked"

I dragged the clotheshorse to the fire and said he could hang his jacket on it.

Not my room – theirs – if I'd lose my virginity it would be on fine linen.

Afterwards, he worried, "We've marked the sheets."

I looked at him with contempt. "This is my room".

"You're kiddin'"

"No, I'm not. I'm really the Laird's second cousin."

He looked at me and laughed. "Come here you little liar" But he didn't remark on marking the sheets after that.

Stella Maris   by   Nan O'Dell

Dennis was away at sea when I discovered I was pregnant. When he returned we were married but he was soon away to sea again.

And that suited me. Do I want Dennis home at 6 o'clock every night? Would I want him with me in bed every night; at the table every meal? At least I can think my own thoughts without interruption, eat or not eat as I wish. So I am forced to go out for adult companionship - but that leaves a lot to be desired too. Because the companions I find are not what I would wish them to be. I'm different from them as well. Different. Always different. Con and I don't resemble each other in thought word, or deed. George, Jim, Eddie. All different. Mother...a religious fanatic. A boarding house keeper. And it was up to her to keep him happy and at home. No wonder he left. Who could stand a lifetime of living with that woman? He was different, too, an artist, and musical too. I wonder where he is - what he's doing? If I hadn't married, hadn't had Stella I'd have written again - "Can I come out to you?" I would have said. "I don't fit with any of these people but from what I remember of you we're alike." Certainly I was the one who loved you. Whose heart broke after you left. And you would have wanted me to come to run your house and be your hostess. "This is my daughter", you'd tell your friends, and I'd have made you proud of me. You used to be proud of me. I was the one you talked to, to whom you told your opinions of what was happening in the world. And yet, I was better than you were for I wouldn't have let myself be so steered into fanaticism over a religion. Yes, I think maybe you and mother are more alike than you know. Both fanatics. Both looking for a better life beyond this one. As if anyone can say with a certainty that there's anything beyond this. I would never have been as fanatic about anything. I don't think anything is worth it. Fanaticism shows a weak mind.

Stella Maris   by   Nan O'Dell

What does Stella feel when she looks at me? Fury, anger, dislike, resentment, death, murder? She has stolen the limelight not only at birth but also since then. Oh God, take her away. I don't want her. She'll always stand in my way; take attention from me – compete. People will notice her first. Oh God, She's ugly. I'll tell her that – whisper it in her ear – you're ugly you bastard – I hate you – if I could get away with it I'd kill you. But are you listening – are you – are you – you are ugly. Hated. Stupid. You appal me.

I wish I could get you out of my sight and my life forever. Oh, I'll never hurt you physically, never, never – you'd just be in the limelight again. No! Lend me your ear, your private ear – see, you're too bloody lazy, defiant to do what you're told – too sure of yourself – well, I'll whisper it – if you won't come to me, I'll come to you;

I hate you.

I'm going to do as little as possible for you.

I'm going to tell you that.

I'll never let you forget it.

Oh, how I disliked waiting on people. Seeing them in big houses – with gorgeous carpets and belongings – all the things I love and that I want for myself. I get to clean them, to lift and look and put them back. Why should they have them? I'm more worthy of them. But I'll see you never have them either. Why should you get the things I wanted? Look – already you are fussed over. I lie here all titivated and they look at you – all the folks about you. All the admiration and here I sit like a fool – a blue ribbon

34

in my hair, a smile on my face, and has anyone seen – cared – admired me? No! It's all you, you, you. But I'll show you, you get[12]. Don't think you'll do this to me and get away with it. Listen, you are so ugly, I hate you – I'd like to kill you but you're not worth swinging for. Oh, how I hate you. I'd like to cover your face with a pillow so they'd look at me. If you died from it, so much the better. I never realised – oh, it's not fair – this thing by my side is going to get all the fuss – I'll be living in her bloody shadow. Oh, I hate you. I like her better when no one's around to admire her.

"Don't break that spirit", he says.

Well, I will. No one can stop me. It would be her neck I'd break if I could get away with it.

However, Stella has a world that her mother can't enter – only those who make life pleasant – who are fun to be with can enter there. No one can stop her from dreaming. She can bob in and out of her own world at will – no one can catch her, restrain her. Her mind is free.

---

[12] Brat, bastard

35

Chapter 7 : Home Alone

The doctor said that Archie had died of a bronchial infection. Rachel told Stella he died of too much kissing from her. "I told you, time and time again, to keep away from him but you wouldn't, even when you were coughing. Well your disobedience cost your brother his life."

Rachel was to tell Stella many times through the years that she would persist in hanging over the basket, kissing wee Archie even when she had the whooping-cough. "You were only three yourself and could hardly be blamed but your Da took it hard. So did I, but a mother forgives more easily."

Apart from reproaches, she spoke little to Stella and any necessary remark was made with eyes averted as though she couldn't bear to look on one so wicked. Stella cried and begged her mother's forgiveness, but Rachel never let on she heard.

Rachel became a pathetic figure. She donned black, used no makeup, and wept copiously. The neighbours in the stair shook their heads. "The poor soul's gone into a decline - fancy not having your man with ye at such a time." They looked at Stella with long faces. "Aye, you'll need to be a big girl now and do everything your Mammy tells you." One woman even wagged her finger when she said it.

Stella felt they must know - that Mam must have told them - what she had done to her brother. She stopped going out to play. She watched the mirror anxiously for the mark to appear on her forehead. The mark that set murderers apart. Granny called it the mark of Cain. When, after several weeks, her skin remained unblemished Stella forgot the mark of Cain and, the dreaded word 'decline' rooted in her mind, started worrying about her mother. What if Mam died and left her alone? Where would she go? Who would take care of her? Who would want a bad girl? Her heart jumped into her throat and stuck there. She stopped eating because she couldn't swallow. She grew thin and had to lie down a lot. When Granny and Auntie Con stopped by one day to enquire after Rachel they got a fright at the change in Stella. Granny, notoriously parsimonious, showed the extent of her alarm by dispatching Con to the chemist for his biggest jar of Radio Malt.

"Nobody ever bought Radio Malt for me," Rachel sighed wistfully as she watched Stella being fed a spoonful.

"Come on then you big wean[13], here's yours," said Granny thrusting the spoon at her.

Rachel burst into tears.

When Granny and Auntie Con left, the malt was placed at the back of the top shelf in the cupboard and not taken out again.

Then one spring day when the sun was pouring through the windows and lighting the darkest corners of the room, Rachel started to sing. Like all the Morrisons she had a sweet true voice and now she filled the flat with it. Stella felt her heart leave her throat and go back where it belonged. Her mother wasn't going to die after all! Suddenly she was hungry. When she went to the kitchen and her mother smiled at her, Stella hugged her. "I love you Mammy."

Rachel kissed the top of her head. "And I love you baby."

---

[13] Baby

Something in her tone made the child look up. Rachel's gaze was fixed on the window. "I have to go out Stella," she said quietly.

"Can I come with you?"

She shook her head. "Mammies have to get away from their wee girls sometimes."

"Where are you going?"

Rachel shrugged, a dreamy look on her face. "I don't know...the end of the rainbow..." Her voice trailed off.

Stella's grip on her mother tightened. "That's too far. Please don't go.'

Rachel peeled her off. "Don't start. It's too nice a day."

"Well when are you going?"

"Not for a while yet. Tell you what..." She tapped Stella's nose lightly with her finger, "...you can watch me getting ready when the time comes."

Rachel said no more about it and as the day passed Stella started to hope her mother had changed her mind about going out, but when the light faded and darkness again filled the corners, she began her preparations.

Stella tried to swallow the lump that was suddenly back in her throat. "I'm feart by myself Mam."

"A big girl like you?" Rachel smiled disbelievingly at her through the mirror. "But you're never by yourself. God is always with you."

"I'd rather have you."

Rachel laughed. "I hope He didn't hear that."

"Why?"

"Because God doesn't like competition. Now stop asking questions and let me get on." She bent to examine herself more closely in the glass. She shook her head. "Sad...sad."

Stella watched in wonder as her mother - the familiar one - emerged from the mother who mourned. Off came the black dress and on went one shot through with pink and silver. It rustled when she walked and the flounces on the skirt swirled when she pirouetted. Carefully she applied pink to her cheeks and her lips, then she brushed mascara on her lashes. Next came a black dot, no bigger than the tip of a lead pencil, which she pressed on at the corner of her mouth. When, finally, she pinned a diamante star into her honey blond hair, Stella drew in her breath and let it out on a long sigh. Her mother was more beautiful than the angel on top of a Christmas tree!

Rachel observed the child's reaction with satisfaction.

"Is your mother pretty then?"

"Oh yes"

"Maybe someday you'll be pretty too." She twirled round, making her flounces swirl. "Now remember - the rules are the same as before. Don't open the door to anyone - pretend that you're just not home. Don't touch matches. Don't light the gas. You've had your tea and you'll find a macaroon in the press[14] and a comic under the cushion. There's not another thing you could possibly need."

"When will you come home?"

Rachel smiled at herself in the glass. "I don't know."

"Will you light the gas before you leave so I can read my comic?"

"There's still some light coming in and there's the light from the fire. If the gas is lit people will know you're here and a bad man might come and get you.

Stella flung herself at her mother. "Oh no Mam, please don't leave me in the dark."

The beads she was trying to fasten slipped through Rachel's fingers. "Now look what you've made me do...you make me so nervous when you start that. I'll put another lump of coal on the fire and that will last you till you go to bed.

Stella knew then that she'd be alone all night and she panicked, "No Mammy no. There's a ghost in this house."

"Who told you that rubbish?"

"Cissie Walker in the next stair. Oh don't leave me in the dark all night."

"The only ghosts here are the ones in your imagination," said Rachel with a quick glance at the pulley hook.

---

[14] Cupboard

Something in that look set Stella screaming. Rachel shook her. "You're not going to stop me going out. If you're feart you can go to your bed and pull the covers over your head. Now - let - me – go." Stella had grabbed her again and now Rachel tried to slap her off. "You're crushing my dress and look you little bitch, you've broken my beads.

I've a good mind to beat you for that." She got herself free and flung Stella to the floor. "Pick them up, every last one. Obedience! OBEDIENCE! it's all I ask from you and what I never get. If you had obeyed me your brother would still be alive."

"I'm sorry Mam, I'm sorry about Wee Tottie." Stella's breath caught in shuddering sobs, "and I'm sorry about your beads too. I'll stop being bad and do everything you tell me but please stay home, please."

"STAY HOME? If you say one more word about that I'll go and I'll never come back and you'll be left here alone forever and ever."

"No Mam, no."

"Yes! And I'll tell you something else... I had just about decided to leave the gas on a peep for you but I won't do it now and you - only - have - yourself - to - blame." She looked at the sodden scrap on the floor. "Oh why do you make life so difficult for me?"

"I don't know Mammy, I don't know."

"I don't suppose you do," said Rachel, quietly now. "You're a sorry looking sight lying there. You'd better get up and give me a kiss but be careful of my makeup."

Stella buried her face in her mother, breathing comfort from her warmth and the sweet smell of her scent.

41

"I'll try to be better Mammy."

"I know you'll try and I shouldn't get so angry with you but you remind me so much of your father. He never wants me to have any fun either. As if I don't know what he gets up to when he's away!" Rachel sighed. "You even look like him sometimes. Oh well, I don't suppose you can help that..." She picked up her coat. "Now chum me to the door and turn the key in the lock behind me. Then I know you'll be safe."

"The gas...please light it for me..."

But Rachel was already through the door and calling back over her shoulder, "Don't open the door to anyone, mind, and remember your promise to be a good girl."

What Rachel hadn't remembered was her promise to put another lump of coal on the fire.

Stella listened with her ear to the door as her mother's heels clicked down the stone stairs. The sound became fainter and stopped. From a great distance came a dull bang as the heavy door to the street swung shut. She was surrounded by silence. The sort that swallowed people up. She held her breath and dashed through the dark lobby to the kitchen where the window still showed cobalt blue against the gathering shadows in the room. She hauled a chair to it and stood on it, looking down at the reassuring oases of the street lights far below. The friendly ladies were already congregating under them. Stella could just make out the tops of their flowery hats and the flare of a match as one lit her cigarette.

She liked the friendly ladies but Mam always made her look the other way when they passed one. Stella was sorry about that for she liked the way they smiled and spoke to people and she wanted to be a friendly lady too some day. Sometimes she practised in her mother's high heels with a pencil for a cigarette.

Now she watched while they drifted off companionably with passers-by. At last only one lady was left and Stella banged the window so she would look up and know she wasn't alone, but the distance between was too great and when, finally, a man came up and spoke to her, they strolled away arm in arm.

Stella realised suddenly that she was cold but she was too frightened to move from the comfort of the window. Behind her loomed a black cavern where ghosts, and maybe monsters, lurked. Her heart was making the only sound in the room when the doorbell pealed. She stuffed her fist into her mouth to keep from screaming and kept it there till the ringing stopped.

When the banging started she panicked and shouted, "Go away, there's nobody in,"

A voice called back faintly and Stella shouted again, "Go away, go away."

The voice kept calling and Stella slowly left the safety of the window to tiptoe along the lobby to hear what it was saying.

Chapter 8 : Tibby

Now it so happened that Rachel wasn't the only one to feel the stirrings of spring that day. A cat, who had lived out of Granny's rubbish bin for months, finished weaning the last of her litter to survive the winter and was ready to sally forth in search of a willing tom on whom to confer her sexual favours. Granny being what she was, the living had been meagre but the cat was grateful and now she showed her appreciation by depositing her kitten at the back door.

Con saw it and was filling a saucer with milk when Granny walked into the kitchen, "What's that for?"

"Oh mother, wait till you see the bonnie wee cat on our doorstep."

"You're surely not going to feed it?"

Con nodded. "It looks hungry and when it saw me it meowed."

"You feed that cat once and it'll be here forever," declared Granny.

"I don't mind - I'd like a cat."

"Well I'd mind," said Granny who thought cats were in some way associated with the devil.

"Oh please mother...it's a lovely wee thing. Just go and look at it and you'll change your mind."

"Never," said Granny throwing open the door, and stamping her feet.

"Oh don't! It's that wee you'll frighten it."

"That's the idea. Scat - get off with you."

The cat shot away and was back within the hour. Granny threw a glass of water on it but this time the cat stood its ground, shivering and meowing piteously.

"Oh don't mother don't. Maybe someone will take it. Why don't I try Mary and Eddie?"

"You can try who you like as long as you get it off my doorstep, and if nobody wants it Eddie can drown it. "

But Eddie, Granny's youngest son, said he'd as soon drown one of his own weans[15] and God knew there were too many of those to take in another mouth to feed. "Mary's got them at the chapel for something or other. They'll be back any minute and if they see that cat they'll want it so get it out o' here."

A fish supper was steaming on the hob and the cat smelled it and started to howl. Con looked at Eddie imploringly.

"Oh all right, I can't give it a home but I can give it some o' my supper."

"Thanks Eddie." Con lifted the kitten from its nest of papers in the shoe box and together they watched it devour the fish,

"Poor wee bugger," said Eddie.

"You'd think she'd take it in wouldn't you?"

---

[15] Children

45

Eddie laughed, "Mother? She's too bloody mean."

"It's not just that. She' s superstitious about them like Rachel is."

What will ye do with it now?"

Con shook her head doubtfully, "Try Jim. He might take it."

"If Ivy'll let him."

"If she doesn't I don't know what I'll do. I can hardly go round the doors asking neighbours and George and Olive are too far away. She's too houseproud for pets anyway."

"Aye for weans[16] too. Her and that bloody bungalow. You'd think it was Holyrood Palace..." Eddie made a dive for the cat who was headed under the bed. "Here, get it out of here before it does its business,"

Con took it from him and tucked it under her chin. "Poor wee homeless cheety-cat."

Eddie looked at her slyly. "There's always Seafield..."

"Never!"

"Good luck then - you'll need it."

Con thought she had it when Jim answered the door of Elm Brae. Ivy was upstairs putting a poultice on Hamish's chest but Jim said they'd be pleased to take the kitten. "It will be company for the wee fella."

"He's not well again?"

---

[16] Children

Jim bit at his thumbnail. "Na ...nothing seems to help him."

"Well maybe this will."

"That's what I think," he agreed.

But Ivy would have none of it. "Have you taken leave of your senses man? A cat might be the death of Hamish with his chest the way it is. You just never think do you?"

I'm sorry sis," said Jim. "That seems to be the end of it."

"It certainly is," snapped Ivy.

Chapter 9 : Tibby Finds a Home

So it was that Con came pounding on Rachel's door, she desperate, the cat demented. She could hear ominous ripping noises as it clawed the box she was now struggling to hold. On the point of setting the kitten free, she heard a faint cry: "There's nobody in."

"Open up Stella," Con shouted. "Come and let me in." "Who is it?" a timid voice called through the door. "It's me, your Auntie Con."

No answer.

"Oh for goodness sake Stella, open the door."

"Is it you?"

"Of course it's me." She knelt down and peered through the letter slot, "Can you not see me?"

"No.

She rattled the flap angrily, "What's wrong with you Stella?"

Silence.

"Where's your mother?"

"I don't know...she says I've not to open the door to anyone."

"Not even to your own Auntie?"

Silence, then "She'll start tying me up again."

"What are you talking about?

"My Mam. "

"Now look Stella, you let me in and I'll make it all right with your Mam. You'll see."

"I'm feart."

"Trust me Stella."

"No."

"Well that's a pity for now you'll not get the present I brought for you."

A pause. "What is it?"

"I can't tell you."

"Can you put it through the slot?"

"It's too big. Ouch." She felt the kitten's claws on her wrist as they pierced the box. "Goodbye then. I'm away."

She waited while Stella fumbled with the lock. The door opened a timid crack and Con pushed through it in case Stella should change her mind about letting her in.

"What are you doing in the dark, lassie?"

"My Mam said I haven't to light the gas."

"Where are the matches kept?"

When the light flared on Stella blinked. "Where's my present?"

"I think you'll find it under the bed."

While Stella tried to coax the kitten out, "Oh come to me wee cheety", Con built up the fire and filled the kettle.

"Just leave it for a while, it's frightened and will come out in its own good time. Now come and get warm and then we'll give it milk on a saucer. They drank tea in front of the fire and Con quizzed Stella. "When do you expect your mother home?"

"I don't know...what's the cheety's name?"

"It doesn't have one yet. What would you like it to be?"

Stella thought for a while. "Elizabeth - like the princess."

"That's a big name for a wee cat. Tell you what...Tibby's a nickname for Elizabeth. Do you think that would do?"

Stella nodded. "Will my Mammy let me keep it?"

"She'd better."

"But she doesn't like cats."

"She'll like this one." "The bitch," thought Con, "the ungrateful bitch." A child like Stella, a cheque every month and a man who was never home to bother her. She sighed. It wasn't fair...it just wasn't fair. "What's this about your Mam tying you up?"

Stella clapped her hand over Con's mouth. "It was a long time ago when I was wee - when I was bad and my Mam said she was sorry she had to do it. Oh please...please don't tell her I told you." The child was frantic and Con gently removed her hand. "Don't you worry, I'll not tell her. Now finish your tea and we'll see about the cat. It's probably under the bed for the night but we'll leave a saucer of milk in front of the fire just in case.

And shred up some newspapers to put in this box and it might do meantime for it to do its business in." Con glanced at the clock and bit her lip." I don't want to leave you here alone but your Granny will be worried about where I've got to."

"Tibby's here too."

"Aye, so she is but I wonder how it would be if I just let on to Granny that we got to talking and I missed the last tram." She smiled. "And that's probably true."

"Are you going to sleep with me?"

"Your bed's a bit narrow for both of us but we can sleep here in the kitchen in the big bed and if your Mam comes in she'll just have to go into yours."

Lying in the warm curve of her Auntie's body, Stella watched the light in the room flicker with the flames of the fire. Home wasn't frightening any more. It was nice. Stella sighed and Auntie Con asked her how she was getting on at the Sunday school. "Dear me, before the year's out I'll be asking you how you're getting on at the school. Such a big girl. Such a good girl."

They lay quietly for a while and Stella heard a little clicking sound from the hearth. "It's the wee cat," she whispered, "it's getting a drink."

Con propped herself up on one elbow. "So it is."

Together they watched till the cat curled up in front of the fading fire and fell asleep. Auntie Con squeezed Stella's hand goodnight and Stella fell asleep too. Sometime during the night Stella became aware of the kitten sleeping in the crook of her knee. Drowsily she hoped her Mam would let her keep it.

When she woke in the morning it was already arranged. Rachel had been blackmailed into not only keeping the cat but buying a bit of fish for it every week as well.

Chapter 10 : Aunt Mary

Shortly after the acquisition of the kitten, Granny suggested Stella stay overnight with her and Con on Saturdays. She merely wanted to ensure that Stella started school armed with Christian principles such as were delivered to herself by the United Free Kirk every Sunday morning but this invitation to start Stella off on the right track was received with suspicion by Rachel. She turned on its bearer.

"You told her! And you promised that you wouldn't let on about finding Stella alone that night."

"I didn't tell her," Con protested.

Rachel swept on, "Have you nothing better to do with your life than interfere with mine?"

"Oh calm down...I promised not to tell her if you kept the cat, and you kept the cat so I kept my promise. Don't make me sorry that I did."

"But why should she suddenly take it into her head to have Stella over to sleep?"

"Why should she not? She's the child's grandmother and maybe she loves her. Did you never think of that?"

"She never loved anybody...certainly not me..."

Con looked at her with disgust. "Oh grow up!"

Rachel stamped her foot. "Stella, always Stella. You'd see me hanged for Stella, all of you."

"You're jealous!"

Rachel shot Con a dirty look. "Jealous...huh."

"You are you know, and it's not normal to be jealous of your own child."

There was no trace of the Christmas tree angel as Rachel sneered, "Not normal? Look who's talking." She paused and looked slyly at Con. "Tell me Con, have you ever...?" She laughed. "No, I can tell you haven't from the look of you." She winked. "It's what you need you know. Try it. Get yourself a man and try it," She placed her hands on her swivelling hips. "I can recommend it."

She dodged out of the way as Con, her face scarlet, lunged at her. "You brazen bitch."

"Brazen yes, but normal." With exaggerated nonchalance, and never taking her eyes from Con, she bit off a hangnail and spat it out. "So you can tell mother thanks, but no thanks. I want my daughter with me on Saturday nights and every other night as well." She measured Con with her eyes. "I'd miss her too much if she weren't here..." She laughed. "...to welcome me home."

"I can still tell mother, and Dennis too, about Stella being left alone," Con shouted, her voice trembling.

"She'd wonder why you didn't tell her before and she wouldn't be too pleased if she knew it was because of a cat that you kept quiet. And as for Dennis...what makes you think he'd care? Tell you what though..." Rachel examined her fingernails carefully. "I'll send her down to you on Sundays. Sometimes."

"So you can sleep off Saturday nights?"

"I didn't say that. Oh don't look so worried." She yawned. "She is my kid after all and I can do what I like."

"No you can't."

"If you're going to bring up the Cruelty[17] again, forget it. It's your word against mine and Stella's kept clean and fed and I care enough about her to discipline her. She looked at Con, smiling slowly. "I'm a good mother. And even if I weren't and it could be proven, what would happen? Dennis might send her to his mother to raise or she'd be put in a home. Either way you'd never get to see her."

"You're rotten."

"Have it your own way." Rachel shrugged indifferently but something in Con's look made her uneasy. "Why do you stare at me like that?"

Con, her face serious, placed a trembling hand on Rachel's arm. "I want you to promise me something..."

Rachel's laugh was almost relieved. "Another promise?"

Con nodded. "I'll do anything you want me to...lie, cover up for you..." She bit her lip.

"Get on with it then..."

---

[17] Royal Society for the Prevention of Cruelty to Children

"...if you promise me that you won't take anything we've said today out on Stella."

"Anything? You'd do anything to spare Stella?" She shook her head in wonderment. "What has she got that I haven't?"

"Innocence for one thing - despite all she sees..."

"You've got a nerve to come here and lecture me."

"I haven't finished yet...she's wee and she's helpless and she loves you and if you ever leave her alone at night again and I find out about it, I'll tell Dennis, mother, anyone who'll listen, and I swear to God I mean that."

"Tut tut, swearing! Goody two shoes swearing." Rachel laughed but she looked uneasy, "Haven't I told you? I'm a good mother."

But in spite of the defiant front, what Con said had registered and she resented it. The accusation that she was jealous of Stella had struck home. And Rachel was still smarting from the way Con had blackmailed her into taking in the cat. Her eyes swept the flat and its furnishings, all leftovers from her mother's boarding house. "Junk" she muttered. "Crumbs from the rich man's table." She kicked the bulbous leg of the old fashioned sideboard. "Ugly, ugly thing. I hate you."

Stella, who was having her breakfast, didn't know if her mother was talking about the sideboard, or Auntie Con, or Stella herself.

Rachel would get her own back on Con for putting her on the spot. Rachel didn't cease her nocturnal activities but she made better arrangements for Stella. Granny's offer was never considered (lest the child get some of the love Rachel felt was rightfully her own) but she talked Mary into taking Stella on the nights she wanted out.

Eddie was dubious about getting involved in his sister's affairs but Mary persuaded him. "That poor frightened-looking wee lassie needs to be with other children more. She's too quiet, too well behaved."

"Just because she's not wild like ours?"

"You know what I mean."

"Aye, I do. She's not like a child at all the way she talks sometimes."

"I wonder if she's ill-used," Mary said slowly. Eddie didn't answer.

"Eddie?

"What?" He spoke absently.

"Do you think Stella's ill-used'?"

"You'd better keep out of it. You've no proof."

"No, there are no marks on her if that's what you mean by proof but there are the things we've just been talking about."

Eddie looked uneasy but he tried to shrug it off. "Rachel's always been odd, Maybe Stella's just like her."

"Life will be hard for her if she's judged by her mother," said Mary reproachfully.

"Look Mary, we've never had to go looking for trouble. It always finds us. Don't deliberately invite it."

"It bothers me..."

"I know it does sweetheart, but you're always bothering about other folk." He laughed as he put his arms around her. "Why don't you just bother about me?"

"Oh you!" Mary gave him a playful slap. "Stella's no folk; she's a child."

Eddie let out a whoop. "Worry - worry - worry." He tickled her with each word and she tried to squirm away.

"No!" she shrieked, running and laughing at the same time.

He came after her, twirling imaginary moustaches. "Ah hah me proud beauty...caught ya!"

He tilted back her head and her eyes laughed into his, "There's too much talking and not enough kissing around here," he said covering her mouth with his. After a minute his lips travelled to her ear "How long do we have before the children get back from the pictures?" he whispered.

Rachel had always despised Mary and looked down on Eddie for marrying an ignorant Catholic girl and thereby incurring Granny's eternal displeasure - not to mention the Almighty's - but it was any port in a storm. With Con's warning ringing in her ears she couldn't afford to take chances too soon.

Stella loved staying with Auntie Mary and Uncle Eddie. Their place was never as tidy as Rachel's, but it was magic to Stella. Whenever she entered she felt comforted and at home. Her favourite place was under the table with curvy legs like Auntie Con's, and a tablecloth that swept almost to the floor – a perfect hiding place for children. Linoleum with a worn pattern covered the floor, most worn between the sink and the table, where Auntie Mary would pace back and forth with her latest baby. There was a rag rug in front of the fire. Next to Uncle Eddie's chair was a smoking stand, but Eddie had stopped smoking for lack of money, so the stand was empty except for balls of stockings to be mended and an occasional penny.

On one end of the mantel was a Statue of the Virgin Mary. On the other end was their wedding picture; Eddie looking surprised that this was happening to him and Mary, clutching his arm, looking unfamiliar in her gown except for the sweet expression on her face. In the middle was the alarm clock, placed there so Eddie had to get up to turn it off.

Sometimes Eddie felt there was no point in getting up but he stuck to a routine as he felt that if he gave in, he'd give up. He gave Mary her tea in bed every morning.

Stella slept the sleep of the unafraid there. It made no difference that the bed was crowded with cousins so they lay like sardines, head to toe, or that wee Joey sometimes wet the mattress when the tales of ghosts and derring-do became too exciting. No matter that when she went home Rachel scrubbed her with carbolic and searched her hair for nits - or that the carbolic stung where the bone comb had scraped. What stung more were the things Mam called Auntie Mary. Dirty! Fat! Pape! And worst of all, a rotten-bad mother,

"Now YOU," Mam would glare, almost hitting Stella with the soap, "I see you're kept clean and I teach you to behave so people will like you, but she, SHE'S raising a mob of snottery-nosed hooligans. THEY'RE taught nothing. Look! LOOK - AT - THAT - I'VE FOUND ONE." Her nails would gouge Stella's scalp before they scraped something along a shaft of hair. Then a cracking sound as she pressed her thumbnails together. "DIS---GUSTING! I've a damn good mind to never let you go back."

Stella's heart would sink and later, in bed, she'd sob out her sorrow to Tibby - quietly, softly, so Mam wouldn't hear. ("You're so ugly when you cry, Stella.") Tensed, listening, in case Mam came in and discovered the cat in bed with her. ("Man was made to have DOMINION over the beasts, not to lie down with them.")

And Stella would wonder why, with a good mother like her own, she wanted to live with a rotten-bad mother? She puzzled over it and worried but could make no sense of it. She put it down to being a bad girl. A girl God would punish. A girl bound for the burning fire. She became glad of the guilt that consumed her whenever she longed to be one of her Aunt's brood for she reasoned that if she kept herself from enjoying these visits too much, God might decide she could punish herself without His help.

But Mam always relented and sent her back and in her joy, Stella would forget, and laugh, and love Auntie Mary more than ever.

To atone, she'd crawl under the table and, hidden by the cover that hung to the floor, she'd sit perfectly still, so no one, not even God, would know she was there.

She'd try to think only good things about her mother and bad things about Auntie Mary, but she never got very far. Someone always crawled in beside her and before long all the cousins would be crowded in and Mam and God and guilt would be forgotten.

"What would you do if you had a million pounds...met King Kong, Clark Gable, Dracula...what would you do?" The clamour that followed the questions, everyone yelling what he'd do, what she'd do, was usually interrupted by Auntie Mary lifting a corner of the tablecover and sliding a soup plate filled with broken biscuits in to them. Oh, it was hard not to love Auntie Mary.

Summer was passing and Da had written that his ship would soon be putting into dry dock for a while. Rachel was, in the meantime, making the most of her chances and, "I'm starting the school soon," said Stella

"I've been at the school a long time," boasted Alec.

"So've I," said Rose.

"So've I," echoed Joey.

Lily spoke up. "You're too wee, Joey. The only school you've been to is the Sunday school."

"Catholics don't go to the Sunday school," said Stella.

"We do so." It was a chorus.

But Granny says Catholics are heathens."

"Granny's just an auld Prodestant," said Alec witheringly

"Aye," shouted Rose, "she's ignorant."

"I heard that," Auntie Mary called sternly. There was silence for a minute.

Myrtle started up again. "Don't we have a Sunday school Mammy?"

"Aye we do but wheesht[18], I'm tryin' to read."

"Then can I come with you the next time you go?" Stella asked

Auntie Mary didn't answer and she lifted the cloth and looked out. Her Aunt was in the nursing chair, the baby at her breast sucking contentedly and the book she was holding drooping in her hand. Her gaze was fixed on the statue of the Virgin that stood on the mantelpiece.

"Auntie Mary, can Prodestants come to your Sunday school?"

"Yes."

"Can I come?"

Auntie Mary lifted her book again. "What would your Granny say, hen[19]?"

It was the way grownups usually answered when they meant "no" and Stella accepted that answer with some relief. The Catholic church held the thrill of the unknown and Stella often stood outside the cathedral and watched folk going in, shivers running up and down her spine lest they never get out again. Granny said, "Awful things go on within the confines of the Catholic Church," and when Stella asked what that meant, Auntie Con laughed and said Granny was a blether[20].

---

[18] Shhhh – quiet!

[19] Affectionate or familiar form of address for a girl or woman

[20] Talked nonsense

But not even Auntie Con could deny that Catholics burned people up. Granny had a book to prove it. The book had pictures of people screaming, their mouths wide open, while flames licked away at them. Stella was feart of those pictures and wondered if that's how she'd look when she was in the burning fire. Granny didn't seem to mind them for the book lay on the table beside her bed between her bible and the container for her teeth.

No, the burnings couldn't be denied but Stella knew Auntie Mary would never burn anyone and she was a Catholic, whereas Granny, a staunch Protestant, might.

And Mam, who never went to church at all... Stella shuddered.

Chapter 11 : Divided Loyalties

"Stella, I'm talkin' to you!"

"What wee Joey?"

"Is your Da bringin' you a present when he comes home from the sea?"

"Aye.

"What?"

"Something good."

"A wee monkey maybe?"

Stella thought for a minute. Her Da sometimes brought her things. Once she got a box of Turkish Delight. That was the time her Mam got Turkish cigarettes and there was a big fight because Mam didn't smoke and she told Da he damn well knew it. Then there was the box of sugared violets and the shells that opened when they were dropped in water and magic flowers came out of them. Yes, her Da often brought her things, but a monkey? "Maybe."

"Can I play with it? Can I play with your wee monkey Stella?" He didn't wait for her answer. "Mammy," he shouted, Stella's maybe gettin' a wee monkey from her Da. Can it sleep with us? Please Mammy?"

Auntie Mary laughed and lifted the tablecover. She ruffled Joey's hair. "You're a wee monkey. You're my wee monkey."

Something twisted in Stella's chest. "My da's got a big ship and it's his."

"Your Da doesn't have a ship," said Alec, "he only works on one."

"Quiet under there, said Auntie Mary "I've just put the baby down."

"You Da doesn't work at all," Stella muttered so just Alec could hear.

"He does so; he worked at the docks last week."

The tightness in Stella's chest spread to her throat.

"What's wrong, Stella? You look funny," said Rose.

Stella's breath caught. "Jenny Blackburn's Mam, in our close, died last week and I saw her coffin going down the stairs. And now Jenny's an orphan and might go to live in an orphanage. She was crying." She said it in wonderment but they didn't notice that and she was glad.

"I'd cry if our Mam died," said Gladys.

"So would I," said Alec.

They both looked at Stella, waiting...

"You look funny Stella."

Her heart was swelling up again. While she could still breathe she said, "I wonder what it's like to be in a box with the lid closed?"

"I wouldn't like it," said Lily.

"Neither would I," Rose agreed. "You get to be a skelton because worms have etten all your flesh."

"They leave the skin though, and that's what skin and bones means." said Alec.

Stella's throat relaxed. "I wouldn't like it either."

"I'd squash those worms and try ta get out," said Myrtle.

"You couldn't, dozey, you'd no be able to move."

"Aye, that's right," said Rose. "Somebody told me about that picture where an alive man got shut in a box for hunners and hunners o' years and when he got out his skin was all wrinkled and he couldn't walk right."

"I mind[21] that," shouted Alec. It was the Mummy." He pulled the skin down on his face. "I AM THE - MUMMY."

The girls shrieked and Joey shot out from under the table, "Mammy, Mammy," he shouted. Molly howled from the pram.

Auntie Mary joined in the din. "THAT'S QUITE ENOUGH!" "As well as wakening the baby you're all scaring yourselves to death. Now finish up those biscuits and come out of there."

In the dim light under the table Stella looked at her cousins. Safe. Secure. Home. Alec lifted the last bit of broken biscuit and suddenly all the envy she had tried so hard to stifle, burst out of her in a cry, "My Mam wouldn't buy broken biscuits."

It was true enough. Rachel thought broken biscuits as demeaning as stale bread and even in her poorest days refused to buy them.

"But they're good," said Myrtle.

---

[21] Remember

"I know they are," said Stella and started to cry.

"Don't greet[22], Stella," said Joey offering her the sleeve of his jersey.

But now Stella had started, she couldn't stop. Tears and words poured out of her. "I like my Mam better'n I like yours and my Mam says your Mam's fat and her house is dirty."

"My Mam is not fat," shouted Rose,

"And our house isn't dirty neither," yelled Alec.

"And my Mam says your Mam's an auld tail[23]," shrieked Lily.

Stella didn't know what it meant but from the way it was said it must be bad.

She hit Lily and Myrtle pulled Stella's hair.

Joey, who had come back under the table, made a dive to get away again and took the tablecover with him. The tangle under the table was exposed.

The baby was shrieking now and Auntie Mary grabbed her up. "Stop it at once you lot."

Alec pointed an accusing finger at Stella. "She started it."

"Aye, she did, Mam," shouted the rest.

---

[22] Cry

[23] An old prostitute

67

"You were all wanting to fight or it couldn't have started," said Auntie Mary, looking grim.

"I wasn't fighting Mammy," cried wee Joey burying his face in her apron.

"I ken[24] ye wasn't pet. It was the big ones that should know better."

"It was Stella's fault," said Alec sullenly.

"Yes, Do you know what she said about you Mammy?"

"If there's anything I can't abide it's folk who clipe[25]" Now get out from under there, all of you, this minute. I'm taking Stella ben[26] the house till you all quiet down. Alec - get that cover back on the table. And Rose - shoogle[27] the pram till the baby quiets down. The rest of you, start setting the table for your father's tea."

Auntie Mary looked at Stella kindly when they were alone and Stella started crying again, her breath coming in deep sobbing gasps. She panicked in case she'd never be able to stop and Auntie Mary held her tightly till she could speak.

"I'm sorry," she whispered between two sobs. Her Aunt nodded and Stella went on, "I...I...I called you fat and I told what my Mam said about

---

[24] Know

[25] Tattle!

[26] Through

[27] Rock

68

your house being dirty." She looked at Mary with swollen eyes. "Did you hear me say those things?"

Mary nodded.

Stella started to cry again. "I'm sorry."

"Wheesht hen[28], I know you are, but we all say things we don't mean when we're upset." Mary looked down at the floor and bit her lip. "Like I said something about your Mam that I regret, something that wasn't even true. But with me?" She laughed. "Well, I know I'm too heavy and I know my house could be tidier so you see, you and your Mam were tellin' the truth. I wasn't."

Stella flung herself at Mary. "No! We weren't. You're pretty - prettier'n anybody and your house is the best." She realised what she was telling her Aunt and she stiffened, remembering. She drew back, the hot tears still stinging her eyes. "I don't love you honest. I only love my Mam."

She trembled, waiting for her Aunt to say she could never come back, but Auntie Mary said slowly, "That doesn't matter hen, for I still love you. Now let me wipe your face and comb your hair, for if your mother comes for you and finds you like this, she'll never let you came back And I wouldn't like that at all."

But Eddie wasn't so sure about Stella's coming back.

When Mary told him, later, after Stella had gone home and their own were asleep, "She went under the table again", he made light of it at first.

69

"Weans[29] all do that."

"I know they do - but this is different."

"How?"

Mary shook her head. "It's hard to say. "She seems to go away somewhere - not just under the table - but somewhere. And it's how she looks. I don't like it Eddie."

"Neither do I. There's a problem there that we can't solve and I don't think we should get in too deep."

"We can't just ignore it."

"We're not ignoring it - we just can't solve it and I think you should stop trying Mary. You looked upset when I got in."

"That wasn't Stella's fault. It was Rachel. She was at me again."

"That bitch...what was it this time?"

"The usual. Her nose in the air."

"That's what I mean, Mary, you shouldn't have to put up with that from her."

"It's for Stella, Eddie."

"Are you sure that's all that happened?"

---

[28] Shush, girl

[29] Children

Mary hesitated..."That was all." But it wasn't, and Mary knew if she told about it he'd never let Rachel back and that meant Stella too.

When she came for her child, Rachel had looked at Mary through narrowed eyes. "You're not looking well and I know what it is." She laughed. "It's that brother of mine. You should chase him the next time he comes near you. You've already got too many and from the looks of you another one would kill you."

Mary's eyes had filled and Rachel spoke as though she were the offended one. "I'm only telling you for your own good. You think about it, and you *could* start thinking about Eddie too. How would he cope on his own with six weans? He'd have to remarry and there would be little choice of women with that army at his back. Oh come on Mary, don't be so dashed easy hurt. Look - I've been thinking. It costs you something to put Stella up so I'll start paying you." Would half a crown be all right for this time?" She put a coin on the table.

"Lift your money off my table and your arse off my chair."

"There's no need to be nasty.", said Rachel."

"I mean it."

"Then it will be a pleasure."

"Wait... you can still bring Stella. I don't want paid."

Rachel shrugged. "Oh well..." She laughed. "You're really quite a good soul you know..." She looked about her, "So where's the brat? It's time I got her home and into the tub."

Mary's face burned at the memory but she knew she'd never tell Eddie about it. Dennis would be home soon and Rachel would have to start behaving.

Chapter 12 : A Loving Mother

The nights were drawing in and lights were coming on now soon after school let out each day. I liked when my Mam sent me to the shops then. They were bright oases in the November dark and if I met someone I knew, we would look into the shop windows and play 'I spy'.

I especially liked being sent to the chemist. He had an open flame on the counter and when he had Mam's purchase wrapped he would hold a stick of wax in the flame till it softened and then he'd press it on to the paper, leaving a blob of red. With the smell of hot sealing wax in my head I'd go back to the darkness where haar[30] and chimney-smoke mingled with a haunting smell of decay that was not unpleasant. And to add to the magic, Christmas lay just ahead. I wished it could always be November.

Then one afternoon the chemist let me hold the wax in the flame and press it to the paper. This done, he took my money and when he gave me my change he placed in my hand what was left of the stick of wax. "Don't say I never gave you anything."

I sniffed it all the way home. I handed my mother her package and told her I was the one who had sealed it. "And see, Mr. Scott gave me a bit of wax to bring home."

My mother looked at me in silence. Then she took the wax. Still she said nothing and the feeling that I had done something wrong crept over

---

[30] Mist or fog

me. My feet were cold the way they always got when I was feart. "What's wrong Mam?"

She looked at me sadly. "There are certain things a mother must do for her child's welfare...even if she doesn't want to... even if it hurts her more than it hurts the child. They say that God chastises those whom he loves. Well a good mother has to be like God and do the same."

She was silent again and my hands became as cold as my feet.

"I'm sorry Mam.", I said not knowing what I had to be sorry about.

Finally she spoke again. "Aye, and there's the hereafter to think of too. I couldn't bear to see you tossed into the flames of eternal fire. God knows the value of punishment but still He shows mercy. It's only the most hopeless cases that are the ones who he consigns to endless torment; the ones who think impure or angry thoughts, who don't like the mothers who gave them birth; who rebel and disobey. Who bring pain to their parents."

I needed to the bathroom now. I started wriggling.

"STAND STILL WHILE I'M TALKING TO YOU", she shouted.

"I'm sorry Mam."

"Do you know what you've done?" I looked at my feet and shook my head.

"You mean you don't remember what I told you about fire?"

I nodded.

"Well why did you do it? Why did you go near the flame at the chemist's?"

"I thought it was just the gas I wasn't to light or poke the fire."

"Ah well, you thought wrong. And I think you thought wrong deliberately. I don't think you realise what an agonizing death burning is...I think it's time you found out... don't you?" I was crying now, "Oh please Mam, don't make me find out."

"I have to baby. Don't you see that? Lessons have to hurt and I care for you too much to let you take chances with your life..."

"... Please no Mam."

"... so lift the poker and stick it between the bars on the grate."

I lifted my eyes to hers. "Please no Mam, don't make me."

"Don't be so silly. I'm not asking you to get it red-hot. Just hot enough to show you what fire feels like."

I became hysterical. "No, I can't do that."

"You can and you will, and the sooner you do it the sooner it will be over. You're acting like a big tumfy[31] so just quiet down and get on with it."

I couldn't stop sobbing and I was aware that my nose was bubbling. I wiped it with the back of my hand.

---

[31] Softie

75

"If you don't hurry up, I'll put the poker in and leave it till it's red hot." She handed me the poker. "Now don't make me do something I don't want to do."

Still I hesitated. • She sighed loudly. "Very well then, don't say you didn't ask for it."

I grabbed the poker from her and thrust it between the bars. She sat back. "That's better...don't take it out already dozey. It's barely had a chance to get warm."

She stood up and covering my hand with hers, pushed the poker back into the fire.

After what seemed like hours I withdrew it and was about to touch it with the tip of my finger when she stopped me.

"Touching it with the tip of finger's not going to teach you much. You have to grasp the end that comes out of the fire."

"Please Mam, I'll never go near fire again if you let me off this time."

"Look," she shouted above my anguished pleas, "I'm not doing this for my own amusement. I'm doing it for your future safety and if I let you off you won't have learned. The poker's too cool now to do any good. Now shove it back in the fire and let's get this over before I lose patience with you. And this time I'll tell you when you can take it out."

The process was repeated and when she judged the poker ready she withdrew it from the fire and held it out to me. "Take it." She spoke quietly now.

"Please please I'll never be bad again and. I'll do everything you tell me."

She started shouting again. "Start now. Get the feel of fire and learn what awaits you in this life and the next if you disobey me."

"I can't I can't," I cried backing off from her with my hands behind my back.

"If you don't take it now I'll put YOU in the fire."

Quickly I grabbed the hot end of the poker and with the first searing pain I shrieked and flung it to the floor.

"Stupid stupid creature you're burning the hearthrug." She lifted the poker by the handle and hit me over the shin with it.

I fell to the floor. She stood over me with the poker. Suddenly she hurled it down on the hearth. "Why WHY do you try my patience? What devil gets into you? " She sank to the floor beside me. "Oh my baby, what have you made me do to you?

I was sobbing. I couldn't stop. My mother started to cry too. "You see why I had to do that don't you? I had to do it... I had to. Now you know how much you mean to me. What I go through for your good. Of course it hurt me but if it will someday save your life it will have been worth everything it cost me." She kissed my burnt palm and murmured endearments while I sobbed. "It hurts Mam, it hurts."

"Of course it does my darling, but someday you'll thank me for it. You'll see. Now come and we'll run cold water on the bit that burns."

"My leg hurts too - I can't stand on it."

"Well the shin is very sensitive. If you hadn't been a silly wee lassie that wouldn't have happened. You see that don't you? Now put your arms round your Mammy's neck and she'll try to ease you into a chair. I'll bring a basin of cold water for your sore hand and then we'll put Vaseline and a bandage on it. You'll need to keep your weight off that leg for a day or two."

"But I want to go to the school."

"What? You don't want to stay home with your Mammy? Don't you love your poor old mother any more?"

"I don't know."

Of course you love me, of course you do. You're just hurting at the moment." She kissed the top of my head. "But I do promise you that I'll never tell a soul what I had to do to you today. It will he a secret between us so don't worry that I'll shame you by telling anybody." She tilted my head up so that I could see she was smiling through tears, "Cross my heart and hope to die."

My leg was throbbing so her face kept getting hazy and I felt sick. I wished she'd stop talking so I could stop listening. I wished she'd go away and leave me. "I'm tired Mam."

"Of course you are and you're as white as a sheet. Come on to your bed. I'll help you to get there and then I'll bring you a cup of hot sweet tea when you're tucked in."

I couldn't help it. I tried not to, but I vomited into the basin of water that held my injured hand.

Chapter 13 : Stella at Age Eight

I was named Stella Maris because my mother had once read that it meant 'Star of the Sea', and since my father was a merchant seaman, the name seemed appropriate. That it was also one of the titles given the Virgin Mary she didn't discover till Granny Morrison demanded that the papish name be changed. I'm glad she didn't.

One spring, when I was nearly three, and we had just settled into the flat overlooking the Eastern cemetery, my father came home unexpectedly one night and found my mother gone. He shook me awake. "Where is she?" he shouted and when I couldn't tell him, he flung me back down. "Bastard", he roared, "What good are you anyway?"

I lay awake for a long time after that for I was feart he'd kill my mother when she came in. He was smashing dishes in the kitchen and shouting that he'd have to get a shore job to keep an eye on the bitch.

But it was the wrong time for changing jobs, and very soon he was away at sea again. However my mother was pregnant and before the baby was born we had to move to a cheaper flat in a bad neighbourhood.

When I was old enough to go to a Sunday school alone, my mother, with no religious affiliation of her own, sent me to the church nearest home. I was relieved to learn there that God loved all little children, even me, for Mam said that was a hard thing to do and she should know.

We lived so close to the Roman Catholic cathedral now that Granny liked to examine me on Sundays to make sure I wasn't breaking out in papist tendencies. I was sorry I couldn't go to their Sunday school because

I looked in the door once and saw a lot of candles burning and it looked nice, like Christmas.

Except for all the questions she asked, I quite liked going to Granny Morrison's on Sundays for my Auntie Con gave me things I liked for my tea. Besides, my Mam thought Sunday was a dead day, fit only to sleep through, so Tibby and I had to keep quiet and still while she did just that.

My Sunday school was changing. Some of the new children had runny noses and scratched their heads and my Mam had to put turpentine on my hair to kill some nits I caught.

Then a new girl called Brenda Docherty joined the class. She was a bully who said she'd kill me if I ever let on I had seen her smoking. *Her* nose wasn't runny and she wore frilly dresses and ribbons in her curly yellow hair. Because she went to dancing lessons her shiny black shoes had cleats in them that made a nice clickety-clack when she walked and terrible marks on anyone she kicked.

Brenda was soon the teacher's pet and got to take round the plate at collection time. The money was supposed to go to the poor children in Africa but most of it went to Brenda. Miss Merry was too short sighted to see what was going on under her nose and we were all too feart of Brenda to tell her.

Miss Merry always said, "The Lord loveth a cheerful giver." as she handed Brenda the plate, and when she got it back she'd peer into it, shoving coins aside as she counted them. Then she'd look at us reproachfully. "When He's done so much for you, is it too much to ask that you give up some of your Saturday sweeties for Him?"

Once when she said that, Billy Fraser stood up and dropped two aniseed balls into the plate.

"No no," said Miss Merry. "I don't want your sweeties. I want the money you bought them with."

"But that's gone," said Billy.

Miss Merry looked pleased. "Exactly! And what you spent on aniseed balls to rot your teeth could have gone to buy nourishing food for a black child."

Brenda's hand shot up and Miss Merry beamed at her. "Yes dear?"

"It could have bought an orange and an apple."

Miss Merry glowed. "Good girl Brenda."

Brenda simpered and I got the boak[32]. Inside I vowed that she'd never steal from me and Jesus again.

Cheered up now, Miss Merry went on, "I have a plan. Starting next Sunday, for every penny you put in the plate, you'll get a picture of Jesus to take home." She held up a picture of Jesus with a black child on his knee. "Would you like that?"

There was a chorus of "yesses" and none louder than mine, for I was collecting Jesus pictures. Granny Morrison had promised me a shilling for every twelve I collected if I could recite the texts on them with my eyes closed. I needed only four more to make the dozen. There wasn't much chance of my Mam giving me four pennies all at once, or even one penny four Sundays in a row but you never knew. She was seldom awake to give me collection money before I left for the Sunday school, but sometimes I got a Saturday penny and could save that.

Maybe I'd even get two if I went the messages[33] without grumbling. Maybe even more if I told her what the money was for. The catch there was that my Mam could read minds and she said she knew I was grumbling even if it wasn't out loud, and then I wouldn't get anything.

---

[32] I felt disgusted

[33] Errands - shopping

Chapter 14 : The Sixpence

The following Saturday Mam said she had no change to give me a penny but she'd get some while she was out.

"I'll run the messages[34] for you."

She smiled at me through the mirror. "It's not messages I'm going for."

I watched her put perfume behind her ears and pat at her nose with a puff. My Mam always smelled good and when she was going out she looked good too.

"Can I come with you?"

The beads she was trying to fasten slipped through her fingers. "Oh you make me so nervous when you start that."

"Please," I said but she didn't reply. "Will you try to be home before dark then?"

"Of course, but if anything should hold me up, remember what I've told you - you must never light the gas while I'm gone. You might blow yourself and the whole house up. I couldn't bear it if anything happened to you. I'd go mad I think. So promise. Promise me that you'll never light the gas when I'm out."

"I promise, but will you *try* to be home before dark?"

---

[34] Errands

"Oh what a worrier you are." She sounded impatient again. "It's not normal for a child your age to worry so much." The beads were on now and she turned her head this way and that to get the effect. She was satisfied for she smiled at me again. "I may not be gone long and if you get hungry there's plenty food in the press[35] and a surprise as well."

She glanced at the clock. "Oh God... I'll never get out of here." She picked up her handbag and turned to me. "Cheer up sobersides. Your Mammy loves you and I'll lock the door behind me so no one can get in to hurt you." She dropped to her knees and looked into my eyes. "Now remember, if anyone comes to the door don't answer it. Just stay quiet like there's no one in and they'll go away. You have Tibby to play with and I'll give you a penny when I get home. Now go and find your cat, like a good wee lassie."

A quick kiss and she was gone. I heard the big key turn in the lock outside. I put my ear to the door and heard her heels click down the stairs. The sound became fainter and stopped. From a great distance came a dull bang as the heavy door to the street swung shut.

I was surrounded by silence. I wondered if silence could swallow people up so that no one would ever see them again. "Tibby," I shouted. "Please come Tibby." But she didn't till I got out her string and wriggled it across the floor. She shot from under the bed and pounced on it. I stopped being feart and went to the press for my surprise. A comic and a macaroon bar. Tib leapt on my knee and sniffed at the shreds of coconut that dropped to my lap as I ate.

---

[35] Cupboard

The macaroon gone, I read her bits of my comic and then we played with her string. When she got fed up with that I told her some made-up stories but she didn't like them much for she went to sleep. I got out my pictures and went over the texts till the light faded and our kitchen filled with shadows. I went to the window then, and watched the street lights coming on far below. I could see the fancy hats of the friendly ladies who said hello to people passing by and sometimes walked off with them, arm in arm.

My Mam didn't like the friendly ladies and always made me look the other way when we passed them. I was sorry about that for they smiled at me and I wanted to be a friendly lady too some day. When my Mam wasn't in, I practised on her high heels and pretended that a nice man would bow to me and lift his bowler hat and take me to Crolla's for ice cream.

Thinking of ice cream made me hungry and I wished I had saved some of my macaroon. There was bread and jam in the press, as well as a piece of fish on a plate and a hunk of cheese. Tibby ate the fish and I had the cheese and bread and jam after it.

By the time we finished the shadows had all run together and I wished I hadn't promised not to light the gas. I got feart in the dark and was glad of Tib to keep me company. But when I tried to carry her through the dark lobby to my bedroom she leapt from my arms and back to the kitchen range, which was still throwing off a little warmth.

I wondered if I should try lighting the gas. Maybe Mam would never find out, but if the house blew up she'd know and then I might just as well have blown up with it!

85

She might start tying me up like she used to when I was wee. She didn't want to and she'd be sad and say, "You should be ashamed. If you weren't such a bad girl I wouldn't have to do these things to you."

And I was ashamed and was always feart that someone would find out that my Mam had to tie me up because I was so bad. My Mam was good to me because she always used wool to tie me so it wouldn't hurt. She said she didn't believe in leaving marks on children like some parents did. The wool would be nice colours too, but I'd still get fed up. Once I wet my knickers and got cold and shivery. When my Mam came home and I told her I was cold she said, "I'll warm your hide", and she did. It stung but my bum did get warmed up so that was all right.

It was better now that I was bigger. Mam trusted me to obey and now when she was out I could walk about the house and play string with Tibby and watch people out the window. I still got feart in the dark though, so I decided to sing and make a noise as I went down the dark lobby and into my bed, and I did, even after I had my head under the covers. "Jesus bids us shine with a pure clear light, like a little candle burning in the night..."

Sleep made the time go quickly for when I woke up it was morning and my Mam had come home. I dressed as quietly as I could so I wouldn't wake her. I nearly forgot to wash for I was worried about a mark on my dress. It was too dark last night for me to notice that I had dropped jam on it. I tried to rub it off with a cloth but that only made it worse so I buttoned up my cardigan high enough to cover it. When I got to Granny's, my Auntie Con would fix it so my mother would never know. So that was all right. It was when I went to get the sweetie box where I kept my Jesus pictures that I realised Mam had forgotten to leave out my penny.

I didn't want to wake her up and make her angry so I stood by her bed and looked at her for a long time without blinking. That was what Tib did when she wanted someone to do something for her.

Mam didn't look like my Saturday Mam this morning. She had a lot of little lines on her face and the black stuff she wore on her eyes had smudged so she had a patch of black on one cheek. Staring at her and thinking her awake wasn't working so I leaned over cautiously and whispered, "Mam, I need a penny for the Sunday school."

She moaned and moved impatiently in her sleep. "Mam." I said it a little louder. "If I take a penny to Miss Merry I'll get a picture of Jesus with an African on his knee."

She mumbled something I couldn't catch • "Please Mam, I'll be late."

I touched her shoulder and she tried to open her eyes. Her voice was all deep and funny and I could hardly make out the words. "What's this about Miss Merry on an African's knee?"

"Not an African's knee...Jesus' knee." I was hopping, desperate to be away.

"Miss Merry on Jesus' knee?" Suddenly her eyes opened wide and she said loudly and clearly, "What the hell are they teaching you at that Sunday school?"

"It's a picture of Jesus with a black child on his knee. I told you Mam, I'll get one if I put a penny in the collection."

"Oh." Her eyes closed again.

"Please...I'll be late."

"Oh go in my purse and stop bothering me." She rolled over to face the wall. "And then get out of here you damned pest."

I looked in her purse. There was a half-crown, three shillings, a sixpence and a ha'penny. "You don't have any pennies Mam. "

She screamed, "I said get out of here, and don't let me see your face again today."

I grabbed the sixpence and ran. On my way out the door I called, "I'll bring you the change."

Chapter 15 : The Best Laid Plans...

As I ran to Sunday school, I thought about Mam's sixpence. Instead of getting five pence change, I could tell Miss Merry I wanted four pictures all at once and only two pennies change. Then after the Sunday school I'd have all twelve Jesus pictures to take to Granny's. I'd learn the four new texts on the way, recite the lot to Granny, and get a shilling. When I got home, I'd give Mam her five pennies change and still have ninepence left for myself. I skipped the rest of the way to the church.

People were already in their seats and the organ tuning up when I got there. When they rose to sing I slipped into the back row behind a lady with a big hat so the minister wouldn't see me. I was just getting my breath back when someone dug me in the side.

"God'll get you for being late," Brenda Docherty whispered.

I pretended not to hear her. She kicked my ankle and I dropped my box of Jesus pictures.

"You're going to catch it," she said.

Without looking at her I said, "Shut up you."

She twisted my arm so violently that I dropped Mam's sixpence. It bounced before it rolled under the seat ahead. Brenda dived after it and I grabbed one of her corkscrew curls and pulled. She screeched and the lady with the big hat whirled round, "Show some respect in the house of your Maker."

Back on her feet, Brenda said, "It was her. She started it."

The lady gave me a dirty look; "I can well believe that."

The hymn ended and the organ and the singing stopped just as she said, "Ye'll not make a silk purse out of a sow's ear."

A lot of people turned around, and burning with embarrassment I sank to my seat. My ankle still throbbed from Brenda's kick. I didn't know what the lady's words meant but I knew what her look and her tone meant. The lilacs and the veiling on her hat ran together in a purple shimmer.

"Bubbly bairn[36]," said Brenda in my ear.

It was all I needed. I stopped caring that she was the teacher's pet and that she had cleats in her shoes. With all my strength I pushed her and as she fell to the floor her head hit the pew an awful thump. The minister stopped talking and people turned round again. Miss Merry got up and started back towards us and the minister made a sign to the organist who broke into 'Onward Christian Soldiers' The choir, unsure as to whether they should sing, straggled to their feet. One or two began, and the rest of the choir and the congregation joined in. The sound swelled till I thought my head would burst from it and from the shame of what I had done. When Miss Merry reached our pew, she pulled me aside so she could help Brenda up. Brenda was crying, "She shoved me."

"She started it," I said.

The lady in front broke in, "I've been watching that one," she nodded her head at me, "and she's been tormenting that poor wee soul since the kirk started. She should be ashamed, a big girl like that picking on a wee-er one.'

---

[36] Baby

Miss Merry ignored her, got Brenda to her feet and led us to the cloakroom where she examined Brenda for damage."

"You seem to be all right," she said, handing her hankie to Brenda. "Wipe your tears with that. The towel in here is filthy as usual." She nodded at me, "Go you and wash. Your face is none too clean."

"I washed it before I left the house."

"Oh". She looked surprised. "You didn't do a very good job then."

"My Mam's sick," I said, holding out my hand for a turn of the hankie but she didn't see me. She was smoothing Brenda's hair and retying her ribbons.

"There." She tucked her hankie back in her sleeve. "Stella, this might have been very serious."

I didn't say anything and she shook her head. "Aren't you sorry?"

"I'm sorry I lost my sixpence."

"God is watching you and He's not very happy," Miss Merry told me. "Now hurry up." She whirled the towel on the roller. "There's a spot there that's not too bad. Just wipe your face on that."

Anxious to redeem myself in Miss Merry's eyes I made a fatal mistake. "That sixpence was for the poor children in Africa."

Now there would be no change to give Mam unless Granny came through with the shilling she'd promised me when I had twelve pictures! "So can I have six pictures today anyway?"

Miss Merry had brightened up and she smiled at me. "I don't see why not. The janitor will find the sixpence when he tidies up, and it will still go to the children in Africa."

I pointed at Brenda. "She has it."

Brenda let out an indignant howl. "She's a big liar. I don't have it. It rolled under the seat."

"She's a liar. She steals money from the plate every Sunday and then she buys cinnamon stick and smokes it."

"This isn't true, is it Brenda?"

"No miss. She's lying."

"I thought so, and that was a very serious accusation to make, Stella."

Brenda started crying again and Miss Merry knelt down and put an arm round her. "There there dear, there's no need to cry."

I wished I could cry, but sometimes when I felt most like it, I couldn't. I gave vent to my feelings in a less attractive way. I shouted. "People will tell you, she's a damned liar and a thief too."

"Stella!" Miss Merry was shocked and in the silence that followed I heard footsteps in the hall and the hum of voices as the congregation broke up into study groups. Miss Merry said, "It's class time and people will be coming in here. While there's noise and confusion anyway, we'll have a quick look for the sixpence."

"I'll look." Brenda shot ahead and before we even reached the back pew, she was coming towards us, holding out the sixpence. "I told you it rolled under the seat."

I turned to Miss Merry, "It did roll under the seat but she stole it from there."

Miss Merry looked at me sternly, "We'll have no more of that. Say you're sorry to Brenda."

"I won't."

"Very well then...since you won't apologise, you'll just have to share your pictures. Brenda, Stella will give you three of the six pictures she gets today."

The sniff that Brenda gave started out to be a sneer but she caught it in time.

Fright made me frantic. If I didn't get a shilling from Granny this afternoon I couldn't give Mam her fivepence change. "Please, let me keep four pictures and give her two. I need twelve to take to my Granny and I only have eight."

"No Stella. You have to learn not to jump to conclusions about people, and three pictures seems the right price to pay for the lesson."

I don't remember the bible story that day or anything else between the times Miss Merry gave me my punishment and the passing of the plate for the collection. When I was handed six pictures I thought fleetingly of running away with them and never going back to that Sunday school. But Mam would want to know why and she might punish me worse for causing trouble. Still, if I made off with all six cards, she'd get her right change and I could just pretend to be at the Sunday school next week.

I became aware that Miss Merry was watching me, waiting for me to give her back three of the pictures. Silently I handed them to her and my heart leapt with relief when she said, "No dear."

But she went on, "No, Stella, you have to give them to the person you wronged." I didn't move and she put an arm round my shoulders and leaned forward to say quietly into my ear, "Our Father in heaven wants us to be humble and admit when we're wrong. Remember that hymn we sing?" She started to sing it softly, " 'I do it all for Jesus, He's done so much for me.' Your pride won't hurt so much if you think of those words. Right?"

When I still didn't move, or agree, she lost patience with me and said out loud, "Think how it hurt Him to be nailed to a cross...and that was for you."

Without a word I took the three pictures over to Brenda and flung them in her face. Then I marched straight out and paid no heed to Miss Merry's shocked, "Come back here Stella."

Chapter 16 : Never Talk to Strangers

I walked slowly to Granny's, memorising the texts on the three new pictures. Even if she gave me only five pence for the ones I knew, I'd be able to go home and face my mother. If she didn't, Auntie Con might lend me the money to give Mam her change.

But when I got to Granny's Auntie Con wasn't in. "I don't know where she is," said Granny. "She's become very secretive about what she's doing and where she goes. It matters not that I'm here alone and might take a bad turn while she's away gallivanting." Granny kept rolling up the corner of her apron and smoothing it out again, as she did when she was agitated.

"Granny, I've brought my pictures and I know the texts, so can I have the money today, that you promised me?"

"You've got the twelve have ye?"

"It's only eleven, but I know every one and it won't take me long to get another picture."

"What's your hurry then?"

"I need it for something."

"Oh? And what would that be?"

"I owe my mother some money and she wants it back."

"Borrowing. It says in the Good Book, 'Neither a borrower nor a lender be', did you know that?"

I shook my head and she went on, "It's a bad practise and not to be encouraged."

"It wasn't really borrowing. I had change to give my Mam and ..." Caution warned me to say nothing to Granny about the carry on at the Sunday school, for she might condemn me too, so I just told her the ultimate destination for the sixpence.

"...I gave it for the poor children in Africa."

"Very commendable," said Granny, "but it was your mother's money and you should have asked her first."

"I did, and she said it was all right, but then I gave more than she told me to."

"Well that's between you and your mother. I don't believe in interfering between mother and child. Now, if you're hungry you'll just have to go into that tin on the mantelpiece and get yourself a biscuit."

I stood on one of the fender-boxes and reached for the tin that showed battle scenes, one to a side. Mons. Gallipoli. Hill 60. Ypres. Men in tin hats carrying bayonets while shells exploded about them. A man with a blood stained bandage round his head, leaning on a Red Cross nurse. I always tried to turn that picture away from me when I lifted the box. Granny liked it and would say, "Might in the right shall prevail."

She was right about my being hungry so I took three biscuits. "Please Granny, could I have eleven pence for eleven pictures then?"

"Are you still on about that?"

"Please...eleven texts for only five pence and I'll be able to give Mam her change."

"When you've got twelve pictures and can say all twelve texts, you'll get your shilling. That was our agreement and I want to hear no more about it."

The biscuits were stale and the cream filling tasted like toothpaste. "Can I put two back Granny?"

"You've handled them so you have to eat them. Wilful wasters come to woeful want, did you know that?"

I nodded. "But they don't taste very good."

"As long as they fill you up that's all that matters. People make far too much fuss over what they eat, and gluttony is one of the deadly sins. Besides, there's little else to eat in the house. She left nothing prepared when she barged out o' here. Aye, she thinks I don't know what's going on, but I often keek[37] in the kitchen when she doesn't know I'm looking and I see the trashy novels she hides behind the cushions. I know fine what goes on in her head too. I know I'm a burden on her; that she wishes me six feet under. I can read that one's mind full well."

I looked at Granny, amazed. "My Mam can read minds too."

"Huh. I don't suppose she went with ye to the kirk this morning'?"

"No, she was tired."

"What doing?"

"I don't know. Granny, when do you think Auntie Con will be home?"

"The Lord knows, for I don't. The Lord Almighty Who shall come in the fullness of time and take us all Home. And it's time *you* were away home. The sky's inky and you might get caught in a downpour."

"I'm feart."

"Feart? What for? Not the rain surely?"

"My Mam.

"Feart o' your Mam? Never! Your Mam would never hurt you. A mother's love passeth all understanding." Granny broke into one of my mother's favourite songs, "She'd sigh for you, Cry for you, Yes, even die for you, That's what God made mothers for."

She gazed into the fire. She was still rolling up, and smoothing out, the corner of her apron. "Aye, and what thanks do mothers get for all their trouble Hmph!? Some would call Constance a dutiful daughter, but little do they know...aye, little do they know..."

"I'm away then Granny."

"If you meet your Auntie Con tell her I'm waiting for my lunch."

But I didn't meet my Auntie though I stood at the stop for a while hoping she'd get off the tram. I wasn't in a hurry to get home but I started to run when the first raindrops fell. I still had the Links to cross and the long stretch of Leith Walk ahead of me.

---

[37] Peek

Maybe when I got home my mother would be in a better mood than she was in this morning. Maybe she'd think I had taken a penny from her purse. Maybe she hadn't heard me saying she didn't have one and I'd bring her change. Maybe she'd be singing.

"Here, ye'd better step in here till the rain stops.", a voice said as I started up the Walk. He was standing in the doorway of a stair, coat collar turned up, and cap pulled low so that his eyes were scarcely visible.

I stopped. "Who? Me?"

"Aye, it's you I'm talkin' to. Ye're like a drowned rat."

I hesitated and he said, "Come on, I'm not gonna bite ye."

I shook my head and he went on, "I have a wee lassie o' my own at home and I wouldn't like her to get as wet as you are. I'd be worried she'd get her death of cold. I'd be grateful if some kind person, man or wumman, offered her shelter."

I started to run again, but he halted me with a piercing whistle. "What's in your box?"

I stopped and called back, "Pictures of Jesus."

"Pictures of Jesus? I'd fair like to see them."

When I didn't move, he went on, "Have ye been at the Sunday school then?"

I didn't answer. "Ah know what your trouble is... your maw and your paw told ye never to talk to strangers. I'm right am I not?" I nodded. "Aye, I thought so. That's what I tell mine. 'Never talk to strangers'. And it's right that ye shouldn't, but it's a pity, all the same for I'd fair like to see those pictures." He fumbled in his pocket and brought out some money. "Here. Here's a sixpence for being such a good wee lassie."

I walked slowly back to him and took the sixpence. I felt sorry I hadn't trusted him. He was a nice man. I started to open the box, but he interrupted, "Not out here. They'll get all wet. Step into the stair." He held open the heavy door. Rain dripped from the ends of my hair and into my eyes.

"Come on then, you're drowning."

I stepped into the stair and he swung shut the door behind me. "Here, let's sit on the steps while ye show me them. That's right, wee lass. That'll do fine."

I looked up and in the dim light of the stair I saw that he had removed his cap, that his hair was red; that between the reddish stubble on his face, his lips were slack and shiny; his teeth uneven, and I knew. Knew that I had made a mistake in finally trusting him.

I started to my feet but he was on top of me, and because of the position I was in, his legs were around my neck and something wet was touching my face.

"Help, oh help, Mammy." My scream echoed round the stair well. Far above a door opened and a voice called, "What's going on down there?"

"Christ!" The man heaved himself off me and was out the door before I was on my feet. I grabbed my box and ran too. Being caught disobeying my mother was more fearful to me than the risk of running into the man in my headlong dash for home. A quick glance in the opposite direction though, and I saw the shock of red hair receding into the distance.

Leith Walk was Sunday quiet, its length unending. I wanted my home. I wanted my Mam. I ran through puddles and didn't feel them wet. I tripped on my shoelace, fell, and was glad of the hard reality of the pavement under me. As I scrambled to my feet, I found his sixpence still clutched in my hand. It burned my palm. I screamed and flung it as far as I could. I didn't see where it fell. I didn't want to see. I still had the box of Jesus pictures too. The man's thing might have touched it, wetting it as it had wet my cheek. Before I pushed open the door of our stair, I hurled it into the gutter where the lid separated from the bottom and my pictures whirled away in the rainwater that gushed towards the drain.

I ran up the stairs to our top flat. "Mammy. Hurry Mammy."

Chapter 17 : Judas Iscariot

In the time it took her to get to the door I had decided not to tell her about the man. She might start tying me up again if she knew she couldn't trust me. She might even kill me. She opened the door and I was glad she wasn't awake enough to see the state I was in.

"Could you not have gone before you left your Granny's? What a damned racket to make and me with a splitting head."

"I'm sorry Mam. "

She walked over to the mantelpiece and peered at the clock. "Isn't it a bit early for you to be home?"

"I left the Sunday school early and then Auntie Con wasn't in so I didn't get any lunch."

"Where was she?"

"Granny didn't know."

"Did she offer you anything to eat?"

"I got biscuits."

"So what's wrong?"

I was startled. "Nothing, there's nothing wrong."

"Yes there is. There's always something wrong when you call me Mammy." Her eyes narrowed. "Step over here into the light. What a sight you are! You're like you had been dragged through a hedge."

I looked at the floor. She knew! My Mam always knew.

"You had a fight with someone, didn't you?"

In my relief I almost shouted it, "It was Brenda. Brenda Docherty. She stole your sixpence."

"My sixpence? Was that what you took from my purse?" "Yes. And I was going to bring you the change."

"I should hope so. Your da's money won't come for another week. And how did she steal it?"

"When she kicked me I dropped it on the floor in the church and she picked it up and pretended she hadn't done it."

"So what did you do?"

"I shoved her and she fell."

"And didn't you try to get the money away from her then?"

I hoped that I'd say the right thing. That I could divert her suspicions away from me. Better to get into bother over Brenda than over the man. "Miss Merry came and helped Brenda up and Brenda was crying, so Miss Merry believed her and not me."

"What did Miss Merry say?"

"She said I was lying and Brenda hadn't taken my sixpence..."

Mam broke in, "My sixpence."

"...your sixpence. She said the janitor would find it and it would go to the poor children in Africa."

"All of it?"

I looked at my feet. "All of it."

"You're hiding something from me aren't you?"

I didn't look up. I shook my head.

"Well if what you have told me is the case, you're not going back to that Sunday school."

When I still didn't respond, she said, "You don't seem very upset at not being allowed back?"

"I don't want to go back."

In one of her bewildering about-faces, my mother said, "Oh but you have to go back. You have to show them that you've nothing to be ashamed of. You have to face up to them and let them see that you don't care. My God, when I was your age, I had gumption. You get your wishy-washiness from your father's side... The Malcolms have no courage. You're off a long line of feardies."

"I'll go back next week then."

"You'll go back now and I'll go with you. They're going to see they can't treat anything of mine like dirt." All the time my mother was talking she was pacing. Now she stopped abruptly. "I'll get ready. Bring me my things."

"But they'll all be away home by now."

"Not if we hurry. You were home early, remember, so DON'T ARGUE WITH ME. GO!"

"Don't Mam please don't." She paid me no heed. She was preparing for battle. I wished I could die.

When we reached the street I saw that part of my box was trapped between a pile of debris and the side of the gutter. The bright anemones on the lid caught my mother's eye.

"That's your box isn't it? And look, there's one of your texts."

It was the one of Jesus on the cross. His outstretched arms seemed to be clinging to the bar across the drain and water swept cigarette butts and spent matches across the bowed head.

"What are they doing there?"

"I dropped them."

"No you didn't. They were flung, and with some force." She teased at the lid with her toe. "See? That corner's bashed in. Did that Brenda character do that too?"

I stood silent. Staring.

"Don't just stand there then. Pick them up. It will give me pleasure to throw them in that Merry woman's face."

I didn't move. I was aware of her eyes searching my face.

"You haven't told me everything, have you?"

I shook my head.

"Right! Back up the stair. I want to know what you're hiding from me."

Once back in the flat, I told her, never once looking at her, knowing already her expression.

"You filthy little bitch. After all I've told you; after all the warnings you got." She grabbed my arm and pulled me to her. I could feel the warmth of her breath, the faintly sour smell of it. "I'm glad your father's not here. He just might kill you and that might not be such a bad thing." She shook her fist in my face. I tried to shrink back but her grip was too tight.

She gave me a look of complete disgust and her arm fell to her side. "I'd like to kill you myself but you're not worth swinging for. No one will ever accuse me of ill-using you. No one will ever get the Cruelty to me, for I'll never hit you hard enough to leave a mark, so don't worry that I'll strike you, you stinking little coward." She flung me from her so that I staggered and nearly fell. "Now get to your room and stay there till I tell you that you can come out."

Glad to escape, I had my hand on the handle of the door when she called me back. "Just a minute. What did this man look like?"

"He was ugly and he had red hair."

"Judas Iscariot had red hair."

Chapter 18 : Suicide

It was the following afternoon before my mother allowed me to leave my room, and almost as soon as I was out of it, I wished I were back in. She never stopped watching me. Wherever I moved, her eyes followed. She didn't speak to me at all. I wondered what excuse the school would be given for my absence. Tibby seemed to sense I was in trouble and wisely disassociated herself from me. I was glad when Auntie Con arrived, all apologies for being out the previous afternoon. She hadn't realised it was Sunday or she'd have stayed home for my coming.

"Where were you anyway?" asked my Mam.

"Wandering. Looking at nothing... listening to silence."

"Are you all right?"

"A lot better after a few hours away."

Mam laughed. "You'll be telling me next you have a hard life."

"I have a hard life."

"Oh come off it. You know you have a good life, Con, just yourself and mother to do for."

"I know, I know. It's just my nerves. They haven't been too good lately. I've been jumpy."

"Have you seen a doctor?"

"It's not a doctor I need, it's a break."

My mother was silent, one eyebrow lifted, waiting. Auntie Con's face got very pink. "Could you and Stella come, for a weekend just, to let me away?"

My mother didn't answer immediately. She studied Auntie Con, a smile on her face. "I don't sleep well in a strange bed."

For just a second Auntie Con looked at my mother as my mother sometimes looked at me. "I didn't know you had that difficulty."

My mother didn't say anything; just looked at her with the same smile on her face, the eyebrow raised again. Auntie Con swallowed, her face pinker than ever. "I'm sorry Rachel - that just slipped out."

"You should be more careful - especially when you're asking favours."

"I'm sorry. Truly I am. It won't be a strange bed. You'd get your old bed to sleep in."

"Thanks, but no thanks."

Auntie Con still had hope. "You could have mother here then."

"No, my hands are full." My mother's look at me was malicious. Without her eyes leaving my face, she leaned towards my Aunt and said quietly, "Do you know what happened to her this weekend?"

I didn't wait to hear what she said. I ran to my room and closed the door. I leaned against it as though to bar it against her words.

It seemed a long time till she called, "Come out of there and don't sulk. Your Auntie's leaving."

Just before I stepped back into the kitchen I heard Auntie Con say, "I still think you should tell the police."

"It's too late now. It was too late when she told me. I had to winkle the truth out of her and he'd be well away then. Besides, he didn't force her into the stair, she..."

Auntie Con saw me and held a finger to her lips, "Sshh." Then she said to me brightly, "Well, Stella, I really came by today to tell you I missed not seeing you yesterday. When you come next Sunday I'll have something special for your lunch."

Mam looked at me as she asked Auntie Con, "Do you think she's to be trusted out on her own again?"

Auntie Con put an arm round my shoulders and squeezed me. I could smell Devon violets.

My mother persisted, "Do you think she's trustworthy?"

"Of course she is, and I think she should chum me to the tram <u>and</u> go to the school tomorrow."

"We'll see about that, but if she'll promise to come right back without speaking to a soul, she can walk to the stop with you.'

"Oh good! Go and get your coat on, pet." As I went to the lobby I heard Auntie Con say to my mother, "My God Rachel, you're cruel." And my mother's reply, "Don't get high and mighty with me. I didn't need the shock I got yesterday. I hope it didn't do damage. Besides," she laughed, "cruelty runs in the family. Hadn't you noticed?"

As we walked to the tram, Auntie Con swung our clasped hands. She asked me questions about the school, and I told her about a boy in our class called Slavery Sandy.

"What a name!" she said. "Why is he called that?"

"Because he slavers."

"It's not very kind to call him that then is it?"

I shook my head, ashamed that I joined in with the others who shouted it at him. Till now, I had felt only gladness that it wasn't I who was being picked on. I must have been silent long time for she said, "I didn't mean to hurt your feelings."

I wondered how often I had hurt Sandy's. Maybe Mam was right. Maybe cruelty did run in our family. Auntie Con had called my mother cruel. My Auntie Mary had called her that too, once. I didn't want to be cruel. When I went back to the school, I'd stick up for him. I'd give him a sweetie every time I had some.

"Penny for your thoughts," said Auntie Con, squeezing my hand. I shook my head and she said, "Oh well, here's a penny anyway."

The tram came, she kissed me, and was gone. I waved her out of sight and wished I were with her. I wished I were going anywhere but home. I was feart my mother would talk to me again about the man. I was feart she wouldn't talk to me at all, for sometimes that was worse. Then I'd have to guess what she was feeling, thinking. I'd have to be careful. I'd have to guess right.

She had called me a filthy little bitch because I went with the man, but I didn't go far. Just into a stair. I had lost my Jesus pictures and the nice box I carried them in; I had even lost the chance of earning a shilling from Granny. I had been shut in my room with nothing to eat, though that was all right for I wasn't hungry anyway. I hoped Mam felt I had been punished enough for disobeying her. I hoped she wouldn't have to punish me more.

I was worried about Sandy too. Worried that I had hurt his feelings as mine got hurt sometimes. Worried that I wouldn't stick up for him when he got called Slavery Sandy; worried that I wouldn't have the courage to go against the crowd. My Mam said I was off a long line of feardies, and my Mam was usually right. Suddenly I hated Sandy because I knew I wouldn't have the courage to be brave.

And all the time that I was thinking, worrying, I was stepping carefully over the cracks between the paving stones. "Step on a crack, break your mother's back," I chanted.

Now, before I could stop myself, I stomped on a crack. Hard. Water splattered my coat. I stomped again and water came through the hole in my shoe. I couldn't stop. I stomped again, again, again. I hoped I'd get my death of cold so I'd never have to go back to that Sunday school, never have to think about the man, never have to worry about Sandy, never have to be feart of my mother, never have to feel guilty about stepping on a crack, breaking her back. Never. Never. Never.

My heart began to beat very fast and I started to run in the opposite direction from home. I wouldn't stop till I reached Granton. I'd jump off the breakwater there. I'd get drowned.

I knew someone who did that. He had been one of Granny's boarders. When another boarder died and left all his money to her, she emptied the rest out. The man who drowned himself had no place else to go, and he had lost his job, and had no money either. I had heard my Mam and my Da talking about it.

"Your old lady's a monster," said Da. "Fancy having to end your days in a model lodging house, and after a lifetime's work too."

"He should have been more careful of his money while he was earning it," said Mam "and look at it from her point of view. She had worked hard and she was entitled to have her house to herself again."

"To herself and that half-daft daughter of hers, the bloody old hypocrite."

"And you're your mother's simple son," my Mam shouted.

"Shut your damned mouth," my Da shouted back, and they were off.

Mam said the man was a weak character anyway to have taken his own life, and God would punish him for it, and my Da said he wished my mother, and my Granny with her, would jump off the breakwater too.

Because the man had no people of his own, my Uncle Jim had to identify the body but he wouldn't tell me what it looked like. When my Mam identified me she'd be sorry I was dead and not just because my clothes would be in a worse mess than they were in now. She wouldn't care about that; she'd just want me back. She would sob and wring her hands and wish I were alive again. When she was just about to end her grief by jumping off the breakwater too, I'd wake up from being dead and catch her just in time. She'd be so glad to see me alive that she'd throw her arms around me and she'd never get angry with me again, never shout at me and call me names, never leave me alone in the dark ever again.

But my Mam had said God would punish the man for taking his own life. I wondered about God. He didn't sound very nice. I hoped my Mam was wrong. I hoped God had felt sorry for him, that he hadn't been punished. I wondered if it hurt to drown. I tried holding my breath to see what it felt like not to get any air, but I couldn't hold it long enough to find out. But if you were in the water and sinking you wouldn't be able to change your mind and take in deep lungfuls of air as I was doing now. You might get feart. I hope the man didn't get feart.

Mam had said something else. She said he was a weak character to take his life. She would think I was a weak character too to take mine. She would say I took after my father's side, that I wasn't strong like her and Granny. And she'd punish me for that...

"Hello hen[38]." I looked up, startled, and saw one of the friendly ladies smiling at me. "Dreamy Daniel, you've been standing there for ages and it's time you were away home. Your Mammy will be worried about ye."

I smiled back and hoped my Mam wouldn't find out that I had smiled at a friendly lady. I had lost track of time and the streetlights were on and there were other friendly ladies under them. Two were smoking and a third was all twisted round trying to see if her seams were straight.

I ran home to the row I knew awaited me, but I was wrong for Mam smiled at me and said she was glad I was home, and would I like toasted cheese for my tea? I nearly didn't enjoy it for thinking about how I had jumped on a crack to break her back.

---

[38] Girl

Stella Maris   by   Nan O'Dell

Then I remembered that was what we said in the old neighbourhood. In this new one the children said, "Step on a crack, kiss a black." So that was all right then.

Chapter 19 : Paradise Lost

Samples of Heaven were handed out on our street every Saturday night. Rain, snow, or shine, the minute the cart carrying the old pedal organ creaked to a stop, children poured out of stairs and closes, jostling to get into the circle of light under the street lamp. Those who got there first handed out the pictures of Jesus. The workers from the Mission led us into the paths of righteousness and we followed joyously. Oh, the glories and the crowns that were promised if we stayed in them! We thought those meetings were for our benefit but I know now that a wider net was cast and the souls fished for belonged to the oblivious drunks who sagged against adjacent walls. "Jesus loves even me," we sang, while the organ, wheezing, struggled to keep up with us. On cold nights our breaths were spirits ascending to Heaven. The evening always ended with a sweetie and a prayer and we'd go home with sweetness in our mouths and in our souls.

It was a Saturday and wet, I remember when a friend of my mother dropped in with Margaret, her whiny little girl. I was sent for teabread and halfway down the stair my mother stopped me. "You keep that brat entertained and out of my hair."

"I'll take her to the meeting with me," I said. She gave me a little push, "Mind then." But Margaret didn't want to go. "It's raining."

Her mother shook her; "A puckle[39] water never hurt anybody."

While the battle raged my mother sat silent, glaring at me. "They'll give you sweeties," I coaxed.

---

[39] Bit of

"I don't want no sweeties," Margaret whined.

Desperate, I remembered, "One night they ran out of sweeties and I got a penny instead."

That got her to the meeting but when she was given a caramel she pointed at me and howled, "She said we should come here for we might get money."

The Mission lady looked at me sorrowfully, "You are not a nice girl to say that. Jesus doesn't like people coming here for money."

I must have slipped and fallen on the wet cobbles as I ran home for when my mother saw me she shouted, "You bad bad girl, you've torn your stockings."

I was glad of the sting of her hand on my cheek. Glad too, of the pain as I picked the torn stocking out of the raw sore on my knee. Those hurts would heal, and for a little while they took my mind off the other. In time that one eased too but I never went back to the meetings under the street lamp. Shame barred me from them as effectively as an angel with a flaming sword.

It was immediately following that incident that I developed one of the mysterious illnesses that plagued me through my growing years and left me so weak I could scarcely walk. To pass the time my mother let me look in the big book of pictures and she told me who the people were. She showed me my brother who died because I kissed him. "You had whooping cough and you wouldn't take a telling and stay away from him. I'd catch you bending over his cot, kissing him, calling him Wee Tottie." Then Mam started to cry, "Poor Wee Tottie. I didn't hold it against you for you were only three, but your Da took it hard. He wanted a son so badly."

116

Stella Maris　　　　　by　　　　　　Nan O'Dell

Chapter 20 : Granny Malcolm

By the time I was better, my Da was home again from the sea and he said he was taking me to my Granny Malcolm in Dumfries. I had never met my Granny Malcolm because she didn't like my Mam so my Mam didn't like her. "The old witch didn't want your Da to marry me. Huh! As though I were getting a prize."

The night that Da said I was going to Dumfries he and my Mam had a big fight and Mam shouted what was wrong with her mother and my Da shouted back, "It would take too long to tell you." But Da won, for he wrote to Granny Malcolm the next day. Then they didn't speak till Granny wrote back and then they started to fight again. I couldn't sleep for the noise but that was all right for Mam said that too much sleep was bad for children anyway. But I was feart when there was a big crash and my mother screamed, "For God's sake...the baby." My Da sounded feart as well when he shouted, "You goaded me you bitch, and nothing must happen to this one."

So then I knew my Da was taking me away so my next wee brother wouldn't die.

I liked the bus to Dumfries and looking out the window but my Da didn't for he wouldn't look when I pointed to some wee sheep with their Mams. Sometimes I saw myself reflected in the window and my good dress looked nice. It had pink stripes and my cousin wore it only three times before it got too small for her.

Granny Malcolm had our tea ready when we got to her house and we were hungry for Da said we had walked nearly a mile from the bus stop. When my Granny saw my Da she kissed him and said, "Son." Then

118

she shook hands with me. "So this big girl is Stella and my, she's like her mother." She didn't sound pleased and neither did Da when he said, "She is that."

For our tea we had trifle, two kinds, and cake and scones and jam. My Mam said Granny's guts were her god and that's why she was so fat, but I thought she looked nice and soft. Not like my other Granny who was hard and flat.

When I had finished my tea, Granny sent me out to the yard to look for eggs and I found three in a bed of nettles. The nettles stung but I didn't mind for she rubbed my arm with a docken leaf and said I could have one of the eggs for my breakfast.

Then it was time for Da to go back to Edinburgh and he kissed my Granny and she said, "Son," again. He patted my shoulder, "You be a good girl to your Granny."

I watched him till he was out of sight but he didn't look back and I started to miss my home. When Granny touched me, I jumped. "I'm late for the hens," she said. "Come and help me feed them."

I liked the smell of their food and how she clucked at them. I tried to cluck too but I wasn't good like Granny. When the food was gone she said I should get ready for bed. I was surprised and said it wasn't even night. "It's bedtime here," she said, "and don't you argue with me."

I didn't want to take off my clothes in front of her, but she stood and watched and tutted. "You're not sleeping with me till you've had a bath." She held up my vest and I saw her eye through the hole in the front where I had scratched too hard once. "The trollop should think black burning shame," she muttered, but I heard and I knew who she meant. "My Mam's

119

been sick," I said, "so I washed myself but the water was cold and I only did my face."

"Oh?" said Granny scrubbing me hard.

"Yes. And the doctor says she's not to sew or she might die."

"Huh." She threw the sponge into the tub with such force that water splashed all over her and the floor. "Did he say what's wrong with her?"

I searched my mind for something I had heard my mother complain about. "He says she has heartburn."

The scrubbing stopped and when it started again it wasn't hard like before, but Granny did take rub-it-off to my heels. While I dried myself she examined my nightgown. "It's clean enough but I'll bleach it white tomorrow. Now hurry and don't get the cold."

I wished she wouldn't talk like I was dirty and my Mam was a trollop. I wished I were home. "Granny, I want home."

She looked at me for a long time and then she said, "Wait till tomorrow. I have your supper ready, and anyway, the last bus has gone."

"I'll go tomorrow then. Is it more trifle?"

"Oh dear me no, not at bedtime, but I've put a bit by for you for tomorrow." Then she brought me some grapes and a pear on a saucer and said I could eat them in bed. "But first you must say your prayers."

I looked at the grapes and wished I could have one now. "You say your prayers at home, don't you?"

I nodded, "And so does my Mam."

Granny sniffed. "She has much need."

I pushed the saucer away. "I don't want those grapes or that pear either and I'm not saying any prayers."

I waited for her to hit me but she gave a quick little sigh, "Oh well...into bed. You sleep over against the wall and I'll sleep on the outside."

I was glad of that for there was a window at my side. When Granny left the room I lifted the curtain and watched the sky darken. In our street, lights would be coming on and people walking up and down. I wondered how high I could count before the bus for home left the next day. One, two, three, four...

I woke up when Granny came to bed and in the light from the lamp she held I saw her hair, long and grey, hanging about her face. I was feart she was a witch like Mam said but when I asked her she replied, "Whatever gave you that daft-like idea?" and blew out the lamp.

When she got into bed my side rose up in the air and I grabbed the edge of the windowsill to keep from rolling against her. She sighed and then she lay still. She didn't say goodnight. I woke up again when she gently lifted away the arm I had flung over her in my sleep. After that I lay awake for a long time, pretending, like her, to be asleep.

Granny was up first the next day, and shivering in the morning chill, I searched the house for her. There was a fire in the kitchen grate but she wasn't there and my clothes were gone. The only room left to try was at the front of the house and there was no life there but the Honesty in a vase on the piano. I touched one of the keys and a tinny twang shuddered through the silence.

I noticed a picture of my Da on the piano beside the vase of Honesty. It was the same as one we had at home, yet different. Then I realised that the half showing my mother had been cut off. Suddenly I knew that I was the only person left in the whole world except for the chickens I could hear squawking outside. "Mam," I shrieked again and again and behind me Granny said, "Mercy me, you're making enough noise to fricht[40] the French. I was in the wash-house with the clothes when I heard you." She put an arm round my shoulders. "Now come through beside the fire and get your breakfast. There's a good breeze this morning and your things will dry in no time."

While I ate my egg she had a cup of tea. "When you're dressed," she said, "we'll do what has to be done here and we'll away into Dumfries to the pictures. Then we'll have our tea in the town and be back to see to things before bedtime."

"But Granny, I'm going home today."

"Oh right enough. I forgot that."

While she went to get my clothes off the line I thought about it. I could see her through the window and she didn't look like a witch this morning with her mouth full of pegs and her cheeks pink from battling the wind for the clothes. "Granny," I said when she came in, "is there a bus tomorrow?"

"There's a bus every day."

"Well maybe I'll wait."

---

[40] Frighten

So began a time that was summed up in the hymn we sang in Granny's church on Sundays.

"Summer suns are glowing over land and sea, Happy light is flowing, bountiful and free, All the earth rejoices..."

And it seemed to me that Granny and I did rejoice that summer. She didn't remove my arm now when I flung it over her in my sleep. She let me take care of the hens all by myself and I learned to cluck even better than she did. On Sundays I cut the journey from church in half by running across the fields so I could be home to greet Granny and her friends who had walked sedately round by the road. I can see them yet, those ladies with beehive hats, corset-stiff from bum to bust, sipping tea and dissecting the minister's sermon. The last drop drunk, the last crumb consumed, and, "Play for us Mrs. Malcolm." A nod from Granny, "Only if you sing." Genteel hand clapping all round while I lift the vase of Honesty lest vibrations topple it. Granny's solo piece first, and we go from a Persian Market to a Monastery Garden, with everyone joining in for, "Oh Lord hear our prayer, Take away all our care, And fill our hearts with love."

"God is Love", said the text above Granny's mantel and this was news to me for He had always been my mother's vengeful ally. And the love of the God the preacher shouted about at the Saturday night meetings was conditional. That One couldn't love me either because, though I tried not to, I still thought bad things about my Mam and my Da. I soaked up this concept learned at Granny's as a parched earth soaks up rain.

It was during one of those Sunday gatherings that someone asked me about my brother who had been born that summer.

"And are you happy to have a new brother, Stella?"

I nodded, but I didn't say it was because my Da wouldn't want me to come home now and I'd get to stay with Granny Malcolm forever.

Then Granny was asked when I'd be going home. "The school starts in September," she said.

"You'll fairly miss her Mrs. Malcolm."

"I will that," said Granny.

"She doesn't take after the Malcolms, does she?" asked someone else.

Granny hesitated. "No, she takes after her mother's side."

This talk of who I took after triggered the memory of my mother getting me out of bed one night to come and hear my Da say I wasn't his. "But you are his," Mam shouted as she dragged me up to him. "Look," she said, "look her in the face and tell her she's not yours."

My Da looked at his feet instead, "There was someone else," he mumbled.

Now I was feart my Granny would say I wasn't hers either. I didn't want to hear that so I ran and locked myself in the washhouse. I had stopped thinking about that night and I had stopped thinking about home too. Now when I got a letter from there I didn't open the envelope unless I felt a sixpence inside. I knew without looking that it would say my Mam was missing her dear wee lassie and was she remembering to say her prayers every night, and hurry back to her loving mother, and lots of kisses darling. Sometimes I felt sick till the torn up letter was buried. Once I even buried the money too in case God punished me for liking sixpence better than my Mam's letters.

124

The first time I got one of those letters I couldn't believe it was from her for I had never heard her talk like that. Now I realise that, like the preacher at the meetings, she was aiming at a wider audience.

Granny was pounding on the door, "Stella, are you in there?" I didn't answer and the door rattled, "I think you are in there. Answer me Stella...are you all right?"

"I can't come out till everyone's away."

"Well they'll be gone in a minute."

"Now," said Granny when I opened the door, "What got into you to make you suddenly run like that?"

"I felt sick."

"You looked more feart than sick."

I shook my head. "I felt sick...Granny, can I stay with you always? Please Granny, please."

She looked startled. "But what about your Mam and da? They'd miss you and now you have a wee brother as well."

"But you told those people you'd miss me." I was half crying.

"And indeed I shall," said Granny, "but you only came to me to get over your illness and be ready for the school when it starts."

"Please Granny, let me go to the school here."

She put an arm round me. "Come and get ready for your bed and we'll talk about it tomorrow."

But that night Granny woke up gasping for air and I thought she'd never be able to talk to me again. When she jumped out of bed I followed her in a panic. Her chest whistled as she tried to reassure me, "Asthma. It will pass."

She filled the kettle and put it on what remained of the fire. As it boiled she gulped in the steam and when she could speak, she told me to make us tea and not burn myself. "Oh dear, what a fright I gave you, but I'm all right now and you're not to worry." Her cup rattled in its saucer and so did mine.

The next day she was tired and short of breath but she told me asthma was just a nuisance that looked worse than it really was. I made her Cornflakes and tea and while she ate them I read her a story from the "People's Friend." "My, I did enjoy that," said Granny. "You're a rare wee help to me."

That was the first of many attacks I witnessed, but I learned to nudge her awake when I heard the short little coughs that preceded one. Granny couldn't send me home now for I knew she needed me. I gathered the eggs, ("I'm not so able to bend any more."); ran the messages[41], ("The road to the shop gets longer every time."), and now I took care of her when she had asthma. I wondered when she would tell me I could stay forever.

Sometimes I'd catch her watching me like she was sad but maybe that was because my Mam must have kissed my new brother and given him her heartburn for he had died already. There was no reason now for my Da to want me away, but he'd be going back to sea and my Mam

---

[41] Errands

wouldn't mind if I stayed here. She often said she wished she didn't have to look after me so she could be free and enjoy her life.

Then one day the postman brought Granny a letter from my Da. He was coming for me before he went back to his ship. The next day, in fact.

I went mad. "No, Granny, no," I shrieked, clinging to her.

"You'll come back next summer so you will." She was crying. "Be a big girl now. Look how you're upsetting your Granny." But I couldn't stop the shrieks from coming. Finally she shook me by the shoulders. "Now," she said firmly, "we'll have no more of this nonsense."

I knew then that nothing would stop her from sending me home. "You're not my real Granny anyway," I shouted.

"What a terrible thing to say!"

"It's true. There was someone else."

Granny let go of me and her face was white. "Who told you that?"

"My Da did."

That night I heard Granny's cough starting and then after a while she jumped out of bed and ran towards the kitchen. I could hear her struggles for breath clear ben[42] the house but I turned my face to the wall.

When my Da came, my case was all packed. He was wearing a black band round his arm and when Granny saw him she kissed him and said, "Son."

---

[42] Through

"Are you ready to go then?" he asked me.

"You'll get your tea first," Granny told him.

"I don't want any tea," I said and ran out to the yard. My Da called after me, "Don't you go away, we're leaving soon."

I went to the places where the hens usually laid and I broke three eggs before I ran to the clump of nettles where I had found some that first day. Gritting my teeth, I plunged one arm into them and then the other. I welcomed their sting as I had welcomed the sting of my mother's slap after I tore my stocking running from the meeting.

About to enter the house, I stopped when I heard my Granny say, "I've enjoyed having the child here, she was no trouble. But God forgive me, I saw Rachel every time I looked at her."

There was a low murmur of voices and then I heard Da ask, "And what do you think made your asthma start up again?"

"I was sore troubled when she asked me if she could stay here. I'll be all right once she's away and it's settled."

Their chairs scraped the floor and I knew they were getting up.

"One minute son, before you call her there's something I must know."

"What's that?" My Da sounded feart.

"Did you ever tell her she wasn't a Malcolm...that there was someone else?"

"Did she say that?"

128

"Aye, she did, and before you leave this house I must know if it's true."

"That one looks like her mother and lies like her mother," said my Da.

"You've set my mind at rest then," said Granny.

I felt nothing when we said goodbye. It was like the time the dentist pulled a tooth and I couldn't feel it coming out. Granny hugged me, "Come back next year Stella. You've been a good girl to your Granny."

I walked away when she hugged my Da. All the way up the road I could hear her calling, "Next year Stella, come back next year." But I didn't look back. My eyes were fixed on the road ahead.

Chapter 21 : Auntie Con Rebels

Back in Edinburgh, it was Auntie Con who took me to buy new shoes for the school. They were a gift from her and Granny Morrison and I was to go home with Auntie Con afterwards for my tea.

On the way to Granny's on the tram, Auntie Con said, "Your Mam's not all that well yet, so you mustn't mind if she's short with you at times."

I wasn't sure what Auntie Con was on about, for my mother had hardly spoken to me at all since I came home. She didn't seem to know I was there. She stared out the window all day, not speaking, seldom moving.

"I wish she would talk to me."

"She will. It will all come right in time, you'll see."

"Was my brother nice?"

"He was a beautiful baby."

"How did he die, did someone kiss him?"

"Lots of people kissed him, I'm sure, but kissing didn't kill him. He just died • No one knows why. Your Mam went to his cot when he slept through his feeding time and he was dead."

"Did Jesus come and get him?"

"I think that was it...Yes, I'm sure that was it."

"Did he have a funeral?"

"Yes. Yes he did."

"Did you go?"

"No. Your Da went and I stayed with your Mam. "

"Did she not want to see him going in a hole?"

"It wasn't your brother that went in a hole. It was just his body. His soul had gone with Jesus to live with the angels."

"Well why didn't my Mam want to go to his funeral?"

"She couldn't go because she was feeling too sad."

"Would she feel sad like that if I died?"

Auntie Con looked startled. "What a question! Of course she would feel sad."

I doubted it, for my Mam told me once that she wished she had never met my Da and been burdened with me.

"And was Tibby glad to see you home?" Auntie Con asked brightly.

I shook my head. "Not at first. She wouldn't look at me and when I spoke to her she turned her back to me. But then she had a daft turn and tore round the house and kept jumping on and off my knee." I didn't tell her that Tibby, that night for the first time, had come willingly under the covers with me, and had gone to sleep with her face cupped in my hand. I wanted to tell my Auntie but she might tell my mother and Tib and I would be in bother.

We didn't talk any more after that for Auntie Con said that between the warm day and the motion of the tram, she was sleepy. But I think she just didn't want to talk about my Mam or my brother any more.

131

Granny Morrison was waiting for us when we got to the house. "My goodness, what a lot you've grown." She clasped me to her and I was surprised to feel how hard she was after my other Granny. Then she turned to my Auntie Con, "What a time you've been. I was fair worried about you."

I saw Auntie Con's face through the mirror on the coat-stand. She was taking off her hat and she didn't look pleased that Granny had been worried about her. I wondered why she should mind.

"I can't see why you were worried... You know how long it takes to fit shoes." Auntie Con rammed her hatpin into the cushion as though she were stabbing someone. "Come on pet," she said to me, "come and help me in the kitchen."

"I'm wanting to hear about her holiday," said Granny holding open the sitting room door and motioning me through.

"You can hear about it in the kitchen while we get the tea ready," said Auntie Con.

I stood in the hallway, wondering which way to turn. Granny was still holding open the door to the sitting room, and Auntie Con, the one to the kitchen. "I have to go to the bathroom," I said, and started upstairs.

I stayed there as long as I could, and when I came back down Auntie Con handed me a stack of plates and saucers, "Set these out in the dining room," she said.

I was surprised at that, for after Granny got rid of her boarders the dining room was never used. It was a cold room. The sun seldom reached it. Auntie Con opened a window. "The air outside is warmer than it is in

132

here, and a lot fresher too. "Let's shift this monstrosity so we can put down the cloth." She lifted the big epergne from the centre of the table and placed it on the sideboard.

"You're setting the table in here!" said Granny from the doorway. "That's a funny thing to do is it not?"

"What's funny about it?" Auntie Con gave the tablecloth a vigorous shake. "We couldn't agree on where we should be so this is the solution."

Granny shook her head. "What gets in to you at times? It's beyond me, and it's too cold in here anyway."

"I could set the fire in here in a minute," Auntie Con spoke briskly as she gave the cloth another shake.

"That would be pure waste when there's a good fire roaring in the kitchen range, and one in my room forbye[43]."

"It's a bigger waste to have a room we never use."

"So that's your trouble is it! You're on about those new bungalows on the West Side. Pasteboard boxes more like."

"No mother, I'm not on about the bungalows. I've given that up. They're too labour saving for your liking. I've accepted it that we'll be here till Gabriel blows his horn."

"There's no need to be irreverent. You ken[44] fine that they're predicting a big jump in value for these houses within the next decade, so why should we sell now?"

133

"Because now is all we have; because I'm getting old and you're getting older. We might not be here in ten years."

"That's no way to talk in front of the child."

"I'm sorry pet."

Granny was right, about one thing anyway, it <u>was</u> cold in the dining room. I saw goose bumps on Auntie Con's arms, but she sat through the meal with her mouth twisted in a funny little smile. She pushed the food on her plate with her fork, but I didn't see her put any in her mouth.

"You're playing with that instead of eating it, and you'll be stuffing your face with cream biscuits tonight," said Granny, but Auntie Con didn't let on she had heard.

I wished they wouldn't argue. I wished I were back at Granny Malcolm's. I felt my mouth twisting up like Auntie Con's from trying not to cry, and I realised she hadn't been smiling at all. I kept my eyes down and tried to think of my new shoes and how Granny and Auntie Con had bought them for me. I thought of Tibby's soft fur and how she purred when I stroked her. She would have missed me if my Granny Malcolm had let me stay with her in Dumfries. When I lifted my eyes, I saw Auntie Con watching me.

"Away you go with Granny and get warm at her fire. I'll bring your cake through to you. Then after I've cleared up in the kitchen I'll take you home."

---

[43] As well

[44] Know

When we were alone, Granny quizzed me carefully lest I should have picked up any false doctrines from my Granny Malcolm. She seemed reassured when I told her I had gone to the kirk with Granny every Sunday, and it was the Church of Scotland. That settled to her satisfaction, Granny Morrison asked, "Your mother would be glad to see you home was she not?"

"She didn't say."

"Well I wouldn't worry about that. Some mothers find it hard to speak their hearts so you're not to take it that she's not pleased just because she doesn't say anything. Always remember that your mother loves you dearly."

I looked at my feet. Granny had asked me to put on the new shoes so she could see that they fitted all right.

"They're bonny shoes right enough; may they aye[45] walk in paths of righteousness."

"Granny, can I go and help Auntie Con with the dishes?"

"Aye, away ye go then."

I could hear a man singing on Auntie Con's wireless, "Somewhere the sun is shining, so honey don't you cry, we'll find a silver lining, the clouds will soon roll by."

---

[45] Always

I pushed open the kitchen door but she didn't hear me and her back was to me. She was gazing out the window and rubbing endlessly at the same plate.

"Auntie Con." I touched her and before she turned round, she rubbed her eyes with the back of her wrist.

"My goodness, you startled me. Here's the cloth - you can wipe for me."

When we had finished the dishes and were drying our hands, she said, "It's nice to have you back helping me Stella, and you're not to think that because your Mam doesn't say much she isn't pleased as well. Some people have trouble saying what they feel. Especially if it's something nice."

Chapter 22 : Who is Joseph Morrison?

I was jealous of my dead brothers. My Mam always said, "They were so good... so good," and when she got to the bit about them being safe in the arms of Jesus, she'd start to cry.

If I were safe in the arms of Jesus would she cry about me? Maybe my Mam only liked dead people. Maybe if my brothers weren't dead she wouldn't like them either. Maybe it wasn't because I was bad that she got angry with me. Maybe it was because I was alive.

My Mam said that the worst part about losing wee Hughie was not knowing what made him die. "It was your whooping cough that did for Archie but Hughie hadn't been sick. No mark on him. Nothing."

I hoped she would never find out that because of something I did at my Granny Malcolm's I was to blame for Wee Hughie dying.

Granny Malcolm always sent me for the messages[46], one mile to the shops and one mile back, but I liked to go for the road was lined with hawthorn and wild roses. One day I picked some and took them home. Granny liked the roses but she wouldn't let the hawthorn in the house. "It's bad luck," she said, and we don't want anyone dying, so run round the back and put them in the bin. And come right in again for you've been away such a time that I've got the baking done and there's a bowl for you to lick."

---

[46] Errands, shopping

This done, she sent me back out with a pan of eggshells and potato peelings. The hawthorn had been in the bin only a few minutes, but already wilting from the walk home, they now bore no resemblance to the flowers I had picked. I lifted them out before I dumped in the rubbish. Then I found a better resting place for them under the lilac bush a good distance from the house.

"I'm sorry for picking you..."

"Stella," Granny called, "it's time to feed the hens."

"...and I'm sorry you've got a bad name..."

"Yoo-hoo Stella."

"...and I think you're too nice to make people die and I'll prove it, see?"

Before I turned and ran to Granny I tore off a sprig and stuffed it in my pocket. She probably flung it out the next washing day without recognising it, for she said nothing to me. I thought no more about it and when news came of my brother's death my father was on its heels to take me back to Edinburgh. It was only when I heard of Hughie's dying so mysteriously that I remembered. I remembered too what Granny had said as she dabbed stuff on the scratches I got from the roses. "There's a price to pay for everything." Did Hughie pay the price of my taking hawthorn into the house?

Mam didn't go out and leave me anymore. She didn't go out at all. When I came home from the school, she'd be sitting at the window where I had left her hours before. She would look at me when I came in, but I couldn't tell if she was pleased to see me or not for she seldom spoke. Sometimes she'd fix me something to eat, but I never saw her eat anything.

Because my father was away at sea most of the time, and my mother had always met her friends outside, we rarely had visitors to the house. Auntie Con came whenever she could manage it, but Granny was going through a bad spell with her heart and needed my Auntie close by, "In case the worst happens," Granny said.

I wondered why she should call dying the worst that could happen, when she was always saying that the world was corrupt and a better life awaited in the sweet by and by. She rarely had visitors either though she had two married sons and several grandchildren in Edinburgh and a married son in Glasgow. In the old days when Mam dropped me off at Granny's for Auntie Con to mind, Mam would always try to skip out before Granny caught her and started lecturing. So apart from Auntie Con I probably saw Granny oftener than anybody did. Talking to her was always hard for she only wanted to hear about the Sunday school and what I had learned there the Sunday before. Since I never went any more it saved a lot of bother just to make something up. She wouldn't have been pleased to know I had got into a big fight, been told off, and never wanted to go back again.

Now, with my mother so quiet and still, I welcomed invitations from Auntie Con, asking me to come for my tea straight from the school and she'd put me on the tram for home afterwards.

It was on one of those visits that I discovered that the gold turnip watch, which lay on Granny's night table between her bible and the container for her teeth, had belonged to my grandfather.

I had always wanted to hold the watch; to feel its smoothness and the whirring of its insides before it chimed the hour and the half-hour, but Granny wouldn't let me touch it.

She seemed tireder than ever that day. Without opening her eyes, she asked me what I had learned at the Sunday school the day before. I closed my eyes too, for I found it easier to make up stories if I couldn't see the person I was telling them to. With my fingers crossed behind my back I said, "I learned that Jesus loves me and a liar is an abomination unto our Father which art in heaven."

"Amen," said Granny, "and what's the text you're to learn for next week?"

My mind went blank and then there flashed into it something that had happened to me once when barefoot; I had been guddling[47] for minnows in the Water of Leith. Ada Bruce and Thelma King were sitting under a tree and giggling over bits they were reading to each other from the bible. When I asked them what they were laughing at, they went into shrieks. Now I told Granny what they had told me. "How beautiful are thy feet with shoes, o prince's daughter..."

"That's enough," said Granny sharply, which was just as well for I didn't know what came next.

"Here, hand me that bible off the table," she said. "Let me see how well you can read." She flicked through the pages till she found what she wanted. "Start there."

---

[47] Catching fish with the hands

I read, "Hear o heavens, and give ear, o earth; for the Lord hath spoken, I have nourished and brought up children, and they have rebelled against me."

Granny heaved a big sigh and I stopped and looked at her. She was nodding as though in agreement with Isaiah. "Carry on then," she said impatiently.

It was a long chapter and I wasn't that fast a reader. Before I reached verse twenty I was yawning and Granny looked like she was away. There was no telling - maybe she was in one of the light dozes that so annoyed Auntie Con who maintained, "She's supposed to he asleep, but she hears better with her eyes closed."

"Granny?" I said quietly but she didn't let on. I moved closer to the table where the watch lay. There were eleven verses to go. I read another two and Granny was expelling little puffs of air between her slackened lips as she breathed deeply and regularly. Another step and I'd be close enough to touch the watch. "Thy princes are re-bel-i-ous, and-com-pan-ions of thieves; every one loveth gifts..."

If I stopped reading the silence might wake her up, yet I couldn't hold the bible and the watch at the same time.

I remembered the "Child's Garden of Verses" I had when I was wee, and slowly I slid the opened bible on to the table. "A child should always say what's true, and speak when he is spoken to." The watch was silk beneath my fingers. I lifted it and weighed it in my palm. Now I knew what 'worth its weight in gold' meant. I held it against my cheek and touched it with my tongue. And what 'good as gold' meant too!

"And behave mannerly at table; at least as far as he is able." I rubbed my thumb across the smooth surface and in so doing I must have touched a hidden spring, for a thin lid flew open to reveal a name engraved inside. 'Joseph Morrison'. Startled, I quickly pressed it shut again and put the watch back on the table, all the while keeping an eye on Granny. "The world is so full of a number of things, I'm sure we should all be as happy as kings."

She stirred and I snatched up the bible and tried to find my place.

"Kings?" she said. "There's nothing about Kings in the second chapter of Isaiah!"

The watch chimed four silvery notes and I was saved. "Ring the bell for your Auntie Con. She's late again with my tea."

Auntie Con and I had ours in the kitchen while Granny ate hers off a tray in her bedroom. "Anything to create work," Auntie Con muttered as she set out the tray. "How can she have heart trouble when she doesn't have a heart?" She looked at me and smiled, "I'd rather have my tea alone with you anyway."

Granny cared nothing for food, but she still liked to be served the best and it was this that Auntie Con gave me. Real butter, honey from the comb, and oranges. "She'll never miss one," Auntie Con would say, rolling a Jaffa across the table to me.

But they were uncomfortable, those teas, for she ate margarine and runny jam of her own making, while my bread was spread thick with butter and honey. And every time I swallowed a segment of orange I'd picture Granny checking on her fruit and calling my Auntie to account. So, to me, stolen fruits were never sweet. Indeed, Granny's oranges seemed invariably sour.

Sometime during our tea that afternoon I asked Auntie Con who Joseph Morrison was. She looked taken aback. "Who's been telling you about him?"

I tried to look innocent. "No one, but I saw that name somewhere."

She didn't answer and I watched her as she scraped a drip of jam off the tablecloth. It seemed to be taking her whole attention. I smelt a rat.

"Who is Joseph Morrison?" I asked again.

Without looking at me, she said, "Your grandfather."

I digested that with my bread and honey. "Is my grandfather your da?"

Auntie Con nodded, still looking at the tablecloth.

"Granny's MARRIED?" It was incredible to me.

"Of course she's married!"

"Oh." I let that sink in. "Where is he then? Did he die?"

Auntie Con pushed back her chair and started to rise, "He went to live in the city of the saints."

Granny's bell rang just then and my Aunt muttered, "Oh, what next?" As she bustled off she called back over her shoulder, "Finish your tea and don't ask so many questions."

Stella Maris   by   Nan O'Dell

I didn't need to ask any more questions. I could see my grandfather in the City of the Saints where the tall spires were made of shining gold; where some had wings and some had harps. In the midst of the multitude stood my grandfather wearing a long white robe like Granny's starched nightgowns that smelled of camphor.

Chapter 23 : Miss Anderson

The days when my mother didn't speak to me were long. To fill up the silence I talked to her and read her stories and once, when I sang a song she liked, she touched my hand and smiled. My Mam and I were becoming best friends and from that moment when she acknowledged me, I'd have gone to any lengths to please her.

Maybe because she was at the window all day now and could keep an eye on me, she didn't seem to mind my going out to play. I'd tell her, "I won't go away Mam. I'll stay where you can see me and I'll wave to you." And I did. Even if she never waved back, it felt good to see her there. She hadn't said anything about it lately so I knew she had forgiven me for going into a stair with that man.

Then one day, shortly after I got home from the school, the doorbell rang. When I answered it I could hardly see the person behind the big bunch of flowers that was handed to me.

"I'm Miss Anderson and you must be Stella. Your mother told me all about you when we were in the Infirmary together. Is she in?"

I nodded and opened the door wider. "She's in there." I pointed her towards the kitchen.

"I bumped into your sister this morning, Mrs. Malcolm, and since I had to be in this area later today, I brought you these flowers from the garden."

Mam was silent, just looking at Miss Anderson. Finally, Miss Anderson spoke again, "And I wanted to tell you how very sorry I was to hear your sad news."

My Mam actually spoke, "Please sit down," she said and started to cry.

Miss Anderson came often after that, and bit by bit, she drew my mother out of herself. She brought nice things for us too; always flowers and sometimes fruit, and once she brought me a slide for my hair and a hankie with my initial on it.

A long time before, I had heard my Mam and my Auntie Con talking about her. She was in the bed next to my mam's when they were both sick in the hospital. She liked my Mam and had invited her to her house for tea once they were well again. But Mam didn't want to go. She told Auntie Con, "She's too fantoosh[48] for me."

"She seemed a down-to-earth woman to me," said my Auntie. "Not fantoosh at all."

"You know where she lives don't you?"

Auntie Con shook her head and my mother mentioned the neighbourhood where she had worked as a table-maid before she married my father.

"You're not holding that against her surely?"

"No... but when people are sick they sometimes say things they regret later."

"Oh, I don't know. She was a nice woman and she's probably lonely. You know yourself she seldom had any visitors."

---

[48] Fancy

"That's true. The only person who came more than once was her minister, and between you and me, I think he hoped to be remembered in her will if she passed on."

Auntie Con sighed. "That could well be. I'll swear that minister of mother's has his eye on the main chance."

My mother laughed. "Maybe it's you he has his eye on!"

Auntie Con looked uncomfortable. "Don't be so daft."

Now when Miss Anderson invited my mother and me to her house, my Mam said, "Yes."

On our way there, she pointed out to me the house where she had worked. "They could be slave-drivers, but I was happy then."

Miss Anderson's sitting room was bigger than our whole flat and when I tilted my head back I could see plaster cherubs trailing garlands of flowers around her ceiling.

There were flowers everywhere so the room looked like an extension of the garden that we could see through the tall windows. Near where I sat, there was a table with a big bowl on it. The bowl had a dragon going clear around it and I thought a faint smell came from it but when I stood up and looked in it, all I could see was a lot of dried up flowers. Mam said later the flowers were called pot-pourri and I had affronted her by being nosy. There was a statue on another table that would have made Granny Morrison's eyes jump clean out of their sockets. It was a man and a lady, bare naked, and the man had hooves and he was looking at the lady like Dracula looked at a lady in a picture I saw at the Salon, except the people in the picture had their clothes on.

We had thin sandwiches and tea out of dishes so fine, I could see my fingers through them. The tea was scented and Mam said it was too weak for her taste. I took the last sandwich and Mam said she thought she had brought me up better than that. "You never take the last of anything in case your hostess thinks she hasn't given you enough to eat, even if that's true."

On the way home, I thought a lot about Miss Anderson and I hoped she would invite us back. Before we left she had sent me out to the garden to pick flowers to take home. Her garden had a wall round it and a stone bench where I sat and pretended it was my house.

We were nearly at our stair when someone called, "Rachel...Rachel Malcolm."

We turned round and there was a woman and a wee girl coming towards us. "I wasn't sure if it was you or not."

"Oh hello Pearl", said my mam, "and is this your Doris then?"

Doris gave my mother a dirty look and her mother said, "Aye, and she's a flamer, always whining about something."

"Oh, they're all the same." My Mam turned to me, "Say hello to Mrs. McKechnie, Stella."

"Hello." She ignored me.

"Well well, fancy bumping into you! Long time no see, eh? How long has it been since ye were at the dancing?" She didn't wait for an answer, "Has your man been home then?"

My Mam dropped her polite accent and started talking like Mrs. McKechnie. "Home and away again. Twice."

"But God, it's been months."

"Aye, I know, and it's been like years to me. I've no been well."

"Oh I'm right sorry ta hear that..."

"I lost a wean[49]."

"Never! Oh I am sorry..."

Doris tugged at her mother's coat. "I'm tired Mammy. I want home."

"Wait the now." Mrs. McKechnie turned to my mother. "There's times I wouldn't mind losing this one."

"Still the same crowd goes then?" asked my Mam.

"Aye, the same weary Wullies." They both laughed.

"...home Mammy, home Mammy, home..." It became a chant as Doris swung against her mother. Mrs. McKechnie aimed a cuff at her and missed. "Devil take ye," she shouted and had another swing. She got Doris on the ear and Doris let out a bellow.

"Oh for the love of God shut up," her mother yelled above the din. "It's impossible Rachel, I'll need to get this one home."

"We live just up the next close," my mother yelled back. "Top flat. Come up for a cup of tea one day."

"Will do..." shouted Mrs. McKechnie as Doris pulled her away.

---

[49] Baby

"She's a nice woman that," said my mother, "a rough diamond but the salt of the earth." Once inside, she stopped at the mirror, ran her tongue over her teeth and patted at her hair. "No nonsense there! All the same I hope she doesn't bring that damned wee pest when she comes."

And come she did, and usually with Doris, whose entertainment became my unenviable lot.

Miss Anderson came too. Just once after our visit to her. My mother saw her from the window. "She's coming here. Well we're just not in, so don't you make a sound."

The doorbell rang twice, and after a pause, a third time. Another long pause and I heard her start back down the stair. I watched from the window as she walked away. I wanted to call her back; I wanted to go with her.

"Get back from there," my mother ordered. "If she turns around she might see you." After a few minutes she sidled up to the window. "Good, she's away. Now I can light the gas."

We met Miss Anderson in the street twice after that but Mam always pretended we were in a hurry to go somewhere and dragged me away. Once I looked back and Miss Anderson was gazing after us with a puzzled expression. Then a card came from Stranraer where she was recuperating from an illness. She'd be back in Edinburgh on the 17th. Could we come to tea on the 20th?

"Dash it all, will she never get the message and stop pestering us? Now I'll have to write to her." Mam grumbled under her breath for a few minutes, then, "I won't do it. We're just ignoring her invitation altogether and that'll be the end of that."

It was. We heard no more of Miss Anderson till Auntie Con brought the news that she had seen her death notice in the paper.

My Mam shook her head. "No wonder! I was chilled to the bone when we visited her. The tea was cold before it reached our lips. When I think of that old maid rattling about in a big house and so many needing homes... I've no time for it at all, all that nonsense that goes on amongst the would-be gentry...!"

"She was good to you Rachel," said Auntie Con quietly.

My mother sneered. "Lady Bountiful."

"I mean the way she helped you to get over the baby's death."

"Hmph."

Later, when Auntie Con was leaving, Mam said, "I think you came here today for the sole purpose of making me feel bad about Miss Anderson."

"Well, if that was my purpose, I'm away home disappointed."

Mam was awfully quiet for the rest of that day and the next time we passed a florist's she stopped and looked for a long time at the flowers in the window. "I haven't seen such a glorious display since the day we went to Miss Anderson's."

The next time the McKechnies came, it seemed to me that she deliberately brought the talk around to Miss Anderson. Mam described her, and the house, and everything in it. "Oh the grandeur! Eggshell china and silver spoons and cold to the bone. I nearly got my death."

"What for did ye go back then?" asked Mrs. McKechnie.

"Oh I didn't. I don't go for all that show and damn all[50] behind it."

"I don't go for that kind of carry-on myself. Naw. I'd go once and if she pulled that fancy stuff on me a second time, I'd never go back. Nobody gets the chance to toffee-nose me. I'm a plain wumman and I've no time for all that folderol nonsense at all."

My Mam nodded. "Quite right!"

But Mrs. McKechnie wasn't finished. "And what right do some folk have anyway to have more than others? We should all have the same. But here kid, maybe ye should've gone back. If she was that bloody well off she might've left ye something in her will!"

"Never occurred to me. Oh my God, what did I not think of that for? Ach, but what would I want that old junk for anyway?"

"Aye. The would-be toffs are all fur coats and nae knickers."

My mother laughed. "We used to call them 'kippers and pianos'."

"Tripe and strawberries," laughed Mrs. McKechnie, wiping her eyes.

"Pride and poverty," gasped Mam doubled up.

"Aw shut up Rachel. You're making me pee ma pants."

My mother dabbed at her eyes. "Oh here, before I forget to ask ye, was Tony at the dancing last week?"

Miss Anderson had been laid to rest.

---

[50] Nothing

Stella Maris   by   Nan O'Dell

Chapter 24 : Betty and Sheila

The nights were drawing in again and lights were coming on quite early. The shops were bright oases in the November dark and if I met someone I knew we'd stand at the shop windows and play "I spy". It was a magic time and to add to it, Christmas lay just ahead.

One day when I came out of our close, I spotted two familiar figures staring at the display in the window of a nearby sweetie shop. They went to my school and the bigger one, Betty, was in my class. They didn't speak to anyone and at playtime they always stood together and apart from the rest of us. The teacher said they had just moved here from England and we should be friendly to them and make then feel happy that they came to live in Edinburgh. I tried to make them feel happy by offering them a shot of my diablo but they shook their heads.

"Watch me then. I can throw it higher than anybody."

They looked at me with expressionless faces. I threw the diablo higher than ever that day but when I glanced over to see if they were suitably impressed they had gone. When they came out of the girls' lavatories that stood separate from the school building, a teacher was blowing her whistle for us to line up and march back to our classrooms.

It wasn't only at school I saw them. They had moved into the caretaker's flat above the burnt-out dancehall across the street from us. We were higher up than they were and when their lights came on I could see right into their house. They were always sitting around their table, having their tea, doing their homework, playing games with their Mam and Da. Then their Mam would leave the room with them and after a while come back alone. She would knit while the Da read. When he yawned and put

154

down his book, the Mam would fold up her knitting. Then she'd bank down the fire while he wound the clock. It was lonely after their lights went out.

"Hello Betty" I said now and joined them at the window. They turned and looked at me. Then they turned back to the window.

"I'm buying one of those boxes of chocolates for my mother's Christmas", I said.

Neither of them spoke. I pointed to the banner across the window that said, "Join our Christmas club now."

"I'm in the Christmas club."

Betty tossed a pigtail over her shoulder. "I'd rather be in the Brownies."

"Ha ha," I crowed. "She doesn't know what a Christmas club is."

"Come on Sheila," said Betty to her sister," don't pay any attention to her. She's common."

"No I'm not. You're jealous because you don't know what a Christmas club is."

She whirled on me. "I do so know."

"Tell me then."

Dragging Sheila behind her, she walked quickly away. I followed on their heels. "All right I'll tell *you*. It's a thing you put money in and when you have enough you can pick anything you want."

They were walking very fast so I danced around them and facing them, started to walk backwards. "I have nearly a shilling in it now and I can have anything I want out of that window."

"No you can't." Betty dropped Sheila's hand and ran back. "You can't have that one." She pointed to the biggest box, which lay on a black velvet pedestal in the middle of the window.

"Ha ha again. That one's empty."

"Well I can have it filled with chocolates. I can have anything I want. My father's rich."

"Liar!"

"It's the truth, isn't it Sheila?'"

Sheila nodded.

"See? I told you."

"Well my father's at sea in his big ship and he's bringing me a lot of good stuff when he comes home."

We all stood and looked at each other. I had their attention at last. In the light from the shop window they looked very clean. They wore white knit caps and gloves and their pigtails were tied with white ribbons.

"What would you like if you could have anything in the world you wanted?"

"A whole shop full of dolls," said Betty.

"I'd have a big car and a crown of diamonds," I said. "What would you like Sheila?"

156

She pointed shyly at a chocolate box with kittens on the lid.

"I have a cat called Tibby," I said. "What's your cat's name?"

"We don't have one, that's why she wants that box with cats on it, isn't it Sheila?"

Sheila nodded.

"Someday you can come to my house and play with me and my cat," I said, hoping they'd invite me to theirs but they were silent. I'll get my Mam that big box like I told you, then I'll get that one for myself." It was a box with coloured daisies on the lid. It reminded me of the box I threw in the gutter.

The truth was I only had sixpence in the Christmas club. I had depended heavily on getting that shilling from my Granny Morrison. When I told Auntie Con about my texts she said I could come and help her with the annual insanity and she'd pay me. That's what she called giving Granny's room a good turning out before New Year's day. My Granny believed that if there were one thing dirty or out of place when the New Year came in, we'd end our days in squalor. However, Granny always cleared out of the way to let Auntie Con get on with it. That meant a hot bottle at her back and a glass of hot water and lemon with "just a bit of whiskey in it" to soothe her insides, and her Bible or the Book of the Martyrs.

Once Auntie Con told me Granny was "a flaming old liar", but nevertheless it was a good way to get her out of the road for a while. So the week after next I was to go to Granny's on the Saturday and help my Auntie. Auntie Con said that if we could get finished on time she'd take me to the Playhouse to see "Son of Kong".

157

"I'm going to see Son of Kong," I said. "And I saw King Kong as well."

"We saw The Bride of Frankenstein, and we saw Frankenstein too."

"That was boring." (It had scared me stiff.)

"I saw the Mummy."

"Our Mam and Da took us to see David Copperfield. And Treasure Island."

I hadn't seen those ones. I preferred to be scared. Nevertheless I knew they were criticising my choice of movies.

"They were boring too."

"You didn't see them."

"Yes I did."

"Tell us what they were about then."

"I can't tell you because they were so boring I fell asleep."

Chapter 25 : Little Doris

Though Mam said Mrs. McKechnie was on the common side, "She's always good for a laugh. The only fly in the ointment is that Doris, and if you kept her entertained, as you should, she wouldn't be such a damned pest. But I must he fair about it, it's not entirely your fault. No, it's Pearl that doesn't chastise her. Oh I know there are some who think I'm hard on you, but I've taught you to behave. The mark of a good mother is a well-behaved child...

My Mam thought I was well behaved! I was glad of that for she was a good mother and I wanted to please her. She often said she didn't enjoy chastising me but it had to be done so people would like me. For the same reason she never left marks on me so they wouldn't know how bad I was sometimes. I wish trying to be good didn't make me feel so tired. Auntie Con said I looked like I never got enough sleep and I was too pale and thin, but Mam told her, "She's growing too quickly - she's outgrowing her strength."

"Then she needs a tonic."

"I'll get her one the next time we're out."

And she did. Mam took me to the chemist and bought me Radio Malt. She said we couldn't really afford it but she got me it all the same because she was a good mother. Because she loved me. I should show I love her too, by trying harder to keep Doris entertained.

Sometimes Mam's face would be white after the McKechnies left and she'd have to lie down with a cologne-soaked hankie on her forehead. Once she even vomited. It was the time Mrs. McKechnie yelled for some caster oil to give Doris. "If ye have any, Rachel, let me administer a dose to this one that'll keep her in the lavvy and out of my sight for the rest of the day."

I was glad my Mam didn't have any, for Doris always wanted me to chum her to the lavatory and if I said no, my Mam would give me the "I'll take care of you later" look. So I would chum Doris and because she knew I tried not to breathe when she did number two, she'd jump off the pan and tickle me till I had to. Then I'd get the boak[51] and she'd laugh. My Mam said I was too easily scunnered[52] and I'd go farther and fare worse. I hoped I wouldn't.

The trouble with Doris always started the minute they arrived.

"Where's yer cat, Stella?"

"She's out." (I hope she is.)

"But I want her."

"Come and play Snakes and Ladders." (Mam's looking annoyed.)

"Ah want to find her first."

"I'll read you a story." (Please, I'm getting into trouble.)

"I don't want no story."

"She's maybe in my room. We'll look and see." (I'm sorry Tib.)

---

[51] Nausea, revulsion

[52] Sickened

"She's not under yer bed."

"She's out. I told you." (Please be out Tib.)

"She's not behind your dresser either."

"Doris! Why are you moving that chair, Doris?"

"To see if she's on top of yer wardrobe. Aye, she is Stella." (Oh run Tibby.)

"Come here cheety. Chee chee chee chee. Come on cat, come to me."

"Leave her Doris. She doesn't like her tail pulled."

"She'll not come. MAMMY - STELLA'S CAT BIT ME."

"I told you not to pull her tail." (I'm for it now.) The door flies open. Tibby flies out. Mam and Mrs. McKechnie fly in.

Mam: "What's going on in here."

Mrs. McKechnie: "What's all the carry-on?"

"I'm bleeding Mammy. Her cat bit me."

"Damn that cat!" (All you had to do was keep Doris happy.)

"I'm sorry Mam. " (I've failed you again and now Tib's in bother as well.)

"Come here Doris and let me put iodine on it." (I'll fix you and that cat when they go!)

"I don't want no stuff on it."

"Do what you're told!"

"No no no."

"Do ye want me to send for the polis[53]?"

"Ah don't want no polis neither."

"Doris. DORIS," my Mam yells above the din, "I'll give you each a penny and Stella will take ye to the wee shop."

Magic! "I want the black sweeties like sugarally[54] and a lucky tattie[55] with the change."

But, the sweeties gone, Doris went right back to being a pest. It wasn't so bad when the weather was fine and we could go out to play, but the day came when the rain was lashing and there was no money to send us to the shop. My mother made tea and I watched her as Doris crumbled a biscuit on the hearthrug and spilt tea on the cloth. Mam's face was getting white the way it did when she was angry. I coaxed Doris into my room and shut the door so my Mam wouldn't hear if she made a noise.

But Doris kept whining to get back to the table. "No Doris, you can't", I said leaning against the door.

"Let me out. What for can I no?"

"Because."

---

[53] Police

[54] Liquorice stick

[55] Potato

"Why because?"

"Because... because you're just a fly in the ointment." Doris stopped trying to push me aside. "I'm not a fly, Stella."

"It doesn't mean you're a fly, dozey. It means you're a pest."

Doris took a swipe at me. "Let me out. I'm gonna tell yer Mammy what ye called me."

I had jumped out the way of her swing and she grabbed the door-handle.

"There's no good telling her," I said, trying to haul her back, "for she's the one that says you're a fly in the ointment."

She wrenched the door open. "MAMMY! STELLA SAYS HER MAMMY SAYS I'M A FLY IN THE OINTMENT."

"What's this?"

Doris repeated it.

"I hope you don't believe that?" If looks could kill I'd have dropped dead from the look that Mam gave me.

"Well I wouldn't like to think ye thought that..."

"That girl's turning into such a liar I don't know what I'm to do with her."

"A cake of carbolic in her mouth should fix her.'

"It's off her da's side. The Malcolms are all liars. They wouldn't know the truth if it bit them on the nose."

"Aye well, ye should see to her before somebody believes her and bites *you* on the nose."

"Come here hen[56]. Let me see what I have for ye in the press." My mother stood on tiptoes and rummaged under a pile of stuff on the top shelf. "Here. Here's a book with nice pictures for ye to look at." She turned to me, "And as for you, you go to your room till I say you can come out."

As I turned to go I got a glimpse of the picture on the cover of the book. It was the same as the picture on the book I had lost a long time ago, the one my Granny Malcolm gave me. It was about the adventures of some children who went for their summer holidays to a farm and at first some of them were feart of the animals but it ended happy with the children making lots of friends and wanting to go back to the farm every year. I had liked that book and when I lost it I had looked for it a long time and Mam said it was my own fault for being too careless with my possessions.

I crawled under my bed beside Tibby, who was trying to hide again, and I thought about the book and I wondered how it had got on to the top shelf in the press. But it couldn't be the same book for my Mam had helped me to look for that one and we couldn't find it. She must have bought one to replace it and was hiding it for my Christmas. That was it! She was a good Mam and wanted to surprise me and now I had spoiled it by not keeping Doris entertained. I'd try harder the next time. I hoped Doris wouldn't hurt the book or get it dirty. I hoped my Mam wouldn't give it to her to take home.

---

[56] Girl

Stella Maris   by   Nan O'Dell

It seemed a long time till she called to me to come out and I was stiff from being scrunched up under the bed. She was at the door saying goodbye to the McKechnies and I was glad to see the book lying on the hearthrug. The corner of the cover was all bashed but my Mam would straighten it out. I hoped she'd let me have it now and not wait till Christmas. I turned over the pages and there were Rory and Joan and Jimmy and Ted just as I remembered them on the farm. Till the last page when they were back in the city and their holidays over for another year. And there too was the moustache I had drawn on Rory's face!

I heard the front door close and I turned to ask my Mam about it. She was upon me in an instant, her face twisted and her eyes like burning coals. "Mam", I shouted and jumped back as she made a grab, but it was the book she grabbed. I shouted again as she flung it on the fire. "Don't, please don't."

"Stupid stupid creature," she shrieked. "How else will you learn that you must not tell what is done or said in this house?"

Chapter 26 : Norah Kennedy

My mother was like two people. There was the self that hated household and family responsibilities and the self that seemed to wallow in maternity and domesticity. These two factions warred with each other, or perhaps the latter was the self that she sometimes wished she could be. Certainly, to some people she showed the second side. And it was to Norah Kennedy that she was the motherly Rachel Malcolm. Norah had come from Ireland to work and lodged with the McGonigals in the next stair. I often looked at Norah with envy – studied her – wondered why she succeeded where I failed. With Norah my mother's patience was endless – her advice on tap – ready to listen, to advise, to comfort or console when necessary. Norah's pale prettiness wasn't unlike my mother's own. The colouring, the features, even some of the mannerisms. I have wondered since if my mother saw Norah as herself – yet someone who had been even less fortunate in life's draw. For Norah hired herself out as a daily, cleaning different houses every day. For her were left the heavy and often distasteful tasks. No light dusting for her. "Why don't you find a place you could go to every day?" But no, Norah could make a few shillings more by working the way she was doing

"You see the innards of everyone's lavatories and dirty ovens. You get the jobs housewives hate most."

Norah knew it, but the extra money was needed for her mother in Donegal.

"I hope you'll be as good to me," my mother would say. "She's so slight to tackle the jobs she does. Let her be a lesson to you. She's carrying out what the bible tells her – Honour thy mother and thy father. And I hope her mother appreciates it."

But she said to Norah, "I can't see that one (this was me) ever doing anything for me. I keep telling her she has it easy."

"Oh, yes," Norah nodded, "she's lucky to have you. I can always tell you everything."

"And I'll always be here to listen," said Mam.

My Mam liked to quote that bit from the Bible about "Honour thy mother and thy father", but I couldn't see her doing it herself. She visited Granny when, as Auntie Con put it, "it comes up your back." More than once I heard Mam say as she spied Granny coming toward the close – "Oh, dear, here's the old lady – tut – old pest."

Chapter 27 : The Hogmanay Bash

My Da was coming home. I had seen him so briefly in the past year that he was like a stranger to me. It was like my Mam and my Da were both single with brief spells of marriage. My Da didn't write to my Mam very often but the shipping company sent his check every month so Mam said that was all right. My mother was out every Saturday again and often through the week as well. The week before my Da got home she was out every night, "For God knows I'll not get out when he's in. I have to live it up when he's gone for there's little joy when he's home. He watches me like a hawk and there's ructions if he sees me smile at anyone of the male sex."

Sometimes my Da brought me presents but after he gave them to me he would be too busy with my Mam to talk to me. He and my mother had lots of fights and once when I got up and went through to the kitchen where they were fighting, my Da said, "This is your fault. If it hadn't been for you I'd never have married the bitch." Then my Mam turned to me, "Haven't you caused enough trouble already...get through to your bed and stay there till we tell you that you can come out."

But sometimes they forgot to tell me and they'd go out after a while and not say it was all right to come out.

They usually made up their fights but they didn't make up with me. This time when my Da came home it would be different. My Mam and I were friends now. Since she had been sick she seemed to like me better and now she didn't go out so much and Mrs. McKechnie came to the house more than my Mam went out. Now she seemed satisfied to stay home more.

My Da was home and away again before Christmas that year. He got his gifts from us before he left. From my Mam, a scarf; socks from Auntie Con that she had knitted herself; handkerchiefs from Granny Morrison, and I gave my Da a packet of cigarettes that he smoked right away. I was glad of that for I got the card from the packet. "Candytuft: a charming dwarf annual in many pretty shades." I already had Cosmos and Salpiglossis.

He gave my Mam and me a box of sweeties between us, and for her special gift a record she wanted called 'Paddy'. My special gift was 'The Schoolgirl's Annual'.

I was glad he left before the Christmas holiday from school started for if my Mam told him about the man I went in the stair with, he'd be angry and might make me stay in my room the whole time. Every morning when I woke up I'd wonder if this would be the day she would tell him. But if she did, he never let on, and when I said goodbye to him a fortnight before Christmas, I was dizzy with relief to see him go.

There was another reason why I was glad he was away before I'd be home from the school all day. It was the way my Mam and Da looked at each other and whispered and touched when he was home. Then Mam would titter and they'd look at me to see if I was watching. If I went away to my room they'd tell me to come out and stop sulking.

"That one's so jealous she hates to see you get any of my attention."

"If I decide to give her some of mine she'll be sorry," and my Da would pretend to be undoing his belt.

Then they'd go back to what they were doing before. Then one of them might say something to make the other angry and they'd be off. Their battles raged right through the night and sometimes one of them would drag me out of bed to come and hear what the other one was saying. Then they'd say they were getting a divorce and which one of them would I choose to go with. Sometimes I'd cry because I didn't know what to say and they'd say, "Isn't she ugly when she cries? Who would want her anyway?" Then they'd make up and they'd be angry with me if I didn't act happy because they were happy again.

This Christmas though, I was safe. I made paper chains and Mam and me hung them from the corners of the room with a big paper bell in the middle.

Granny and Auntie Con came on Christmas Eve and Granny was in her Sunday best and Auntie Con wore her new angora cardigan and the pearls she had bought for a Christmas present to herself one year. They gave us presents and we gave them presents and Auntie Con and Mam talked about the old days while Granny dozed and I pretended to read my Schoolgirl's Annual.

Granny and Auntie Con were invited to Uncle Jim's and Auntie Ivy's on Christmas day and Granny wasn't looking forward to it.

"My children are dutiful when it comes up their backs and they always put a face on things at Christmas."

"Oh for goodness sake mother," said Auntie Con, "are you never satisfied? If they didn't invite you you'd greet[57] about that too."

"Hmph."

"You'll never find George and that one he's married to putting a face on anything," said my Mam.

"You might be seeing Eddie and the children the night[58] now that you're so close to the chapel," said Granny to my Mam. "They'll be at that papish midnight mass. She'll not be there though for I hear tell there's another one on the way."

Auntie Con laughed. "Eddie says they're trying for a football team."

"They must be nearly there then."

---

[57] Cry

[58] Tonight

Granny tutted. "Just about."

"How did you find out Mary's expecting again? Has Eddie been by?"

"Not him. He knows better than to come to me with news like that. He knows my feelings about him turning to please Mary."

"You miss a lot, mother. Mary's a canny[59] soul and the children are bonny."

"A snottery nosed lot," said my Mam, "and their house is Paddy's Market[60] from one year's end to the next."

Auntie Con looked at the clock and started to roll up her knitting. "It's time we were away, mother."

"Oh by the by," said my Mam, "would you mind if I drop Stella off to spend the night on Hogmanay[61]? I've been invited to a "do" put on by the shipping line for wives of the men who'll be away."

It was the first I'd heard of it and I was glad Granny and Auntie Con said "Yes", so I didn't have to be by myself that night.

On Christmas day my Mam roasted a chicken and we had plum pudding though there were just the two of us. She didn't talk about being bored like she usually did if there was just her and me. She asked me questions about the school and what I'd like to be when I grew up and I felt shy like my Mam was a new friend. Then we played Snap and Snakes and Ladders and I won more times than my Mam.

---

[59] Good

[60] Untidy

[61] New Year's Eve

171

She tucked me in bed that night and as she bent over to kiss me, I said, "I love you Mammy."

"You're a good wee lassie."

Then it was Granny's ginger wine and black bun in front of a big fire on Hogmanay, Auntie Con watching the clock and Granny holding the turnip watch. Twelve deep boings and twelve silvery chimes and it was the New Year. We kissed each other and Auntie Con went to the piano, and with many pauses while she hunted for the right keys, we sang, "A good New Year tae yin and a' and many may ye see." We sang it loud to cover up Auntie Con's mistakes, as she had asked us to do.

I went to sleep that night warm with ginger wine and contentment.

It was the third day of the New Year before my mother came for me. Though she was several years younger than Auntie Con, she looked much older that day.

"I'm tired. Dennis came home after a shorter run than he expected. That's what he said anyway. I think he was home to spy."

"Surely you weren't doing something you didn't want him to know about?" Auntie Con asked dryly.

My mother glanced at me. "Wheesht[62]." Granny walked into the kitchen just then. "Fancy mother, Dennis is home unexpectedly and that's why I'm late in picking up Stella."

"I'm sure I don't mind. The child was welcome."

I hated saying goodbye to Granny and Auntie Con for my Da was still at home and wouldn't be rejoining his ship for several days. It sounded like he and my Mam were fighting again and they'd be asking me to decide which one of them I would go with when they got divorced. And I

---

[62] Shhh – quiet!

didn't want to go with either of them. I was for it on the Day of Judgement when God opened the big book at my name! I wondered what my punishment would be for not wanting to live with my Mam and Da.

I went home with my heart in my mouth and my bowels like water. My Da said it was those silly women with their ginger wine and black bun that had made me ill.

But my Mam and my Da weren't fighting and I felt even more wicked, and guilty now as well, for not wanting to live with either of them when they got divorced. I had never seen them so polite and it began to dawn on me that this was another way of fighting and I might still be asked to choose between them. They didn't talk much to each other and they didn't talk to me either.

I waited for something to happen and it was only when I saw my Da take his bag out, ready to pack, that I felt safe. My Mam started packing it for him and she put in Granny's hankies, the socks Auntie Con had knitted for him, and her own gift to him, a scarf.

My Da took the scarf out again and laid it on the bed. "I'll not take that."

My Mam snatched out Auntie Con's socks and waved them under his nose. "But I suppose you'll take her socks?"

He just nodded and resumed packing his bag.

Mam started to cry. "I'm damned if you will."

"Give me those socks!" He tried to grab them but she dodged around him and flung the socks on the fire, still crying that he liked Auntie Con more than he liked her.

My Da was angry when he saw his new socks burning and they burned slow and smelled because they were made of wool. He opened the window but the smell wouldn't go away and he got angrier and angrier thinking about his socks.

Then he took the record he had bought my Mam and broke it across his knee. I felt sorry about that, for I liked that song, especially when the gramophone ran down before the song was finished. The man's voice would get very deep and slow, "And I state sure as fate any man who meets you, Paddy, is b o u n d t o b e f a l l i n g i n l o v e.

"Rotten bitch," he yelled. "Whoring in your own house, but I've had enough. Let one of your fancy men keep you for I'm through!"

"You wouldn't dare desert us," Mam screamed. "I could have gone far in the world If I hadn't been trapped into marrying you, so it's your duty to keep me."

"Gone far in the world? That's a laugh. As far as the lamp-post down there!"

"Swine. Swine. Rotten swine."

"You couldn't even take care of my son. You let him die. Don't think I've not had my thoughts about his death and your part in it."

"The police said there were no suspicious circumstances, and you know that. He was my son too...why would I kill my own son?" Mam looked like she would fall down and her face was a funny grey colour.

My Da was shaking and his face was red like it would burst. "Why do you do any of the hellish things you do?" He grabbed up his bag and his coat. "If I don't go now I'll kill you and one murderer in the family's enough."

"You have to keep Stella. The law will demand it."

"Her? Let the man who fathered her keep her, and you too."

My Mam lifted a vase and hurled it as he went through the door. "Do you think if I had to murder one of my two children it would have been him?" she shrieked, not caring that I heard; not caring that I knew.

174

It was only later that I realised they hadn't made me choose between them.

Chapter 28 : Pearl McKechnie

When the door slammed behind Da, Mam turned on me. She thrust her face against mine; "I'm free now except for you."

Suddenly she started screaming, "Damn you, damn you, damn you."

I jumped back but she grabbed my hair and pulled me forward. "Don't back away from me while I'm talking to you. When I speak you will listen. Do you understand?"

I nodded, crying.

" Well why are you trying to escape, you snivelling little coward. Why? Why? Why?" With each word she jerked my head back and forth. "Why?"

"Because I'm feart."

"Feart? How dare you say that to me! Have I ever left a mark on your body or ill used you?"

Between sobs I whispered, "No."

Mam pulled my head back so I was forced to look into her eyes. At what I saw in them I screamed, "No, Mammy, no, please don't kill me."

"You're not worth killing. You're not worth God's notice. Oh you're his all right. Every rotten bit of you. There's nothing of me in you. Nothing." She started wrenching my head back and forth again. "Why did I have to be the one to bear such a loathsome creature? Why couldn't it have been one of the tarts he picks up on his travels? Why me? Why?"

"I'm sorry Mammy. I'm sorry."

"So you should be." She released me suddenly, flinging me back as she did, so that I staggered and fell against the metal fender. "Now get to your room and stay there till I say you can come out. I don't want to see your ugly face again today."

I struggled to my feet, my eyes never leaving hers. Slowly I backed from the room, pain pounding at my back and catching at my breath; fear of my mother keeping me mobile.

At the door I panicked and turned and ran, frantic lest she follow. I crawled into the safe darkness under my bed. I stifled a scream when I encountered something warm and furry. Only when I felt claws did I realise that Tibby had sought refuge there too.

I lay under the bed a long long time, tense, listening. Only when I heard my mother leave the house did I relax.

Then the pain started tearing at my back in earnest but I was alone now and could scream out loud. Tibby scooted away in a fright but now the screams had started coming I couldn't stop them.

It was all a mixture of pain and nightmare for I seemed to sleep and when I awoke it had settled to an ache that was bearable as long as I lay on my stomach. I could see under the door that the kitchen light was on and Mam was home.

It was the following morning before I ventured into the kitchen for a drink. And all the time I watched my Mam who ignored me as though I didn't exist. I could lie on top of my bed now but was still frightened to sleep in case my mother crept in and killed me. The house made noises in the dark, or when the fire had burned itself out. The best times were when Tibby came in beside me and curled up against my sore back.

One day Mam caught me filling a hot water bottle and demanded to know what it was for.

"My back's sore."

"Well that's not going to help it," she said, taking it from me.

Those days following my father's dramatic exit were so quiet that I could hear my own heart pounding. I was frightened my mother would hear it too and emerge from the world into which she had shut herself. I felt fairly safe as long as my Mam stayed there.

On the 10th of January Mrs. McKechnie showed up. "He's away again then?"

"Damn fine ye know it," said Mam, speaking at last.

"Was it bad, hen[63]?" Mrs. McKechnie's eyes were eager and the poppies on her hat trembled in anticipation of Mam's reply.

"What do you think? If I find out the bitch that told him..."

"Ye can't be sure it was one of the lassies."

"Well I can't see Tony nor Bill nor Norman spilling the beans. No, it has the earmarks of a spiteful wumman, but mark my words well, she'll not live to tell the tale once I get my hands on her."

"Don't look at me. I had nothing to do with it."

"I'm not saying ye did so why are ye acting so helluva touchy?"

---

[63] Girl

"I get insulted every time I come here. I don't know why I bother."

"Because you're nosy, that's why." My Mam laughed and Mrs. McKechnie turned brick red. Mam went on, "Oh stop feeling sorry for yourself and have a cup of tea."

Mrs. McKechnie sniffed and started to unbutton her coat. "I can only bide a couple minutes. Doris'll be coming in from the school."

"You're not usually that bothered about Doris."

Mrs. McKechnie started to look huffy again and Rachel said hurriedly, "Any word of Tony or any of the crowd?"

"None whatsoever. Things is awfully quiet the now." She laughed. "The after season slump has set in and everyone's broke forbye[64]."

My Mam snorted. "Hung over ye mean, though more like they're all frichted[65] to death and lying low after Dennis barging in here the way he did."

"By God aye, caught in the act right enough." The poppies started trembling again. "Oh kid, was it awfully bad?"

Mam turned to me. "Away you in my purse and get tuppence for teabread."

Mrs. McKechnie looked at me suspiciously. "What's she doing home?"

---

[64] As well

[65] Frightened

"She says she has a sore back." Mam started filling the kettle.

"I noticed her hirpling[66] when she let me in, and she's awfully white."

"She's swinging the lead[67]."

Mrs. McKechnie ignored my Mam and asked me, "What's wrong with it?

"I fell on the fender."

"How did ye do that?"

"She was being' her usual clumsy self." Mam looked at me with dislike. "Get out of here," she yelled, "and get that teabread."

I did as I was told. There was only a sixpence and a threepenny bit left in Mam's purse when I had taken the two pennies from it.

I liked going to the baker's. Liked the smell of the baking bread, and the fat lady behind the counter who was always smiling. Now as the lady put the teabread into a bag she asked, "Did Santy come down your chimney this year or are ye too old for Santy?"

I nodded and the woman twirled the bag shut and handed it to me. "I thought so but ye're not too old for a lucky poke[68]?"

---

[66] Limping

[67] Loafing, evading duties

[68] Bag

As she spoke she was scooping up the tiny silver dragees and bits of cherries that had fallen from teabread and fairy cakes. She put them in a twist of paper, which she handed to me. "Here hen, and you tell your Mammy that she has a good wee lassie."

My mother would never believe that! And I knew the lady was wrong and hoped she'd never find out and stop giving me pokes of dragees and cherries and sometimes coconut. I never ate the dragees. They were too pretty and too tasteless. I kept them in an empty Zube tin and they made a pleasant sound when I shook the tin.

When I got home Mam was mopping her eyes. She was telling Mrs. McKechnie about mother love and accusations.

"But he's not the only one. I know there are those who wonder how a baby could die when nothing's wrong with it. I see the looks. I know what they're all thinking. Do they never think of me? What I felt like when I touched my baby's cheek and felt marble? I hope in all my born days never to feel the like again. There are times I think I'll go crazy wondering what happened.

But how do ye find out? What can ye do to find out?"

Mrs. McKechnie took a deep breath. "Ye go to a Spiritualist meeting, that's what ye do."

My Mam stared at her.

"I'm telling ye. A Spiritualist meeting and there's a rare medium at the Tuesday night one."

"How do you know?"

"Because I've been."

"Ye never told me that."

"I only thought of it the now."

"A Spiritualist meeting?"

"Aye, and this medium, Jessie Bowden's got the gift. She'll put ye in touch with the ones ye've lost."

My mam was indignant. "If my babies wanted to get in touch with me why would they go to her?"

"I told ye. She's psychic and can see things you and me can't see."

Mam shook her head unbelievingly.

"Well then, how many spirits have you seen?" Mrs. McKechnie demanded to know.

Mam laughed. "Very few since the New Year!"

"Aye well, ye'd be laughing on the other side of your face if ye'd been at the meeting I was at. She told old ma Finlay about her man and the two laddies drowning. 'I can see them', says she, 'they're wearing fisherman's boots and jerseys and one of them's smoking a pipe...' What the hell are you laughing at?"

"You! Fancy swallowing that stuff."

Mrs. McKechnie's face was the colour of her maroon coat. "Are you calling me a liar?"

"Not you. Them. The Spiritualists. Fancy telling the old body a tale like that!"

"It's no skin off my nose if ye don't go. It was for your sake I mentioned it."

"Oh I know it was kindly meant but to tell ye the God's honest truth, I'm a wee bit feart of it. It's not meeting my babies I'm feart for. Naw, it's not that, but my father used to say that spiritualism was the work of the Devil." She laughed again. "And I wouldn't care to take the chance of running into Old Nick."

I stopped counting the dragees in my Zube tin and pricked up her ears. My mam never talked about Grandfather Morrison and I was more interested in hearing about him than in hearing about the Devil. I knew all there was to know about the Devil from Granny Morrison who kept abreast of all his doings.

But Mam said no more for Mrs. McKechnie had jumped to her feet and was buttoning up her coat. "All I've got to say to you is, if it's the work of the Devil an awful lot of us are headed for the hot place."

Hurriedly my Mam said she'd attend the meeting on the following Tuesday and peace was restored. "Wait till I get my coat and I'll chum you to the tram. Stella, you wash up the dishes while I'm away."

Mam didn't see the look Mrs. McKechnie gave her while her back was turned, but I did, and I shivered.

"I'll not be long," Mam told me "but if anything should keep me, mind and not light the gas."

Stella Maris   by   Nan O'Dell

I knew then that my mother might not come back that night or even the next day, but it didn't matter. My mother was talking to me again and my back had stopped throbbing.

I was able to go to school the next day and, come Sunday, to the Sunday school as well. I had decided to go back and was ashamed that it wasn't because I loved Jesus or had forgiven Brenda but because Sundays were long if my mother was sleeping, hazardous if she was awake.

All the children talked about what they had received for Christmas. Miss Merry said she hoped they hadn't forgotten Whose birthday it was; that they had taken time out from all the fun to thank their Heavenly Father for sending His Son to redeem them; that the exchange of gifts was to commemorate the gifts the Wise Men gave to the Christ Child.

"Now," she said, "each of us will tell, not the gifts he got, but the love he got this Christmas. Who would like to begin?"

The first hand up was Brenda's. "Please miss, we sang carols every night and my Mam and dad told us about Christmas in the olden days. And my Granda gave me and my sisters a half-crown apiece."

"We weren't supposed to tell about the material things we received," Miss Merry chided gently.

Billy Fraser jumped to his feet. "My father says Christmas is just a commercial enterprise set up by the Jews and only fools fall for it."

Quickly, Miss Merry pointed to another of the waving hands. "Yes Stella?"

I had stuck my hand up like the rest and hoped Miss Merry wouldn't acknowledge me.

"My Da had to go back to his ship before Christmas but..." I remembered presents weren't to be mentioned but my imagination, which was to save me many times in my life, came to my rescue now. "...but because he loves my Mam and me so much he left his ship and came home for Hogmanay." I sank to my seat and waited to be struck dead for telling lies in the House of the Lord, but nothing happened. I wondered about that going home. Maybe I was still alive because I hadn't told a lie after all. Maybe my Da <u>had</u> come home because he <u>did</u> miss us. Yes, that was it. My Da loved Mam and me and had been missing us.

I skipped the rest of the way home and nearly bumped into my Auntie Con who was coming out of our stair. "Hello pet. I've just been up to tell your mother that there might be a job for her at Fairley's. I hear they're looking for waitresses."

"Don't go home yet Auntie Con."

"I have to. Granny's not well again."

"Can I come with you then?"

"Not today pet. As soon as Granny's better we'll go somewhere nice."

"Where?"

"Maybe for our tea. We'll see. Now off you go and your Mam will tell you about the job." She kissed me and hurried off to catch the tram that would take her back to her prison.

"Mam", I called as I jumped the stairs two at a time.

"How often do I have to tell you?" Mam flung open the door "You should go before you leave the Sunday school."

Chapter 29 : Depression

"Cheer up. I told you I could get along without your father. Well this will prove it.

She was right. Her experience as a table maid got her that job and many more, jobs waiting tables at private functions. Before long she didn't have to go looking; jobs came to her. The hours were sometimes long, and often in the evening, but the days were lengthening so I didn't mind being left alone. I had found a way to pass the nights when I waited in our darkened flat for my mother to come home. I pretended I lived with the Willises across the street, that I was Rebecca Willis. When their light went out at night I'd call goodnight from our flat. "Goodnight to you too dear," Mrs. Willis would say as she tucked me into my bed.

I looked forward to Mam coming home and watched from the window so I could have a basin of warm water ready for her to soak her feet in. She always brought me good things. I liked when she came home with her pauchle[69], which in those days meant the untouched remains of the feast. Dainty sandwiches or French cakes and if she had been at a wedding there would always be the bits of cake that had crumbled in the cutting. Once she even brought me a miniature bouquet of pink carnations and white heather. "There was one at every place," said Mam, and they all matched the flowers the bride carried, except her carnations were white. I might have had a white wedding if it hadn't been for you."

---

[69] Parcel

I didn't know what Mam meant but she didn't sound angry or unfriendly. "Fill up the basin with hot water," she said now. "You're a good wee lassie to have a basin ready for your Mammy to soak her feet in when she comes in."

I was glad these carnations were pink for the sprigs of white heather showed up better.

I think she enjoyed those evenings. They reminded her of the old days in service in Inverleith Place.

"Oh what toffs they were. The bride's dress was satin with seed pearls sewn round the neckline and I heard one of the guests say her veil was real Chantilly. Oh, if I hadn't had to marry your father! I might have had a wedding like that. It's too bad that the bride today had a cast in her eye. It spoiled the whole effect. The groom's mother looked a bit common and the bride's father had a roving eye. I caught it looking at me more than once." Mam laughed. "Oh that water feels good on my feet. "You're a good lassie to your mother having this ready for her coming in."

As she dried between her toes she said, "Do you know we're nearly through the woods? Isn't that great? I've managed to pay back your Granny what I owed her and I only have to finish paying for my uniforms now.

After a busy month, however, there was a lull in the work and we were once again "in the woods."

I didn't mind being in the woods with my mother for I felt close to her again, and when she brought me things I knew she was thinking about me while she was out. I was happy to hear her talk.

Then something odd happened to me. Something I had never experienced before. The elation I felt at my mother speaking to me again was replaced by a feeling that was akin to horror. The horror I had felt that time I saw "The Mummy", but more than that.

A cold black cloud seemed to have enveloped me, hampering movement and even speech. Not even Tibby leaping on my knee and singing the happy song helped. The cloud came between us and though I saw my cat I felt nothing but the horror. Sometimes I couldn't hear either, and twice I got the belt for not listening to the teacher. When I tried to tell Miss Johnson what was wrong, my jaw felt so heavy, and my lips so stiff, that they couldn't move to say the words.

Mam told me, "Cheer up sobersides. You'd think the worry and responsibility were yours, but God gave me intelligence and I'll get by without your father."

The job at Fairley's seemed to prove it. Mam's experience as a table-maid stood her in good stead and soon she was again in great demand to wait tables at functions.

So the dark cloud lifted and speech and easy movement returned and it was many years before I learned that the cloud's name was depression. But by that time it had enveloped me so many times that I lived in dread of its coming.

189

Chapter 30 : Mrs. Bowden

When Mam finally went to the Spiritualist meeting, she didn't take me, but when she got home, she told me all about it.

"It's maybe a load of rubbish, but the medium's a nice enough woman all the same. She came up to me after the meeting and it turns out her man's in the navy too. He's a petty officer. I wish your Da was a petty officer but he'll be an ordinary seaman till the day he dies, for he's like the rest of the Malcolms - no ambition."

She went on about the Malcolms and their faults, the meeting forgotten, till she saw my eyelids begin to droop. " And you might as well go to your bed for all the company you are to me. Sitting there sleeping while I'm talking to you."

"I was listening Mam. "

"You're a liar like the rest of the Malcolms. Now get to your bed."

When I was in bed I heard her muttering under her breath and I lay tense for a long time, waiting for her to pounce as she sometimes did when I had made her angry. But then there were no sounds from the kitchen and after a long while I fell asleep. Then Mam woke me up.

"Wake up Stella, wake up," She was shaking me. "Sometimes I think your mother's crazy. Do you know I forgot to ask her what ship her man's on. Ach well, never mind, McKechnie will know." She kissed me and tucked in the blankets around me. "Goodnight my baby, sleep tight."

But Mrs. McKechnie didn't know the ship Mrs. Bowden's man was on. "I don't even know his first name. She just always calls him the P.O.

190

'The P.O. this, the P.O. that.' They must get along alright together or she wouldn't mention him so much."

"Yes", said Mam "that was my impression too. I can ask her the name of his ship when she comes to her tea on Sunday."

"Bowden coming to her tea on Sunday? My, my, it didn't take you long to get in thick."

"You sound fair annoyed" said my Mam.

"I notice you haven't asked me."

"Well - I'm asking you now - can you come to your tea on Sunday?"

"Is that an afterthought?"

"Not at all. You're invited to your tea but I'm not begging you to come."

"Thanks very much," said Mrs. McKechnie.

My mother gave an impatient sigh, "What the devil's got into you lately?"

"It's what's got into you. I think you forget you were just the maid and not the mistress of that house where you worked."

Two red blotches came up on my mother's cheeks and her eyes were angry. "I'm never likely to forget that. God no! My humble beginnings are paraded before me every time I see a member of my family. No, they'll never let me forget who I am, but that doesn't mean I can't try to be something better."

"Now *you're* in the huff," said Mrs. McKechnie.

"Well are you coming to your tea on Sunday or are you not? You'd better make up your mind for I'm not asking you again."

"Oh I'll come," said Mrs. McKechnie grudgingly.

Before she left, my Mam told her, "Oh, by the by, it'll be just the three of us on Sunday. You, me, and Mrs. Bowden. Stella will be at her Granny Morrison's."

It was the first I had heard of it.

"I think you're telling me not to bring Doris?"

Doris started whining and swinging against her mother. "I want to come too, Mammy, I want to come with you."

"You can't Doris," said Mam, "this is adults only for a change."

"Oh please, Stella's Mammy, please let me come."

Mrs. McKechnie butted in. "With Archie working at the weekend and the school out, what am I supposed to do with her?"

My mother said something under her breath that sounded like "Drown her,"

"What was that - you - said?" asked Mrs. McKechnie, knowing fine what my Mam had said.

"I said, the same as you do with her the nights you're at the dancing. If you can leave her for that, you can leave her for this."

"Come on hen[70]," said Mrs. McKechnie to the now whimpering Doris, "you're not biding where you're not wanted. But mark my words Rachel Malcolm, you'll rue this."

"I doubt it," said Mam.

"Shit, you rotten bitch," was Mrs. McKechnie's parting shot.

Many times during that week my mother said, "She'll come alright! There couldn't be a show without Punch and that one's nose will be bothering her sore come Sunday."

But Mrs. McKechnie didn't come and I didn't have to go to my Granny Morrison's. Mam told me why. "I only said that so I'd have an excuse to tell McKechnie not to bring that damned wee pest. I can't be bothered with it at all, the way some folk take their brats with them everywhere they go. I wouldn't dream of letting you be a nuisance, always interrupting adult conversation, sticking your cheeky nose in." She was setting out the tea as she talked. "You see that stain on the cloth? That's where that little bugger skailt[71] her tea. I can't get the mark out and why are you standing there doing nothing? Get out the good dishes and see you don't drop them."

The good dishes were a measure of my mother's esteem for Mrs. Bowden. Mrs. McKechnie always got the cracked ones. I liked our good dishes. I had helped my mother choose them from the Littlewood's

---

[70] Girl

[71] Spilled or splashed

catalogue. Red, yellow, and purple tulips standing soldier-straight around the rims. There were only three cups left.

"I wish to God your father wouldn't throw the good dishes when he's in a paddy. We've plenty of the other kind, the Lord knows, but that's your father! Selfish, like all the Malcolms. No thought for anyone but himself. Come on then, move. You're standing there in a trance."

I was uneasy about our impending visitor. "What's Mrs. Bowden like?"

"If I've told you once I've told you a hundred times. Oh, Her man's a petty officer. She's not fancy like Miss Anderson, but definitely a step above McKechnie..." She was interrupted by the pealing of the doorbell.

"That's her now...go you and answer it while I wet the tea."

I grabbed her arm. "I'm feart Mammy."

She tried to shake me off. "What on earth for?"

"Ghosts. I'm feart she'll bring ghosts."

"Don't be so daft. Will - you - let - me - GO?" One by one she peeled my fingers off her arm and made for the door. "Oh hello Mrs. Bowden, I wasn't sure if I heard the bell or not. Come away in... it's a gey[72] cold day."

"It is that," said Mrs. Bowden, sweeping in on a blast of cold air and musk.

---

[72] Very

I loved Mrs. Bowden from the moment I saw her. She was Santa Claus and all the friendly ladies in one. She was the fattest woman I had ever seen. She wobbled when she walked and her colourful dresses were merely tents with holes cut in the top for her head. And such a head it was! Her high piled hair was the colour of a new penny and the long earrings she always wore nearly brushed her shoulders. Her teeth were white and even and the lips around them were always smiling even when they were holding a cigarette. She had a fat woman's laugh, rumbling and resonant. She laughed often, and coughed often too. After that visit my mother always said, "As sure as a cat's a beast that cough will get her if the fat doesn't get her first".

Oh the hours I practised smiling round a pencil. She smoked even when she talked, one eye screwed shut against the smoke from her cigarette.

"Here, let me take that." Mam held out her hand for the fox fur that lay like a listless snake across our visitor's bosom.

With ring covered fingers tipped the same scarlet as her lips, Mrs. Bowden disconnected the fox's jaw from its tail and handed the fur to my mother. I was glad she didn't give it to me for the fox's pointed chin and glassy stare gave me the grues[73].

"May I take your hat too?" Mam asked politely and shot me a dirty look.

I realised I had been staring for, put our guest under a street lamp and my mother would have made me look the other way. A large beauty spot looked very black against the bright pink of her cheekbones and over all a bluebird with outstretched wings, perched precariously on a nest of golden hair.

It was a hat that would have overpowered anyone else, but Mrs. Bowden had both fox and bluebird working for her and the result was majestic. Even without them she was an eye-catching figure. The high-swept coppery hair matched her amber earrings, which swung to and fro with every move of her head.

"Thank you dear but it's so much bother to put on, I think I'll just leave it where it is."

Had the bird ever been alive? Was it once able to sing... and fly? I swallowed hard and decided not to look at it while I was eating.

Mrs. Bowden leaned to the mirror to tuck up a wayward lock of hair. My eye caught hers in the glass. She winked at me. "Bluebirds for happiness but I wouldn't set any store by this one. It's a fake."

To my surprise I winked back. Suddenly I was hungry for my tea.

"Come on then," Mam told me sharply, "you're blocking the door."

Mrs. Bowden laughed. "She's wondering if I can get through it, aren't you hen[74]?"

When I nodded she laughed again. "Aye, that's what I thought."

---

[73] Horrors

[74] Girl

She dismissed my mother's polite protests by sweeping ahead of us into the kitchen. The eyes that smiled at me now were as blue as the bird on her hat.

When she saw all the nice things we were having to eat she said, "Oh my! What a lot of bother you've gone to."

"No bother at all," said my mother insincerely. "Now do sit where you can see the fire." While Mam fussed and Mrs. Bowden got herself settled, I studied her without anyone seeing. I decided that it wasn't just the way she looked that made her seem like a friendly lady. It was the way she made me feel. Like she really liked me and thought I was nice.

As she poured tea into the three tulip cups, Mam asked Mrs. Bowden, "I hope you don't think you were invited here because of your psychic powers, to hold a seance or anything like that. What I mean is, I wouldn't want you to think I was using you."

Mrs. Bowden denied any such thought and Mam went on, "It was just with your man in the navy I thought we'd likely have a lot in common."

Mrs. Bowden looked puzzled. "The navy? My man in the navy?"

"Aye. You kept calling him the P.O. so I thought he was a navy man."

Mrs. Bowden let out a whoop. "The P.O.? You think the P.O.'s my man?"

My mother nodded.

"Lord love ye, no. The P.O.'s my guide. The poor soul was drowned at Jutland."

"Never!" said Mam, pouring tea into Mrs. Bowden's cup. "You're not married then...oh but you must be, you're 'Mrs.'"

"Aye, I am, but in name only. Bowden took off one day and I've not heard eechie or ochie[75] from him since."

"Fancy! Where did he go?"

Mrs. Bowden shrugged. "I haven't a clue. He could be dead and buried for all I know."

"Oh, surely not...do help yourself...that plate's tongue and the other's salmon..." Mrs. Bowden took one of each. "... did he not leave a note?"

"Nothing", said Mrs. Bowden, quite joco[76].

"But that's terrible. Maybe he met with foul play. Some awful things go on you know."

"Oh I know that right enough but if he had been bumped off his body would have turned up long since. He's away two years past."

"You would have seen his ghost," I said.

---

[75] Anything at all

[76] Pleased (jocose)

198

My mother gave me a look. "What have I told you about interrupting adults? Another word out of you and you're away to your room."

Mrs Bowden said, "But the child's right. I think he'd have got in touch even if it was just to gloat over the fact that I couldn't lift a penny of his insurance without a death certificate."

"Was he an awkward man then?"

Mrs. Bowden took a bite of sandwich and winked at me again. "That's putting it mild."

"Maybe he's got insomnia," I said. Mrs. Bowden spluttered into her teacup.

"What did I just tell you?" shouted Mam.

"Leave her," gasped Mrs. Bowden, wiping her mouth.

"I'm sorry Mam, I forgot."

"You'll be a lot sorrier if you don't watch."

"For goodness sake...it was just the thought of Bowden having insomnia...pardon my French but that lazy bugger could sleep on the edge of a razor. But I know what you meant, hen. Amnesia..." She started laughing and spluttering again and when a crumb caught in her throat my Mam had to thump her back. When she could speak she mopped her eyes and said, "It's a sad heart that never rejoices." She looked like she might go off again and my mother thrust a plate of buttered scones under her nose. "Thanks," said Mrs. Bowden, "I'll just take two while they're here.

Mind you, the thought did occur to me that he might have lost his memory. Did you make this jam yourself? It's lovely."

"Did you not go to the police?" asked Mam, ignoring her question.

"I thought of it but decided against it."

"Oh?" said Mam, "why was that?"

"They might have found him and brought him back."

"Eh?" said Mam.

"What was the use of putting them to a lot of bother when, if the truth be told, I didna want him back. Mind you, I didn't come to that conclusion right away. At first I missed him the way ye'd miss anything that had become a habit. It was when I realised I was singing and enjoying my food that I decided to keep my mouth shut and count my blessings." She laughed and took another bite of scone. "No no, I have no regrets. I get on far better with the P.O."

My mother looked stunned and Mrs. Bowden went on, "Sorry, but it's true. He was a pure pest at the hinderend[77]." She lowered her voice and leaned towards my mother, "Forbye[78] everything else."

"Oh I'm not condemning you," said Mam. "I've got one myself that sounds very like Mr. Bowden." She turned to me. "If you're done with your tea, away ben[79] the house and shut your door."

---

[77] Towards the end

[78] As well as

[79] Through

200

I didn't want to go now. I wanted to stay and hear more about Mr. Bowden and the P.O. "Can I have another biscuit?"

"Take one with you."

"I'd like more tea as well."

"No. Take the biscuit and off you go."

Slowly I slid from my chair hoping my mother would change her mind.

"You're doing that in slow motion," she said.

Halfway across the room I turned back. "I forgot my biscuit."

Mam was refilling two of the cups and Mrs. Bowden was rummaging in her outsized bag. "I have a cigarette lighter in here somewhere but this bag's a wide address."

"I'll get you matches," I cried and darted back to the fireplace before my mother could stop me. I stood on tiptoe on the fender box and felt for them, my eyes on Mrs. Bowden all the while. From this angle I could see that her bottom overlapped her chair and the lock of hair was hanging loose again. For all that, she was so splendid and alive I wondered why she surrounded herself with dead things like the P.O. and the fox. The bird didn't count - it wasn't real.

My mother caught my eye. She was frowning. "You're going head first into that fire if you don't pay attention to what you're doing."

My fingers made connection with the matchbox and I climbed down.

"Would you light my cigarette for me please?" asked Mrs. Bowden.

I nodded and struck a match. The cigarette I held it to wasn't like the kind my Da smoked. It was thinner and there was a gold band around the bit she put in her mouth. She took a deep draw and started choking. I ran and got her a glass of water. When she had her breath back and the cigarette lit she said, "Oh dear that was a carry on. I'm glad the doctor wasn't here to see. He keeps telling me if I don't stop cigarettes they'll stop me. Thank you hen." She handed back the glass to me and I wondered if she had a little girl at home to bring her drinks when she choked. I wondered if she'd talk nice to her little girl and like her. Be glad that she had her. As though she knew what I was thinking she said, "If I had a girl like you to call my very own, I'd ask for nothing else in this life."

I felt my face grow warm and I looked at my mother to see if she was pleased too. She was still frowning at me. "You shouldn't tell her that. She's conceited enough."

Mrs. Bowden didn't say anything. She was puffing hard on her cigarette to bring it back to life.

"Can I go out to play instead?"

"You can do anything you like as long as you get out of here and stop interrupting."

The end of Mrs. Bowden's cigarette was glowing now but she must have pulled on it too hard for when she tried to speak she took a great fit of coughing and spluttering. Her face got very red and Mam jumped up and thumped her on the back. "Away you go then," she said to me.

Chapter 31 : The Willis Family

I was sorry to go before I saw what would happen but this was my chance to visit Betty and Sheila Willis who had moved into the caretaker's flat above the burned-out dance hall across the street.

As I crossed the street and climbed the stair I rehearsed what I would say. Mrs. Willis answered the door.

"Hello," I said, "I'm Stella Malcolm from across the street and I'd like to visit with Betty and Sheila, if it's all right."

She said I was welcome and led me through to the kitchen.

"Hello," I said to Betty who was still at the table.

"Hello." She didn't sound very pleased to see me.

"You're Stella," said Sheila.

I nodded, wondering what I would do next.

"Have you had your tea?" said Mrs. Willis.

I nodded again, and remembered what Auntie Con had told me. "Thanks."

"Well don't be shy," said Mr. Willis. "Nobody's shy in this house."

"Can they come out to play?" I nodded towards Betty and Sheila. They just looked at me.

"Out to play?" said Mrs. Willis. "At this time? It's dark already and as soon as they've finished their tea and done their homework they were to go to bed."

The fire crackled and sputtered and hissed. It sounded very loud.

"What time do you go to your bed Stella?" asked Mrs Willis.

"Anytime. Except when my Mam's angry with me. Then I have to go early."

"And is your Mam often angry at you?"

I didn't answer. I looked at my feet. I started to trace one of the flowers in the hearthrug with my toe.

Mr. Willis cleared his throat and Mrs. Willis said, "Will your mother be worried about you if you stay long enough for a game or two of Snakes and Ladders?"

"She said I can do what I like."

"Right," said Mr. Willis, "we'll get the board out."

Chapter 32 : Letter From America

I had graduated from A Child's Garden of Verses and visited Treasure Island before I heard any more about my grandfather.

"The old man's coming home. Ma's had a letter. I was there when it came," Uncle Eddie told my mother.

Her hand flew to her mouth, "Oh no ...how is she taking it?"

Uncle Eddie shrugged, "Like she takes everything. She started searching the bible for ammunition, then she changed her mind and said she was going to ignore the whole thing, so..." Uncle Eddie mimicked Granny, "I don't wish to hear or say another word about this." He laughed. "Then she tore the letter into bits."

My mother sucked in her breath. "When's he coming?"

"As soon as we send his fare."

"The old blackguard can whistle." Mam wrung the dishcloth as though it were someone's neck.

"Who?" I asked. "Who can whistle?" They ignored me.

"He has enough to get to New York. He needs passage from there."

"Let him swim," said my mother.

"I've spoken to Jim and George...they're willing to help." He whistled softly between his teeth, all the time watching my mother.

"So...?" said Mam.

Uncle Eddie stopped whistling and I saw his Adam's apple jump up from behind his collar and sink back down again.

..."Well, speak up. I know you're not here for the pleasure of my company."

Uncle Eddie looked at his shoes, pulled a handkerchief from his pocket and started buffing up the toes. "How much can I put you down for?"

"You can put me down for bugger all[80]. After what he did to me it's no wonder you can't look me in the eye when you ask that."

Uncle Eddie straightened up. "Oh come on now, you weren't the only one to be affected by his leaving. George had to leave school and he was the brightest of us all..."

"No he wasn't. I was.", said my Mam.

Uncle Eddie shrugged, "I didn't give a hang about school myself so I won't argue with you about that."

"See and don't then."

"Will you let me finish?" Uncle Eddie looked annoyed, and after a second's silence he went on, "Look at Jim then. He was the one who tried hardest to please the old man, but never could. Damn near had a breakdown."

"Don't dramatise... he was only ten."

---

[80] Nothing at all!

"He started wetting the bed."

"I don't remember that."

Uncle Eddie laughed. "You didn't have to sleep with him."

"You're breaking my heart"

"I'm trying to touch it, not break it, but so far I haven't seen any evidence that you even have one."

"You'd better give up then and go home."

Uncle Eddie ignored that. "And Con ...look at poor Con. Dried up before her time; a right old prune she's become."

"That's because she has no guts. She should have got out like I did."

"You were always good at getting out of things."

"None of what happened was my responsibility. Father was the one who got out of his. Well now he's coming back let him and mother remember they're still married and responsible for each other."

Suddenly I realised who they were talking about. "My grandfather! But he's dead."

I wasn't ignored that time. "Ears! Honest to God, this one's all ears." My mother turned on me. "What have I told you about listening to adult conversations? Now march right outside or I'll tan your hide."

"I have to go to the lavatory first," I said. The window there was always open a crack and because the day was fine, the adjacent window in the kitchen was open as well. No one would tell me about my grandfather, so I'd find out for myself. If I balanced on the rim of the toilet bowl my ear was almost level with the opening and my Mam's voice was loud when she was in a state.

She was saying, "So what reason did he give for coming back?"

"He said he had thought he was going to Zion but it turned out to be Babylon." My mother laughed scornfully, "Huh! I should have thought Babylon more to his taste."

Uncle Eddie laughed too. "I'd make a bet that's not the reason."

"And that's one bet you might win," said my Mam.   "How many have you lost lately?"

"Don't try to change the subject. How much?"

"I told you, bugger all. How do you think ma will feel if she finds out her family sent him money to come back?"

"Don't kid me that you care about her, especially since it was her fault he left. She never stopped nagging him and the quarrels went on half the night.

"Con and I used to call them the 'Religious Wars'," said Mam, laughing.

"Oh, said Uncle Eddie, "and I thought they had something to do with sex."

"Is sex all you think about?"

"Just about," said my Uncle and they both laughed.

"You're shameless," said Mam.

"Look who's talking," said Uncle Eddie.

There was a silence and I was about to get down from the toilet when my Mam went on, "Consider this then. . . if you send him money he might expect lodging from you as well."

" A lot of good it would do him. There are eight of us in three rooms and there'll soon be nine. Even with the most careful packing we couldn't fit him in."

"You would marry a pape[81] so don't expect sympathy from me."

"I'm not after sympathy."

"No - you're after money, and ...I refuse to get mixed up in this."

"God - you're hard Rachel. A few pounds wouldn't break you and don't forget - you were always his favourite. His 'wee lassie with the toy hair...'"

"You'll be asking me to put him up next..."

"...the one he took on his knee; the one he loved more than all the rest of us put together..."

"Shut up damn you."

"Do you remember what he used to sing to you?"

"I said, shut up."

---

[81] Catholic

I nearly fell down the hole when I realised my mother was crying. But Uncle Eddie was relentless. He started to sing "Bonny wee thing, canny wee thing..."

The kitchen window slammed shut and I heard no more. When Uncle Eddie left, I was outside playing peavers. He was whistling and I ran to catch up with him. "Can I chum you to the tram?"

"Come on then."

I skipped along beside him. "Can I come and visit you?"

He shook his head. "Your Auntie Mary's not well but you can come when she's better."

"Can my cousins come and play here then?"

He shook his head again. "Oooh...I don't think your mother would like the noise."

"She would so," I lied.

He laughed. "She only likes the noise she makes herself." He fumbled in his pocket and brought out a penny. "Here." He tossed it to me.

"Let me come with you...please Uncle Eddie."

"Here's my tram, I'll have to run for it."

I called after him, "What's my grandfather like?"

As he swung aboard the moving tram he called back over his shoulder, "Me. He's like me. A no damn good scoundrel." I could see him laughing.

Stella Maris   by   Nan O'Dell

I walked slowly home where I found my mother pacing.

Born in August she said she had a compulsion to pace. "I can't help it," she'd say, "I'm Leo the Lion."

It was always a bad sign. To me it signalled a storm and if I kept very quiet and very still it might pass without sucking me in. Never taking my eyes off her I slid sideways into the armchair my father usually occupied when he was home. It had a high back and lugs so some concealment was possible.

"Why?", she was saying. "Why in God's name did I give him money to help bring that old swine home? Now they want me to take him in." One of her fists pounded into the palm of her other hand. "Oh, Christ, why?"

I slid further down into the chair and the movement caught her attention. She whipped round on me. "As if it's not enough I'm stuck with you, I'd be stuck with him too. And look at you - all staring eyes and bloody cheek." She leaned over me, supporting herself on the arms of the chair so that her nose was nearly against mine. I could feel the warmth of her breath. "That teacher of yours has your head swollen like an inflated balloon." Hand on hip she began to mimic Miss Johnson. "Stella shows great promise but she seems tired all the time. Does she get enough sleep? As if I keep you up at night! No, I could tell her those circles under your eyes are from too MUCH sleep. What your fancy teacher doesn't know is that the balloon on your shoulders is empty. Shall I prove it?" She darted to the dresser drawer and brought out the bread-knife. She laughed, "Let's just prick it and see, shall we?"

Stella Maris   by   Nan O'Dell

I closed my eyes and scrunched my head down between my shoulders. I didn't breathe. Her hand was on my head when I heard the knife clatter onto the hearth. I opened one eye.

She started pacing again. She was talking about me as though I weren't there. "Clever! Huh! I was far cleverer than she'll ever be. I won a scholarship and would have won more but I lost the chance because of him. Because he found religion." She laughed and my spine tingled. She turned her attention back to me and once more I held my breath. "Your Granny tried for years to get him inside a church but he'd have none of it. Then one day two Mormon missionaries came to the door and succeeded where she had failed. He said he had found the true faith. He outscriptured her and outchurched her and it was priceless to watch." Mam's laugh was part sob and part scream. It stopped abruptly. In the echoing silence she walked over to the window above the sink and gazed intently into the backgreen. "That one's washing again," she said.

I let my breath out silently. "I don't understand the washer—wife mentality myself," she murmured almost absently. "But then, I was cut out for finer things." My heart knocked against my ribs and I gasped for air once more. I was thankful she didn't seem to notice.

"He had beaten her at her own game." It was said so softly that I barely caught it. At any moment she might shoot a question at me, and woe betide me if I couldn't answer. I gripped the arms of the chair and willed myself to die, but I couldn't die. "He <u>had</u> found what he was looking for; that much was true." She turned and looked at me • "Do you know what it was?" I shook my head. My mouth was so dry that I couldn't have spoken. "An excuse to get away from a wife and five children. Con had just turned sixteen and Eddie was ten. There were three of us between; I was right in the middle...." The rest of her words were lost to me. I had never known my mother to cry; yet she had cried when Uncle Eddie was here and now she was crying again. Slowly I moved towards her, not believing what I saw. I reached up and touched her cheek. It was wet. The tears were real.

"Mammy," I whispered"

With all her strength she hurled me from her. I staggered backwards but righted myself and made to run to my room. She lunged and caught me. She bent forward till her eyes were level with mine. "Listen you bastard, and listen carefully." She shook me. "Are you listening?" I nodded and she shrieked, "Say it then, say you're listening."

"I'm listening."

"Never expect me to do anything for you. Never. I shall never help you so don't expect it. Never. Never. Never. Now get to your room and don't let me see your ugly face again today." She started laughing again. "Do you know how ugly you are when you cry?"

But I hadn't been crying. She had.

Thankfully I went into my room and crawled under the bed beside Tibby who took refuge there at the first sign of trouble. I wanted to hold her, to bury my face in her soft fur, but she was spooked and wouldn't let me. I thought about Daniel in the lion's den and how he hadn't been feart.

The song we learned at the Band of Hope said that. And the Sunday school Jesus loved little children but Mam said he didn't love me because I was bad. Because I had bad blood in me from my da's side, that I was a mistake but she had wanted me anyway but my Da hadn't. I pulled at my hair to try and stop the thoughts but they kept coming. "I hate you Jesus and I hate God too and I hope you're both listening. Kill me if you like and see if I care." I kept tugging at my hair and the light faded and the room was dark. There was no sound from the kitchen but I was feart to look and see if Mam had gone out. Then I saw a strip of light under the door and I knew she was in and had lit the gas. I crawled out from under the bed when I heard her start to sing. She'd be coming for me soon and if she caught me there I'd get a row for sulking. "Big tumfie[82]," she'd call me and she might scream at me again. She liked me to he smiling when she came for me. She liked to look at a happy face and not at a big tumfie who didn't know how lucky she was to have a home and a mother who cared for her enough to chastise her.

My mother had second, and then third, thoughts about taking my grandfather in, but when she tried to back out of it Uncle Eddie told her that it was too late. The money had been sent and my grandfather would arrive in April.

She went to Granny who behaved as though she didn't quite know what my mother was talking about. "I didn't invite your father back, so what does where he stays have to do with me?" It was all she was ever to say on the subject and then she leaned back and closed her eyes. A sure sign that as far as she was concerned the subject was closed.

On our way out Mam stopped in at the kitchen to talk to Auntie Con, but she wasn't any help either. "I don't have any say in who'll stay here and who won't."

---

[82] Stupid softy

"You're not bloody dumb, are you?" Mam's temper was rising. "You could put in a word and point out to her that they're still married, and therefore still have some responsibility to each other."

"Isn't that what *you* just did, and from the look of you, you didn't get anywhere." Auntie Con smiled sweetly and my mother went mad, "You were listening, you must have been listening at the door you snoopy old maid."

"I didn't have to listen," retorted Auntie Con. "You never come here unless it's to hand someone a burden."

"Do you mean Stella?"

Auntie Con did what my mother did when she was caught unawares. Her hand flew to her mouth. Then she put her arms round my shoulders. "Of course I didn't mean Stella. You know, don't you pet, that your Auntie likes to take care of you?"

Before I could answer, my mother jumped in "Of course she meant you. She thinks you're a burden. What do you think of your beloved Auntie now?"

Auntie Con pressed me close and I was painfully aware of a corset stay pressing into my cheek. "As a matter of fact," she said, "I knew you'd be round, for Ed told me you were frantic to get out of your promise, and we knew you'd have a go at mother."

"So you all talk about me behind my back - I might have known. I've never fitted in with this family, and you've all been jealous of me because of it. You've resented that I am intellectually superior to all of you."

Granny's bell started ringing impatiently. "Now look what you've done," snapped Auntie Con. "She's heard your carry-on and now she'll be having a bad turn."

"Come on, we're leaving," said Mam to me as she shot out the door. I had to take little running steps to keep up with her. Behind me, Auntie Con called, "Don't believe her Stella. It's to her you're a burden, not to me."

Without turning round my mother shouted, "Devil take the lot of you."

During the months that followed she reproached herself constantly, "Why did I let myself get talked into it? I must have been insane." She told me, "First I'm stuck with you, and now I'm stuck with him, but I'll get out of it, you see if I don't. Jim would like to but that Ivy wouldn't hear of it and she has him firmly under her thumb."

"And that George – so superior and that timid frightened creature he's married to. No! George wouldn't have him. It's mother who should do it. It's mother's duty. And for all her so-called Christianity she's the most unforgiving woman in God's creation."

"Eddie can't but he needn't think he can pull his charm on me. No! I shall tell him I won't listen to whatever he says. Let him save his breath. I'll say, 'Don't think you can come here and work on my good nature. Don't think it. Just don't think it."

Chapter 33 : Rachel confronts Mary

One day Mam saw Uncle George coming up the Waverley Steps, just off the train from Glasgow. When she got home she was still fuming so I got a blow by blow description of the encounter.

"I told him *he* should take in the old man. He was the oldest son and the only one with enough room. He refused to discuss it! So I told him, 'You only come to Edinburgh to check up on mother's health, to see how long you might have to wait for her money.'"

"He didn't like that at all. He forgot to be fancy. 'Don't be such a bloody keelie[83],' he says to me out the side of his mouth, 'folk are looking at us.'"

"'And what's wrong with the truth?' I demanded to know and with that he was back down Waverley Steps like a shot. I fixed *him* all right. Oh, there's something about me that puts people in their place. Not many will risk my wrath."

She began to laugh. "I'm Leo the lion, after all." She lunged at me, growling. I jumped back. "You see, that's what I mean, people are frightened of me."

In all the years that have passed since then I have never heard the human voice contain such satisfaction, the human look such delight.

It was as well that she turned her back on me then, for with her uncanny ability, she might have read my thoughts in my eyes. In my mind

---

[83] A tough

Stella Maris   by   Nan O'Dell

I was back at Uncle Eddie's where I was to spend the night while she was away somewhere. I liked sleeping with my cousins though I was always scrubbed with carbolic when I got home. We would sit under the table, which was covered by a big cloth that hung to the floor, telling each other stories. .

Sometimes ghost stories, sometimes monster stories, made up, sometimes true stories, preferably scary ones. On the day I was remembering, Auntie Mary, without saying a word, lifted a corner of the cloth and slid a soup plate full of broken biscuits to us.

I wanted to be under Auntie Mary's table now, hidden by the tablecloth, eating broken biscuits, telling stories. I wanted to be lying in the box bed in the recess watching the shadows on the ceiling cast by the last flickers of the kitchen fire; listening to the latest baby's small sucking sounds as Auntie Mary murmured softly to him.

But I was drawn back to our own kitchen by my mother's voice, "... and that Olive! George has her frightened to death. She's a mouse that one. Huh! Scared rabbit would be more like it. And your Granny for all her so-called Christianity is the most unforgiving woman in God's creation. She'll never have him back. No it will fall on me, just you see..."

Her voice trailed off. She crossed to the bunker and leaned on it with her elbows, chin cupped in hand as she gazed out the window.

"The green's full again. Some women do nothing but wash." She said it almost absently, then she straightened and stretched. "Oh why do I worry about it? None of it is my business." I wasn't sure if she meant the green being full or my grandfather's return. When she turned to me I hurriedly closed my eyes.

218

"Have you been listening to me?" she asked.

I nodded and opened my eyes. She was looking at me with scorn. "You're like a damned old woman. When I was your age I was never tired. You should be out playing - having fun."

"Can I go out then?"

"No you can't, you're coming with me. I've made up my mind what I'm going to do so get your coat."

All the way to Uncle Eddie's and Auntie Mary's she outlined her strategy. "I'll take the war into the enemy's camp; put him on the defensive. I'll say, 'I demand my money back. I won't be party to your schemes!' I'll say, 'You and Jim and George can be fools if you like but I'll be like mother and have nothing to do with it.' That's what I'll say. I'll say 'Don't come crying to me when the old man lands on your door step.' How dare any of them expect anything from me."

As her words came faster, so the speed of her walk increased till I had to take little running steps to keep up with her. We were well past the tram stop when she realised it. "Could you not keep your wits about you and see where we were? Honest to God, everything's left to me." I turned and made to walk back towards the stop. "Come back stupid, we may as well keep walking now."

Down Leith Walk she muttered about what she'd tell Uncle Eddie, but when we got there, he wasn't home. Auntie Mary met us at the door with an infant under her arm and another whose birth seemed imminent. Joey was standing on a stool at the sink, skiddling. The front of his jersey was soaked and his nose was running. Auntie Mary greeted us with a harassed smile. "Come in if you can get in." She shoved a pile of dirty

219

clothes aside with her foot and nodded at the cluttered room. We followed her over an obstacle course of clothes and toys. "I was sorting the clothes for the wash when the baby got unwell." She tried to bend over to move a pile of magazines from a chair but couldn't manage it. "Here", she said to me, "lift those so your mother can sit down."

My mother ignored her and swept them on to the floor. "What I have to say won't take long." She perched herself on the edge of the chair, being careful not to lean back. "Where's Ed?" she asked.

"He's away out with Rose and Alec."

"When do you expect him back?"

"Oh, just when he gets here. He's got them away to the docks to see the boats." While she was talking, Auntie Mary crossed to the sink, and still clutching the baby, she turned off the tap and fumbled in her pocket for a piece of rag to wipe wee Joey's nose. He pulled away and she followed. Indignant, he batted the water in the basin and splashed Auntie Mary's bump as well as the baby, who let out a howl. Auntie Mary boxed Joey's ears and he started howling too. Over the din, she shouted at me, "Take the wean[84] while I make a cup of tea."

My mother gave an ill-concealed shudder and shouted, "No thanks, don't bother making tea for us."

I took Sammy anyway. He smelled but his cheek against mine was even silkier than my Granda's gold watch. I kissed him and he grabbed a fistful of my hair. "Ouch," I cried, eyes watering.

---

[84] Baby

"Stop trying to get attention," my mother shouted at me.

"It's all right hen[85], I'll take him." Auntie Mary pried open his fingers and freed my hair. He let out another howl.

"Please let me keep holding him," I pleaded.

"He needs changing," she yelled above the din.

"Never mind me," My mother shouted it with such wrath in her voice that both children stopped howling and looked at her. Joey ran to his mother and held on.

In the resounding quiet my mother said, "That's better, my head was beginning to throb."

"Let me make you tea then," said my Auntie.

"I couldn't swallow anything in this midden[86]."

"There's no need to he nasty." Auntie Mary looked more hurt than angry.

"When did they leave?" (My mother tapping her fingers impatiently on the arm of the chair.)

"Two hours since. I expected them back by now."

---

[85] Girl

[86] Shambles, dunghill

"It was Ed I really came to see but it would be hard to find anyone in this clutter. They could be back and buried under one of the piles." My mother laughed.

"There's no need to be nasty," said Auntie Mary again.

"Oh you're too sensitive." Auntie Mary was silent and Mam went on, "The direct approach is always best so I'll come straight to the point. I've changed my mind about taking father."

"Ed told me you wanted out of it."

"Yes, well, I meant it. The ones who put up the money to bring him home will have to take the consequences. I'm having nothing to do with it."

My Aunt looked around the room. "Where would we put him?"

"You should have thought of that before you sent the money. How much did you send anyway?"

"We each gave what we could afford and ours wasn't much. We really couldn't afford anything."

"Well more fool you," said Mam.

Auntie Mary's eyes filled up with tears. "It was what I had saved towards a new hearth rug and the weans' Christmas.

"How much?"

"Twenty-five shillings." Auntie Mary whispered it as though stunned by the amount.

"Tell you what then," said Mam, "I'll give you your twenty-five shillings back, plus a pound and you take him in. And I think that's generous. I'll even give you an idea for replacing the hearth rug that won't cost you a penny."

"What's that?"

"You have fire insurance don't you?"

Auntie Mary nodded.

Mam went in her bag and brought out a pound note and two half crowns, which she laid on the table between a bottle of H.P. sauce and a soup plate of broken biscuits. With great deliberation she brought out a second pound note. "There, just say yes to my proposition and it's yours. The idea for getting a new hearth rug free, of course."

"You want me to cheat the insurance company don't you? To burn a hole in the rug and say a coal jumped out the grate."

My mother laughed. "McKechnie did it and she got a lovely new rug in the sales and enough left over for a night at the pictures."

Auntie Mary stood looking at my mother and her face was expressionless. I wished my mother would stop what she was doing. I wished my Aunt Mary would put her out. But then I'd have to go too and I didn't want to go home with my mother, angry as she'd be. I wanted to stay here with Sammy and Joey and Auntie Mary. I laid my cheek against Sammy's silken one. "I love you," I whispered to him, "I love you baby."

My mother was still going on. "You're overcrowded as it is and if you take in the old man your name might be moved forward for a council house. They're putting up some lovely ones. You might get a main door and a bit of garden for the children to play in." All the time she kept her gaze fixed on my Auntie's as though trying to hypnotise her. "You're not scared of what Ed will say, are you?" Aunt Mary still didn't answer and my mother said impatiently, "Oh for God's sake, don't be so timorous. She lifted the money off the table and waved in front of my Auntie. "Take it - come on - it won't burn you. Mam laughed again. And if you're worried that burning the rug will sin your soul, I'm sure Father Bathbush will absolve you at confession."

Auntie Mary drew herself up as erectly as she could in her condition. "This is my home," she said with great dignity, "and you've no right to come into it and talk to me as you've done today."

"Shit then," said my mother, beaten, and turning to me, "Come on you."

Chapter 34 : Granda Morrison

Unwilling though my mother had been to take my Granda in, the time arrived when she needed the money she intended to ask for his keep. My father had been gone for several months by then, and the occasional work my mother had found lately wasn't enough to keep us. As far as I knew my father had contributed nothing.

Granda arrived on a day in early spring when the clouds chased each other across the sky and the wind blew my skirts around my neck in playful gusts. My mother called out the window for me to come up at once for I was a perfect disgrace but I pretended not to hear and kept skipping along a peavery bed, one eye all the time on the corner round which I expected my Granda to come momentarily.

Finally I tired of both waiting and skipping and when a missile, weighted down with pennies landed at my feet I was glad of the diversion and I waved up to my mother who had flung it. "Read it, read it." she shouted and I unfolded it to find that I was to "Take the money to the wee shop for a quarter pound of boiled ham and hurry up for your Granda's here and waiting for his tea."

When I got back from the wee shop, I took the stairs two at a time, only stopping for breath when I reached the top landing. I could hear my mother's company laugh. The one she used when she wasn't sure of herself. Then I heard a man's answering laugh and I turned on my heels and started back down the stairs.

"Stella, where are you going? Your Granda's here," said my Mam from our open door. I looked back at her, panic-stricken.

"Come on then," she said impatiently, "he won't eat you."

I followed her into the kitchen, all the while watching my feet. The toe of my left shoe was scuffed. I hoped my Granda wouldn't notice. Silent, I stood stork-like with my left foot tucked behind the calf of my right leg. I could hear my mother making excuses for my bad behaviour.

"It's I who should apologise to Stella," my grandfather was saying. "I walked by her without realising who she was."

Startled that someone should apologise to me I lifted my eyes and was caught in the kindest gaze I had ever seen. I walked towards it and into my grandfather's waiting arms. He was home! So was I.

Within the week my grandfather was installed and though the trumpet had gone towards his fare, his throat produced sweeter sounds than any instrument I had ever heard. And everything, it seemed, reminded him of a song, something that delighted me but was to prove an annoyance to my father. But that didn't happen for a while, and meantime, there was the joy of his presence and the happy realisation that he liked me.

My mother couldn't understand it. "You're the only one he has any time for. I can't see what's so special about you."

I couldn't see either, but maybe it was something to do with my eagerness to share his life, and to hear about the one he had just forsaken. In the long days that I spent alone with my grandfather that summer, without moving from a grey Edinburgh tenement, he took me to Salt Lake City and showed me the scarlet maples in autumn. With him I saw the tall poplars called Mormon Elders because each one represented an elder of the church at the time they were planted. Together, we smelled the white rambler roses that were scentless in the daytime but sweated sweetness on hot summer nights.

"Aye, the desert blossomed as the rose, just as Brother Brigham prophesied it would," my grandfather told me. He taught me the hymns sung by Mormon pioneers on their long and hazardous trek to he Valley of the Salt Lake.

It soon became apparent that my grandfather was not the solution to our financial problems. He couldn't find a job and what money he may have brought from America was running out. He still managed to put ten shillings on the kitchen table every Monday morning but our outings had to be kept within walking distance for the day had come when on a trip to Cramond I had to make a choice between an ice cream cone and the tramcar home. The day being exceptionally hot I chose the ice cream, eating it ankle deep in the River Almond. Since we were both going to walk home, Granda had an ice-cream as well. Enjoyable as it was at the moment of eating, the choice was unwise in a climate such as ours because the day deteriorated into a sullen sky and a slate-grey sea. My grandfather, who had been asleep, sprang to his feet when rain splatted on him. He made abortive attempts to dry my feet with his pocket-handkerchief but the socks stuck to my still-damp skin as I tried to pull them on. Finally he stuck my socks into his pocket and I stuck my bare feet into my sandals and we sprinted for the street that led to the tramlines. It was only when we reached the stop that we remembered. "Well," said my grandfather as rain dripped off the ends of our hair, "we shall just keep in mind those poor souls in Africa who are dying from drought. So give us your hand wee yin[87] and we'll just go singing in the rain."

And we did. All the same I think he was relieved that my mother wasn't in when we got home for she was critical of my Granda and wouldn't have let him away with getting me wet. The fact that it was the rain and not him wouldn't have made any difference.

One day when Mam and I got up, Granda was already dressed and about to leave.

"Don't set for me," said Granda. I've had mine."

"It couldn't have been much," said Mam.   There's only a dirty cup in the sink."

"Tea was all I wanted."

---

[87] Little one

"Don't tell me I hurt your feelings yesterday when I said about not contributing to your keep?"

Granda shook his head. "I didn't want anything this morning. I'm going out directly."

"Where?" asked Mam.

"To follow up on some of the jobs I've applied for."

"Oh," Mam's voice was flat. "So I did hurt your feelings."

I heard my grandfather's sharp little sigh, "That's not the point. You were right anyway... I have to find a job."

"Well, you would choose today to go out. I had plans." She spoke as though my grandfather was going out just to spite her. He asked what her plans were. "Oh what do you care?" she said. "What does anyone care? Well, she'll just have to be locked in. I'm tied in here from one year's end to the next and I won't give up today. I'm going out." She had crossed to the window above the sink and stood gazing out silently for a minute or two. Then, "Oh, how I long to be free. I won't he able to cross the door once he gets home."

All the brightness went out of the day when my Mam talked about wanting to be free. I wished I were old enough to run away. Maybe Granda and I could go together and not bother my Mam any more. I realised I was holding her dream book. I edged backwards into the lobby. Then I went to the bathroom, tore the dream book into little pieces and flung them into the toilet. It took two flushings to get them all away.

Stella Maris   by   Nan O'Dell

I marched right back into the kitchen in time to hear my Granda telling my Mam that it wasn't right to go out and leave me locked in by myself.

"You're the last one who should say anything about right and wrong. Look what you did to yours." She glared at my grandfather, who turned on his heel and walked out. I heard the front door bang behind him. I watched my Mam's face and I was feart. But my Mam said, "Come on, we'll get our breakfast." We sat down in our usual places and Mam said, "Where's the dreambook?"

I jumped up and pretended to look for it in the bookcase, but all the time my eyes were screwed shut and my mind was saying Granny's text.

"The Lord is the strength of my life; of whom shall I be afraid?"

"Oh, come on, never mind it. I'll try to remember my dream and look it up later." When I turned round Mam said, "Why is your face so white? Are you not feeling well?"

My teeth had begun to chatter but I managed to say, "I'm cold."

"Hurry then, drink up your tea and I'll tell you my dream." She took a bite of toast, chewed it carefully, and once it was gone, said, "It was a strange dream. A very strange dream. I was walking on water! Thank goodness it wasn't still water. There was a slow, easy swell. Just enough to keep it from being an unlucky dream. I could see you and your grandfather in a rowboat away in the distance. Ever so far from me. I was calling you to come back, not to leave me alone, but neither of you heard. Then I caught your eye and waved and you waved back. I started to run - still on the water, mind you and when I got closer I heard your Granda say, "Leave her. If we let her in she'll sink the boat. And suddenly it was your Da and

229

not your Granda who was saying it, but it didn't matter anyway. You held out your hands to me and I was trying to grasp them when I woke up. I was glad to be awake. Even if I had the dreambook, I wouldn't know what to look up first. Boat? Water? Father?

One day when my mother was out my grandfather showed me a picture of the Mormon Temple, which only the faithful were allowed to enter. "That's the angel Gabriel on top, calling believers to Zion." He started to sing. "Come, come ye saints, no toil nor labour fear, But with joy, wend your way, though hard to you this journey may appear..." The song petered out and he was silent for a long time. Then, "I am like Moses looking at the Promised Land and forbidden to enter." A tear trickled down the side of his nose.

I lifted Tibby from the hearthrug and placed her on his knee. "Stroke her Granda, she'll make you better." His eyes were fixed on something I couldn't see and he seemed not to breathe. I was feart he <u>had</u> gone to the Promised Land, and had got in. I grabbed his hand and ran it along the length of the cat's back. "Feel how soft," I said.

He gave a jump and his blue eyes focused on me, "Where were we?" he asked. I didn't want to go back to the place where I couldn't follow so I pointed to the mountains behind the Temple. "The Wasatch Range of the Rocky Mountains," he said, and started, once more, to sing - a joyous song this time. "Oh ye mountains high, where the clear blue sky arches over the vales of the free, where the pure breezes blow and the clear streamlets flow, how I've longed to your bosom to flee."

I could see that, for my Granny had no bosom to speak of. She was like a board in front and when I was wee and sat on her knee, I didn't like to lean back. Maybe the Wasatch Range was more like Miss Walker who lived in the next close. My mother always made me look the other way when we passed her. "Street Walker," she would hiss, and I'd be feart Miss Walker would hear her and start a row, but nothing had happened so far. If I managed to see out the corner of my eye Miss Walker would be struggling to anchor the skimpy little fur she wore, even in summer, to her massive bosom.

Her nails and lips always matched the bright red of her hat and I liked the click-click of her high heels on the pavement. She was nice and once she gave me a sixpence for running a message[88] for her. I would have liked to say hello when we passed her on the street.

But now I looked at my grandfather who had risen to his feet and was letting it rip. "Oh my own mountain home, unto thee I have come, all my fond hopes are centred in thee." Was there ever anyone as handsome and noble looking as my grandfather? His slim erect figure gave the illusion of height and the silvery hair, that he washed over the sink every morning, shone like a halo in the soft evening light. He was as fastidious in his clothes as he was in his person. His suit might be glossy from wear, but the crease in the trousers was sharp from its nightly press under his mattress. A king. My grandfather looked like a king.

"Come on wee lass, join in." I got to my feet too and together we sang, "Oh Zion, dear Zion, land of..."

The door opened with a crash that knocked the text off the wall and I knew, before she was through it that my Mam was in a bad mood. "Couldn't you at least start the tea? You're not doing anything else!"

---

[88] An errand

"Granda was telling me about Salt Lake City," I said.

"Filling your head with a lot of lies and rubbish." Mam spoke as though my grandfather weren't there. She rattled the poker in the grate and a spark flew from between the bars and landed glowing on the hearthrug. Mam stamped on it with her foot. "What" – stamp - "good" - stamp - "is he" - stamp - "to anyone!" - stamp.

Tibby shot under the sofa and I flew to my grandfather and held on.

"Stop it Rachel," he said quietly to my mother.

"Don't tell me what to do," she shrieked. "Why did you come back anyway?" She pointed to me, "As if that's not responsibility enough, I have to put up with you, too."

I could feel his hand tremble as my grandfather pressed my face into his waistcoat and the sweet smell of his tobacco. He bent and whispered, "Away ben[89] the house." But my mother knew what he was saying, "No! She'll stay here and listen. She thinks you're so wonderful and it's time she learned the truth."

I let go of my grandfather and clapped my hands to my ears. My Mam pulled them away. "No, you'll listen and you'll hear about him and his escapades. Then see if you think he's so great."

She turned to my grandfather. "Why don't you tell her why you went to Salt Lake City?"

---

[89] Through

232

My grandfather took me by the shoulders and turned me around to face him. He tilted my chin so I had to look in his eyes. I closed mine. I wanted to be sick. I didn't want to hear.

"I went to Salt Lake," said my grandfather slowly and quietly, "because I believed it was the home of the true church of God."

"Liar," my mother sneered. He wanted away from his responsibilities – six of them."

"No," said my grandfather, "I wanted all of you with me, but your mother wouldn't consider it."

"What a relief that must have been!" said Mam.   "Oh, yes, we found out about the winsome widow he met at a Mormon Meeting. She turned her husband's insurance money into a one way ticket to Utah and there was just enough left over to help pay for your grandfather's company on the journey."

I wished my Mam would stop talking at me.

"Not true," said my grandfather. "It was a business arrangement and I paid her back with interest."

My mother laughed. "Interest? So that's what he calls it!"

"I wrote and told your grandmother I wanted her to change her mind. I said I'd save all I could and when I had enough money I'd send their fares."

Now they were both talking at me. "Stop it. Please stop it." I said and started to cry.

"Then why didn't he? Why didn't he send our fares? Ask him. Ask him that", my mother shouted at me.

"Because I was foolish. I saw a way of making it happen faster so I gave what I had to someone to invest for me. I never saw the money – or the man – again."

"A Mormon?" asked my mother.

He hesitated, then nodded.

"Hah," said my mother, "the Saints aren't so saintly after all."

Chapter 35 : Miss "Walker"

On fine days, when he wasn't out searching for work, my grandfather would take me to the park. He'd buy a paper from Mr. Gentry, the newsagent, and while Granda sat on a bench reading the advertisements I'd play on the swings. Mam said we needed Granda's money but I hoped he wouldn't find a job and go and leave me. The days were long when Mam had to go away, and Tib and I were locked in the house. When she was home, I got out to play, but never to the park. Mam said she was looking after my welfare, for bad men sometimes hid in the bushes and waited for wee girls. Since my grandfather had been taking me I had never seen any bad men in the bushes, but Mam said that sure as fate, the one time I went alone would be the very time one would catch me.

It was a hot summer day, I remember, when my grandfather forsook his usual bench for a seat on the grass beside the duck-pond, "because it might be cooler there." The park was quiet. The quiet air was still and there were no shadows. Half a dozen boys half-heartedly dribbled a ball in the playing field. One by one they collapsed on the grass, wiping their faces. Sweat prickled my back. My Granda shook out two sheets from his newspaper and with dexterity fashioned a pair of cocked hats. "Here," he put one on my head and the other on his own, "these will keep the sun off our heads."

When we rounded the path that led to the pond I saw Miss Walker feeding the ducks. I recognised her by the little fur draped over her arm like a listless snake. I stared with envy at the thick coppery waves of hair usually hidden by the red hat that now lay at her feet. Her hair was the kind that Mam told me I would get if I ate my carrots.

When I recognised her I glanced at my grandfather, unsure of how I should behave, but he was smiling, and when we got close to her, my Granda said, "Good morning," and raised his paper hat. Miss Walker smiled back and Granda went on, "It's hard to keep cool on a day like this."

Miss Walker nodded, and looked at me with eyes that were even bluer than my grandfather's. "Is this your little girl?"

"My granddaughter."

"You live near me. I've seen you often," she said to me. I looked at the ground. I had hoped she wouldn't remember me, for I was ashamed of having to turn my head away when Mam and I passed her. But when I looked up, Miss Walker was smiling at me and her eyes were smiling too.

"You ran a message[90] for me once," she said. She didn't mention the sixpence she gave me.

Granda held out his hand, "My granddaughter is Stella Malcolm and I am Joseph Morrison." Miss Walker held out her hand too, "I'm Nettie Vincent."

I should have known, from the way Mam hissed it as we passed her, that Street Walker wasn't her real name. It would be hard now to remember that she was Miss Vincent.

My grandfather spread the rest of his paper on the grass.

"Would you care to sit down?" he asked her.

Miss Vincent hesitated and looked at her feet. The ankles above the perilously high heels were puffy and her feet had swelled around the straps of her shoes. "I'd love to sit down," and added ruefully, "It's the getting up."

My Granda bowed gallantly, "My grand-daughter and I are here to assist you."

Miss Vincent handed me her bag of bread before she collapsed onto the newspaper. "Would you like to feed the ducks?"

---

[90] An errand

I nodded and took the bag. The ducks squawked as they followed me in convoy and their squawks drowned out what my grandfather and Miss Vincent were saying. I'd rather have stayed and listened to them talking. While I was feeding the ducks I thought about the time I ran a message[91] for Miss Vincent. It was a package from the chemist and when I delivered the package to her flat I had a good look around.

The flat, really just a long room, was partitioned off by a screen that hid the bed from the rest of the room. The screen had a cavalier on it flanked by two busty women. Under the picture were the words, "Between two fires." The Cavalier was ogling the two women.

The dressing table was a clutter of china ornaments and cosmetics; a child holding a cat, a figure sitting on a po[92], with Miss Vincent's hat covering all but his nether parts, a cupid with a broken arrow, a posy of forget-me-nots, a comb with teeth missing, a wrinkled hair ribbon, and her fur draped over the mirror.

An arm chair had papers and magazines sticking out from behind a cushion. An Indian shawl covered the table with its fringe touching the floor. On it were the remains of a meal, in fact, the remains of several meals. Auntie Con would have called the room Paddy's Market.

The screen would have been better off hiding the dressing table but then, maybe the bed was worse!

I hoped Miss Vincent didn't mind me staring.

I had hoped to see the picture of a soldier. He'd have been killed in the war so Miss Vincent would have a reason for the clutter. She didn't care any more. The heart had gone out of her. Somewhere there would be an empty chocolate box – a lady with a wistful face on the cover. Inside a bundle tied in ribbon. Letters from the front. The last one saying he

---

[91] An errand

[92] Chamber pot

wouldn't mind dying were it not for her. Death and carnage all around – his friends killed or maimed. The thought of her gave him courage to fight on – to keep the enemy away from our island home – "No Hun shall have you.", he'd say, and as Miss Vincent read them a tear would run down her deathly pale cheek.

When the bread was gone and the ducks had swum off I heard Miss Vincent ask my grandfather, "What brought you back?"

They must have been talking about Salt Lake. I skipped over to them and pretended to be absorbed in picking daisies.

"The depression," said my grandfather.

But that was a lie! I knew depression when I saw it. Mam got depressions all the time and sometimes she sat for hours, not moving, and if she spoke at all, the words were flat and slow like she had trouble getting them out. My grandfather was never like that. Even when he was silent and still, there was colour and movement and sound all about him. Depression was a black bog that sucked you in, Mam would tell me when it was over. I noticed now how quickly my grandfather turned the conversation back to Miss Vincent. "Do you go out to business?" he asked her.

Miss Vincent started picking daisies too. "No. I work at home."

"Oh?" said grandfather.

Her head was turned away from him. She started picking the daisies on my patch of grass. "I give readings."

Grandfather looked puzzled. "Oh.", he said again.

Miss Vincent dropped her daisies and looked my Granda straight in the eye. "Some people call it fortune telling."

"I'd ask you to tell mine," said Granda," but I'm not sure I want to know what's ahead."

"It might be something good," Miss Vincent gave a half-hearted little laugh that sounded like she didn't believe it.

My grandfather fixed his eyes on the horizon, "Maybe...but forward though I canna see I guess and fear." He looked at her again. "Can you make enough at that to live on?"

Miss Vincent picked up her little pile of flowers and counted them carefully before she replied. Her cheeks were very pink. "I have a regular clientele," she said.

Granda nodded and looked back at the horizon. "I suppose that sort of thing is popular with the ladies."

The air was very still and heavy with moisture. A swarm of gnats hung above the gravel path. No one spoke. Suddenly thunder rumbled in the distance and a cold breeze lifted the corner of the newspaper.

"Rain," said my grandfather and leapt to his feet. Miss Vincent tried to get up but rolled backwards on to her daisies. The daisies were done for. "Here," my grandfather held out his hands and helped her to her feet. Freed of its burden, the paper lifted with the wind and whipped away in all directions.

We ran, but the rain caught us. Before we reached the park gates, Miss Vincent's hair was in dripping strands and the black stuff had washed off her lashes and was streaking down her face. My dress clung, sodden, to my legs and Granda's jacket was wet across the shoulders. We parted without ceremony at Miss Vincent's close, and once indoors, my grandfather built a fire with sticks and paper. I was shivering. Hurry and dry yourself off," he said, "while I fix a hot drink." When I came back, he had pulled a chair close to the blaze for me. "I hope you haven't caught your death," he said.

But for the next few days I was feart that my Granda had caught his death. His barking, breath-catching coughs woke me up at night. The skin beneath his eyes became blue and papery and the veins on the backs of his hands stood out.

My Granda never ate much but now he hardly ate at all. He was always thirsty, though, and drank a lot of tea. Sometimes Mam was gone when he got up and I fixed it for him. My Granda never complained like my Mam did when there were tealeaves floating on the top.

Granda's coughing bothered my Mam. "Can't you control it? I wake up every morning with a splitting head." She pressed a hand against her forehead. "Oh, why did I let myself get into this?"

Granda knew what she meant. "As soon as I get a job I'll find another place to live," he said quietly.

Mam ploughed on as though he hadn't spoken, "When I think of mother and Con rattling around in that big house. Just the two of them. They could take you in and you'd never be noticed in a house that size. Ma had to take that place after you left. We had to take in boarders to survive, and I had to give up my bursary and go out to work..."

I looked at my grandfather but I couldn't tell anything from his face. "I'll find a job," he said again.

"But you're not even looking now," said Mam.

"I haven't been able for the last fortnight."

"One excuse is as good as another, but I'm warning you. Dennis is due home soon, and he won't take kindly to your being here if you're not contributing to your keep. That coughing won't endear you to him either."

They said no more about it then, and the next day my Mam brought in a half bottle of whiskey with her groceries. She presented it to my grandfather as though it were an apology, "Make yourself a hot toddy."

My grandfather thanked her. "It was kind of you, Rachel."

That night the bottle was still sitting unopened on the sideboard where Mam had placed it. "What's this then?" She rapped on my grandfather's door, which he had just closed, and called, "Did you forget about the toddy?"

Granda opened the door; "I'll try and do without it."

"No you won't. You'll drink it and let me get a night's sleep."

240

He was silent. Mam said, "Oh I see! She laughed. "Hah! It's against your religion to take a drink. You old hypocrite! You drink tea like it was going out of style and you foul this flat with the reek of your tobacco, and they're forbidden too." Still no response. "Well aren't they?"

He nodded. "But that's not the reason."

"Damn the reason," Mam shouted. "You'll drink that or you'll get out."

I flew to my Granda, "Please don't get out. Please stay here." My mother aimed a blow at my ear and I ducked.

"Very well," said my grandfather, "I'll drink it."

The next morning he was dressed and had the fire going by the time Mam and I were up.

"You see," said my Mam," that whiskey did you good. I didn't hear you once."

I had heard him, but I didn't say anything. My Granda was still there and my Mam was singing that the sun had got his hat on and was coming out today. It was a good sound and if I were very careful, it would be a good day too.

"Come on then," she said to me, "You set the table while I fix the toast.

Chapter 36 : Granda meets Granny

My grandfather had been with us for almost three months when a message came from Granny. "My, my," said my mother as she read it, "the ice is cracking. Your Granny wants us over this coming Sunday and we're to bring your grandfather."

I hoped Granny wouldn't take a fancy to my Granda and invite him back to live with her. I hoped he would think she was an old prune. That's what my Da called her behind her back. But my curiosity about their meeting outweighed my fears, and the days dragged till Sunday.

On the tramcar going to Granny's I watched my grandfather out the corner of my eye. He shone from the top of his silvery head to the toes of his dubbined[93] boots. I couldn't imagine my Granny shining, though she'd look tidy enough in her black bombazine that she kept for Sundays. She always tied a silk apron over it to keep it clean, but Auntie Con said that was just for show since she never did anything that would get her dirty. Granny's hair was in two colours. Auntie Con called it salt and pepper. She wore it pulled straight back into a skimpy bun but maybe today she'd have it fluffed out a bit at the sides and wear her tortoiseshell combs to show this was a special occasion.

My grandfather would bow and kiss her hand. I couldn't imagine my Granny letting him kiss her anywhere else. While they reminisced, Granny's fingers would roll up the corner of her apron, smooth it out, roll

---

[93] Dubbin: a grease preparation to soften leather

it up, and smooth it out, the way she did in times of agitation. She might even faint when he kissed her and Auntie Con would have to run for the smelling salts.

"Wake up, dreamy Daniel," said my grandfather.

I came to and saw the Firth[94] just ahead. I hoped Granda hadn't guessed what I was thinking. I pointed to a tanker that sat on the line between sea and sky. "There's my da's ship."

"Your Da should be in Abadan by now," said my Mam. She examined her fingernails carefully; "I wonder what he's doing."

The tramcar rattled round the corner. "We're nearly there, Granda." He was staring straight ahead and didn't let on he heard. I said it again, louder, and tugged at his sleeve. He shook me off impatiently. "Stop pulling at me."

I pretended to be looking at something in the opposite direction. "I didn't mean to hurt you Stella," he said, "but you were talking too much."

That was funny, for a minute ago he had wakened me out of a dream I was enjoying. Now he said I talked too much. I thought about that as I walked along the street behind my Mam and my grandfather. Suddenly Mam looked round; "That pair of shoes has to last you, so stop scuffing the toes."

I hadn't realised I was doing it. I ran to catch up with them and my grandfather took my hand as we walked up to Granny's door.

---

[94] Firth of Forth, the mouth of the Forth river

Auntie Con met us there. "Con?" my grandfather said with a question in his voice. My Auntie Con nodded and held out her hand. "Hello father." My grandfather shook it politely and we all walked in. Oh well, I hadn't expected any kissing till he got to Granny. I nearly tripped him up in my haste to reach the parlour before he did. I wanted to see their faces when they met.

But my grandfather was taking his time, asking Auntie Con how she was. Then she asked him how he was. I wished they'd hurry up. But finally he was coming, rubbing his hands as though they were cold; shrugging his shoulders as though he were shrugging on the coat he had just removed.

I flung open the parlour door and it was a good thing that my Granny was looking over the top of my head at my grandfather, for my eyes jumped clean out of their sockets. Behind me my mother made a gurgling sound and I heard her footsteps run back across the lobby to the kitchen.

Something was far wrong with my Granny. Her hair had gone all striped like a football jersey. The colours reminded me of the chestnuts on the tree in our school playground *and* the pillar-box at the end of the road. The bun had been replaced by fat sausages and some of them were scorched. And black bombazine my foot! She had on a maroon dress and the longest string of beads I had ever seen.

When my Granda said, "Aye Alice," she blushed. It looked funny with that hair.

"Run and tell your Auntie Con to bring in the tea," she said to me.

I couldn't move for looking at her. "Hurry then," she said.

I still clung to the door handle. My grandfather turned to me. "Do as you're told," he barked.

I found my mother, doubled up, in the kitchen. "Whose hand was responsible for that desecration?" she gasped.

"Mine." Auntie Con sounded annoyed. "And she'll never let me forget it, so don't you start. It was too late to get in touch and tell you not to come."

"I'm glad it was too late to stop us." She started laughing again.

"Here", Auntie Con handed me a little bundle of rice paper flags. "Stick these in the sandwiches."

"Whose idea was it?" asked Mam, wiping her eyes.

"Her own and she was too damned mean to go to a hairdresser. That mess came out of a bottle."

"Granny says you're to take in the tea now," I said.

They ignored me. "You should have refused to do it," said my Mam to Auntie Con.

"She makes my life miserable when I cross her," said my Auntie.

"She'll make it more miserable now," said Mam.

"I'm damned if I do and damned if I don't. Sometimes I wish..." Auntie Con's voice trailed off.

"Are you well enough?" my mother spoke sharply. "You're looking awfully old."

"Thanks," said Auntie Con.

"No need to be offended," said my Mam. "It's a fact, and you should see a doctor."

"It's not a doctor I need," said Auntie Con.

My Mam shrugged, "Oh well, suit yourself."

"I wish I could," said Auntie Con.

I took advantage of a pause in their conversation; "I'll take the sandwiches in now."

"I have another job for you first." Auntie Con turned to my mother who had seated herself on the drainboard and was swinging her legs. "There's a job for you too... if you're not too busy doing nothing."

Mam didn't move. "What's got into you Con? You never used to be like this. You were always the sweet-natured one in the family. Everyone liked you."

Auntie Con walked into the pantry without answering, but Mam didn't take the hint. "I *know* she's difficult Con, but look at it this way. You never have to worry where you're next meal's coming from."

Auntie Con came back and handed me a clean tea-towel. "Wipe those dishes off. They haven't been used in a long time and they might be dusty.'

My mother pressed on doggedly, "Look at the life I have. Dennis gone all the time, and when his ship was re-routed this last time, his check was held up and all we had to eat one day was cabbage. Yet you don't hear me complaining. And now I have father as well."

"Care to change places with me?" said Auntie Con. My mother ignored that.

"Can I go into the parlour as soon as I've finished?" I might as well not have spoken.

"What brought the old man back anyway?"

Mam nodded at me, "Ask her. She's the one he talks to."

I wondered about it too, and I wasn't going to tell them about the tear that ran down the side of Granda's nose when he said he was like Moses looking at the Promised Land and forbidden to enter. I just shook my head.

Mam slid off the bunker and lifted one of the cups I had wiped. "Isn't this their wedding china?"

Auntie Con nodded and Mam went on, "Is she hoping to revive fond memories? Surely she doesn't want him back?" It was more an exclamation than a question.

Auntie Con shook her head, "No, but she wants him to want her back."

My mother laughed. "Fat chance with that head of hair." She held the cup against the light. "Eggshell china. Nice... You'll probably fall heir to it."

"I've washed it often enough."

The doorbell rang and my mother went to answer it. A minute later she stuck her head round the door, "It's Jim and Ivy and they have Hamish with them."

Auntie Con wrung her hands. "Oh no! You know how bitter Jim has always been about father. I couldn't take anything more today. Where are they?"

"Ivy's in the bedroom combing her hair and Jim and Hamish have gone up to the bathroom."

"Well go and see that nothing happens," Auntie Con wailed.

"Can I go too?" I said.

"You stay here and set this table for you and Hamish. And see that he eats. He never looks well, that boy."

When we were seated at the table I looked resentfully at Hamish. Were it not for him, I'd be having my tea with the big ones now and keeping an eye on my Granny and Granda as well.

"I have a new engine Stella," he said through adenoids and a mouthful of cake. I didn't say anything. "It's not here," he went on, "it's at home."

"Don't speak with your mouth full," I said.

He helped himself to another cake. I'd never get out of this kitchen! "I'll tell Auntie Con you took two cakes," I said.

"Clipe[95]," he said and a crumb flew out of his mouth into my tea. I looked at him with disgust and he stuck out his tongue. It was coated with cake. Auntie Con appeared and filled a plate with biscuits, "I always forget something and she always notices."

"Can I come into the parlour now?" I asked her.

"You haven't finished your tea."

"I don't want it."

Well, you can come as soon as Hamish finishes his."

"Hurry up you," I said to him and Auntie Con heard me, "Oh that's not nice - he's just a wee boy." She hurried out the door.

"Granda lives with me," I said.

"He's coming to live with me too," said Hamish.

"You're a liar, Hamish Morrison. Your Da said he didn't want him."

"My Da changed his mind and we're taking Granda home with us tonight."

"Liar,"[95] I shouted, and hit him.

He let out a terrible wail and Auntie Ivy rushed in. "She's hitting me, ma," he whined.

Auntie Ivy looked at me with dislike, "I'd give you what-for if you were mine. Come on son, you can sit with me at the big table.

Left alone, I wanted to cry. How could a day that held so much promise hold so much hurt? My grandfather had snubbed me twice, Auntie Ivy had told me off and Auntie Con was too busy to be bothered with me. Mam said I was ugly when I cried, so I wouldn't. I went over to the mirror

---

[95] Tattletale!

above the comb box and stuck my tongue out at the Lizzie Misery I saw there. Then I marched right into the parlour.

Uncle Jim was holding out his packet of cigarettes to my grandfather. "Smoke?" My Granda patted his pocket. "I have my pipe."

"Do you still smoke Irish Roll?" asked Uncle Jim. My grandfather nodded. "You used to send me for it." He looked thoughtful as though he were adding up something. "That was 16 years ago." He sounded startled.

There was suddenly a great flurry of activity round the table - everyone but Granny moving and talking at once. She sat like she was turned to stone, and her face, under that incredible hair was impassive. Only her lips showed what she was feeling. They were pressed together in a straight line.

There was a discordant crash from the piano where Auntie Ivy and Hamish were jammed together on the stool. "Play for Granny", she was saying. "Show her what you learned this week."

Hamish mumbled something and Auntie Ivy said, "You know it. Come on - 'A fairy peeped from a purple flower,'" she half sang it.

I looked at my grandfather. His eyes were closed. Uncle Jim was looking daggers at Auntie Ivy. "For God's sake Ivy, there's enough confusion without that racket. And who the hell wants to hear a kid thumping the piano anyway?"

Auntie Ivy got up. Hamish looked defiantly at his father and gave the piano an almighty bang. Uncle Jim flew at him and aimed a cuff at his ear. Hamish howled.

My Granda went to the piano. "Move over," he said to Hamish and squeezed in beside him. "I'll play a song that I know about fairies."

I didn't know my grandfather played the piano! I came out of my corner and went and stood behind him. "The fairy dream-boat's in the harbour anchored to a white moonbeam. All the crew is waiting for you, they're ready to sail, so hurry up do," my grandfather sang.

Hamish wriggled off the stool, "I have a new engine," he shouted above the singing.

Uncle Jim jumped up again and he shouted too. "This is impossible, we've got to go." Auntie Ivy started shouting too. "Don't take it out on Hamish because your father's back."

Uncle Jim shot through the door with Auntie Ivy on his heels and Hamish being dragged forcibly. I covered my ears to shut out the racket. My mother followed them to the door and Auntie Con raised an eyebrow at me; "Come and help me tidy up the kitchen," she said.

There was silence from the parlour and I wondered what was happening. Then I heard the piano again. My grandfather sang, 'Bonny wee thing, canny wee thing.' But that was the song he sang to me! I sagged against the table that still held the debris of our tea.

"You're tired," said Auntie Con. "Come and have a wee lie down on Granny's bed."

She tucked a quilt around me and kissed the top of my head. I must have fallen asleep for when my mother's voice woke me the room was dark. She was just outside the door.

"I'll wake her," she was saying, "It's time we were away too."

"Have you forgotten what day it is? Scripture reading."

"Why do you think I'm running?"

"Oh, she might not, since father's here."

I'm not taking any chances." Mam laughed. Eddie says she's been collecting ammunition from the bible ever since she heard he was coming back. Well, if she isn't already letting him have it, she'll have to hold her fire a while longer"

"But we haven't finished clearing up" said Auntie Con. "And I'm tired"

My Mam spoke consolingly, "Leave it till tomorrow when you're rested." She raised her voice. "Come on, father. Time to go."

As we were leaving, Auntie Con handed me a bag. "You didn't eat, so here's some cake home with you."

I walked down the street backwards, reluctant to take my eyes off the square of light in which Auntie Con stood. She kept waving, though I know she couldn't see us in the dark.

The bells in a distant church started playing, "Now the day is over, night is drawing nigh, shadows of the evening steal across the sky."

It was a melancholy sound that made me think of dying. I turned round but the dark had swallowed my Mam and my grandfather. I started to run and cry at the same time, "Granda!"

He stopped me in my headlong rush. "Easy there, easy."

I wrapped myself around his neck. He was silent while I sobbed, "Oh, Granda!" again and again.

My mother called back, "What's going on? We'll miss our tram."

My Grandfather took my hand and when we caught up with her, my Mam took the other hand. They swung my arms up and down as we walked to the tram stop.

Chapter 37 : Miss Vincent

Grandfather and Miss Vincent and I seemed to have found a unique friendship. It was not "Excluding". I was an important part of it. It was like Cinderella in a way. Only the transformation was in Miss Vincent. Her weight on the too high heels caused her to walk with an unsteady gait. The shoes were replaced with sturdy, medium heels. The little fur acquired a certain dignity. It was no longer the seedy souvenir of better times. Her handbag was still big enough to hold a bag of bread and a sweetie for me. Her warm brown eyes no longer shut out the world but took it all in.

We met Miss Vincent several times after that. Though the weather had broken, there were still a few fine days left in summer. School started soon and the good days had to be seized with both hands. It was never hot enough again to wear paper hats but it was, to me, preferable that the wind should have a snap in it. My Granda was quieter now and he didn't sing so often. We stuck to the paths. Skipping and paper hats and daisy chains belonged to a time that had passed. My Mam always said, when she was chastising me, that I was a big girl now and should have known better. Well now I felt like a big girl, like a girl who had got big too soon. I sometimes caught my Granda looking at me with a sad look on his face. Always when he caught me watching him he'd smile, but his eyes still looked like he was thinking about something that made him sad.

Miss Vincent always had her hat and fur on now when we met her. The only thing different about her dress was her shoes. We didn't sit on the grass. We'd join her on a bench. Sometimes my grandfather and Miss Vincent didn't talk much at all and when they did, it was mostly about things like Miss Vincent's shoes.

"Now Stella here won't need high heels. She'll carry herself tall and proud. Like a queen."

They both smiled at me and Granda's eyes were sad, hers were tender. I liked Miss Vincent to look at me. And she was always the same. I never needed to worry about annoying her.

Sometimes I took her hand walking along the path and when grandfather took the other, I would feel that I could never be feart again.

"Do you like the school?" she asked one day.

"Sometimes," I said, "when we get composition and poems.

"Oh," she said, "I like poetry. I like it a lot."

Granda asked, "Do you ever write any?"

"I used to but I had to get rid of them."

My grandfather raised an eyebrow. "Oh? Why was that?"

"I shared a flat with someone then. We split the rent 50-50. And it was the rent that trapped me. I never really liked her. I should never have put up with her. I thought I couldn't manage the rent on my own so I put up with her. One night I came home and she was in my room. She had my poems out and she was reading them and laughing." Miss Vincent was quiet for a long time.

"What did you do?" prompted my grandfather.

"I flung her out first and then my poems, too." My grandfather made a sorry sound. Miss Vincent continued, "They weren't good poetry but they were my feelings." She stopped walking and looked at Granda. "Don't you think laughter can be more cutting than words?"

"Infinitely," said my grandfather. They stood for a long time looking at each other, not talking.

I began to feel funny inside, like I shouldn't be watching. I felt lonely and my heart was beating fast. I started to scuff the gravel with my feet. I didn't know what to do. If I hid in the bushes, they wouldn't know I was gone. I couldn't look at them. My breath came in big gulps. Suddenly Miss Vincent was kneeling in front of me. "Stella," she said, "is something wrong?" I was going to shake my head, but the look on her face made me nod it.

"What is it? Can you tell me?"

"I'm feart." It came out as a wail. Miss Vincent didn't say anything but put her arms went around me and she pressed me into her cushiony front. It felt safe and warm, and the fright went away.

There was just one more really warm day that summer. Granda and I met Miss Vincent in the park. Granda and Miss Vincent sat on the grass by the pond while I fed the ducks.

When the bread was all gone and I turned back to Granda and Miss Vincent, she was reading Granda's hand! I ran over to them. "You have travelled to far places and you have another move coming shortly. But you won't cross deep water again. There's a woman in your life. You met her recently. She's short and fair and I can see she brings you great joy and happiness through stormy days where you and she stand on happy ground."

Granda looked over at me and winked. Miss Vincent's head was bent over his hand so she didn't see the wink.

"Tell mine, please?"

Miss Vincent gave Granda back his hand and took mine. "I can see lots of parties in your hand and a journey across water soon."

My Granda butted in. "That's right! We're going over to Burntisland on the Willie Muir next week."

It was the first I'd heard of it. "When, Granda, when?"

"On your birthday." I'd be 10 next Friday.

A cool breeze had sprung up and was riffling the top of the pond. Miss Vincent shivered. Granda jumped up and took her hand. "You take her other hand, Stella." He said. Together we pulled Miss Vincent to her feet.

We said goodbye at the park gate. Miss Vincent had business to attend to and was going in the opposite direction.

"Have a happy birthday," she said, "Burntisland was my favourite place when I was your age."

When Miss Vincent smiled at me her eyes smiled too.

But when my birthday came, my Granda wasn't well, and we had to stay home.

"It's just as well," said my mother, "your grandfather's spoiling you." I didn't say anything. "And nobody likes a spoiled child," she went on.

I still didn't speak. "Oh," said Mam, you don't need to sulk. Be happy that I care about you enough to discipline you." I tried to look happy so she'd stop.

"That's better," said Mam.   "You mustn't be miserable on your birthday or you'll be miserable all year. And after I've gone, go into my top drawer. You'll find a present from me. Now give me a kiss – I've got to hurry"

All the time she was speaking she was putting things into her bag. Comb, lipstick, hanky. Before she tossed in her little coin purse she opened it and handed me a threepenny bit. "That's to go with your present."

She was off, calling over her shoulder as she went; "I don't know when I'll be back, so fix something nice for your tea. Granda's not eating today"

Bang – the door closed behind her, but she didn't lock it with the big key now that Granda was home to protect me.

I went into Mam's drawer and took out my present. It was the little handbag I had seen at Woolworth's. She had remembered I wanted it. Inside was a birthday card that said:

"I did not choose my daughter,

But had that been mine to do,

And worlds of daughters I had met,

My choice would still be you."

I wished Granda would get up so I could show him. There was no sound from his room. The bag was blue with red and white stripes cutting diagonally across it. The red and white stripes separated to show a secret pocket where you could keep things you didn't want anyone to know about.

I put the threepence in the bag, put on a pair of my mother's shoes, and went to the street swinging my handbag. I saw Miss Vincent's red hat before she saw me. I swung my handbag higher, and it caught her eye. "Stella," she said, surprised, "I thought you were off to Burntisland today."

"My Granda's sick." I said.

"Oh, dear, I hope it's nothing serious."

"I don't know. He's in his bed."

"You tell him I hope he'll soon be better. Here," she opened her bag and fumbled inside, "this is for your new bag." She handed me a sixpence, and wished me many happy returns.

I walked to the sweetie shop backwards, watching Miss Vincent as she got smaller and smaller. Her little fur looked smaller than ever on the broad expanse of her back. My Mam was slim and neat and had lots of blonde curly hair, and she wore nicer clothes than Miss Vincent did. But though I wanted to look like my Mam, I wanted to be like Miss Vincent. If she had any children they'd be happy.

When I got home my Granda was up and dressed. He was awfully white and when I held out my poke of sweeties he said, "Please, no."

"I met Miss Vincent," I said, "and she gave me sixpence for my birthday."

"She's a nice woman, Miss Vincent," said my grandfather. He was quiet while I put the kettle over the fire. "I'm sorry about Burntisland. It was to be your birthday present from me."

"I bought something for our tea with some of my money." I showed him two fairy cakes.

"Can I keep mine for later?" said Granda. "But while you eat yours I'll sing you a birthday song if you like."

I nodded and Granda began to sing. He started with "Happy Birthday" and went through all our favourite songs. I pretended I was in a teashop and Granda was the orchestra. The table looked nice with my new bag on it.

When I had finished my cake he said, "My throat's dry from singing. Maybe I could handle a cup of tea now."

When he had finished his tea he went back to bed, but not before he had broken up the fire with the poker and put a new lump of coal on. "That should keep you for a while – maybe till your Mam gets back. Where did she say she was going?"

"She didn't tell me. She was wearing her earrings that my Da brought from Persia. She looked nice."

Granda nodded and said something I couldn't make out. "I'll away ben[96], Stella, but you call me if you need me."

---

[96] Through

Stella Maris   by   Nan O'Dell

I spent the afternoon happily pretending that my Granda and I were away in Salt Lake City and my Granda had a shop that I got to serve in. I was the customer, too, who kept opening her bag searching for things. "I know it's somewhere in this bag," I'd say to me behind the counter.

The lump of coal Granda had put on was nearly burned away, and as the flames died down the room got darker. I wished Granda would get up and light the gas.

"Granda," I said, sticking my head round his door. He didn't answer or move. "Granda." I said it louder. I tiptoed to the bed and gave his shoulder a little shake, but I couldn't rouse him. "Granda!" I screamed it. I ran from his room, out the door, down the stairs and to the next close. I pulled the bell that said "Vincent" above it and went running up the stairs. Miss Vincent was peeking round her door, her face looked all streaky. "You can't come in – I'm giving a reading," she said.

My Granda's dead," I shouted. She opened her door wider and I saw she was wearing a silk kimono that she clutched around her.

"You go back and I'll come over right away."

I stood at the foot of her stair crying with fright, hopping from one foot to another, and chewing my nails. I heard her say to someone, "You'll have to go." When I heard her door bang I thought she was coming but a man brushed by me in the dark and he was swearing. When Miss Vincent came running down the stairs I could see she was dressed. As she passed me she took my hand and I ran with her. For all her weight and age, she was going faster than I was. I had left our door standing open and Miss Vincent shouted "Is this it?" as she shot through it.

261

Stella Maris   by   Nan O'Dell

My Granda called from his bedroom, "Who's there? What's going on?"

Miss Vincent stopped dead in her tracks. "Oh, my god, what a fright!" She was shaking all over and I was still crying. My Granda walked unsteadily from his bedroom. "What's all the carry on?"

I flung myself at him. "Oh, Granda, I thought you were dead."

"She came for me," said Miss Vincent, sinking into a chair. Her coat fell open and in the last sputter of the fire I could see right up her leg. Somehow it fitted in with the rest of the nightmare.

"Steady on, steady on. I'm sorry you had such a fright. Here," said Granda, I have a drop of brandy in my case under the bed. You get it, Stella." I hauled out my Granda's suitcase and found a flat bottle tucked in with some letters and winter underwear.

"And get some glasses. I think you could use some, too, but just this time." He handed me his glass and I was about to tip it up to my mouth when my mother came in.

She said what my Granda had said but in an angry voice, "What's going on here?"

Chapter 38 : Two Sisters

It was just three days after that, on a day when my grandfather was out looking for work, that Auntie Con dropped by with socks that she had knitted for him, and a pot of home-made strawberry jam.

My mother raised an eyebrow when she saw them. "Is this your contribution to his keep?"

Auntie Con's face grew very pink. "I'm knitting a pullover for him as well"

Mam lifted the socks and examined them carefully. "I hope you didn't join the wool at the heel like you did on the pair you gave Dennis at Christmas. After they were washed he said it was like walking with a stone in his shoe. He had to throw them out."

"I don't remember joining the wool at the heel," said Auntie Con. No wonder she didn't remember! My Mam was telling lies.

I was there when she put them in the fire because my Da liked them so much. She was crying when she did it and she shouted that he liked Auntie Con better than he liked her for he had worn the socks a lot but not once had he worn the scarf she gave him.

Now Auntie Con was saying humbly, "I'm not much good at making things."

"Mmmm," said Mam "I'll be curious to see the pullover when you've finished it." She put down the socks. "These seem to be all right."

As though encouraged by Mam's approval, Auntie Con took out her knitting. I waited for my Mam to say something sarcastic but she was tilting the pot of jam to one side, "It's rather runny."

"Strawberry used to be father's favourite." Auntie Con sounded defensive.

"Hold it to the light Mam, it's the colour of rubies."

She nearly bit off my head. "Don't you interrupt while adults are talking and get your nose out of that book and take your Auntie's coat."

"What are you reading pet?" Auntie Con squinted at the title. 'When knighthood was in Flower'. Isn't that a bit old for you?"

"She reads too much, that one. I keep telling her she'll get St. Vitus' dance."

Auntie Con smiled at me. "Oh I doubt that."

"That's right, side with her even if it means contradicting me."

I took the coat to the lobby before Mam got angrier. Auntie Con must have left home before the rain came on for she didn't bring an umbrella and her coat was damp. The artificial violets that she wore on the collar were bedraggled and they smelled like the inside of an old church. I tried not to breathe while I hung it up.

When I went back to the kitchen Mam was filling the kettle. She banged it on to the gas ring. "I wish father would move before Dennis comes home and makes him. I think ma should take him back." Auntie Con was silent. "Does she show any signs of relenting?"

"She never mentions him."

"Oh well, she'll not want to see him again till that terrible hair grows out." Mam started to laugh. "Has she forgiven you for that yet?"

"She never forgives me for anything", Auntie Con said quietly and I wondered why she should need forgiveness for something Granny had made her do. "Has father had any work at all?" she asked.

"Nothing," said Mam. "No one wants him."

"That must be hard,"

"Oh it is. I'm fed up with it."

Auntie Con's knitting needles clicked faster. "I wasn't thinking about you."

"No, I don't suppose you were. No one thinks about me."

"You could be worse off. You could have mother."

"Maybe...but it galls me to have him here after what he did to me. My life could have been different...so different."

"And mine, not to mention Jim's and George's and Eddie's."

Mam ignored her. "I could have gone on to university. I'd have met a better class of people. I'd never have mixed with the likes of Dennis Malcolm."

I was pretending to read my book but out of the corner of my eye I saw Auntie Con shoot her an admonishing glance. "Rachel!" she said.

It didn't stop Mam. "It's true. The teacher used to tell me that I'd go far if I kept on the way I was doing. Then he went away and I had to leave school and go out to work."

"I wish I could have gone out to work," said Auntie Con.

"What could you do?" Auntie Con kept her eyes on her knitting, and said nothing. "Anyway, you were needed at home."

My Aunt laid her knitting in her lap and looked at her hands, first the palms, then the backs. "They're so rough they keep catching the wool."

Mam had a look at them. "It's sheer carelessness to let your hands get in that state. Buy yourself some glycerine and rosewater. That's what keeps my hands looking nice."

My mind slipped into a trick I had discovered that made me feel better when Mam hurt my feelings. In this trick my mind would hear my mother telling Auntie Con, "You should have a girl like Stella. She does the dishes a lot." Then Mam and Auntie Con would smile at me and Auntie Con would say, "I wish she was my girl; I'd take her home with me," and Mam would say to her, "You can't have her; she's mine."

When my mind came back to the kitchen Mam was gazing into the fire and half-singing, under her breath, "I wished on the moon, ta ta ta ta ta tee-ta." Auntie Con's needles clicked busily and her face was expressionless. Suddenly I remembered something I had seen her do when I was staying with her and Granny one weekend. Granny was going over the schedule for the day to make sure Auntie Con wouldn't be neglecting anything if she took me to the sands in the afternoon.

"Don't forget it's the day for clean sheets and turning the mattresses." Auntie Con gave a resigned sigh and Granny heard it.

"Oh I know you grudge doing anything for me, you know how my back bothers me if my mattress isn't turned regularly."

"Yes mother," said Auntie Con. Her expression was blank as it was now but her eyes made me think of a magazine I found under the bed at Uncle Eddie's one night I was sleeping with my cousins. There was a story in it about a man who could zap people with his eyes. I waited for Granny to be zapped but nothing happened.

"You come and dust Granny's dresser while I do the bed and we'll get away faster," said Auntie Con.

"Be careful with my ornaments," said Granny.

While we worked I could hear Auntie Con muttering away to herself and I don't think she knew she was doing it for she was answering her own questions. "Why do I put up with it?" She shook her head and drew in her breath with a hissing sound. "Because...I have no choice: I'm not trained for anything and there's not one of them would take me in while I learned a skill."

The muttering stopped and I looked at her through the dresser mirror. She was staring at something on the corner of the mattress. "A pin?" She sounded puzzled. "What's it doing there?" She touched it as though to make sure it was real. Then she straightened up, comprehension on her face. "The old bitch. The rotten old bitch. She'll be checking tonight to see where the pin is, and if it's still on the top she'll know I haven't turned the mattress."

She laughed and I got the grues. I looked down at the china pig I was holding in case she caught me watching her. "Well we'll just take care of that." When I glanced through the mirror again, I saw her remove the pin, lift the far corner of the mattress, and secure it to the underside. Then she became again the Auntie I knew, the one who was sitting with us now, always dependable, sometimes vague, and never unkind.

I studied my mother and my Aunt over the top of my book. My mother was small-boned and neat. Her hair, the warm amber colour of honey, fell in loose waves almost to her shoulders. Her skin was clear and soft and her face had a chocolate-box prettiness. The only feature that didn't fit the rest of her was her eyes. They had a cold constancy that made me want to cover my own. Even with the tendency of the young to see one's parents as old, I often felt that I was the adult and she, the child. Yet, at that time, she was thirty, and I was just ten.

My Aunt, only three years my mother's senior, might have belonged to Granny's generation. Her straight fly-away hair was what my mother called mousy brown. In a vain attempt to keep it tidy, it was secured by outsized kirbigrips. Except for a propensity to blush when she was embarrassed, Auntie Con's skin had the dull look that is associated with poor diet and a life spent indoors. Her eyes, which were large and luminous, spoke more than her tongue. As she kept them cast down most of the time, she had a diffident look. Her figure had the cushiony appearance that comes from too many thick soups and steamed puddings, and her clothes did nothing to minimise her size. They were the sort that were advertised in magazines for "the fuller figure". Perhaps this was a carryover from her boarding house days. Granny put great store on keeping people filled. She demanded fattening fare, though she herself only picked at it, and stayed thin and flat. "Eat it up," I often heard her say to Auntie Con, "we can't have waste in this house." Then she, and my mother, would chide my Aunt for letting herself go. At the thought of this injustice I heaved a great sigh and Mam and my Auntie looked up at me. Quickly I lifted the book closer to my face but not before I had spotted a difference in the two sisters that I hadn't noticed before. My mother seldom smiled! Not for her the little darting glance, such as Auntie Con was giving me now, that says "I like you."

No – my mother's smile was usually the prelude to a cutting remark.

"Are you reading that book, or just pretending to read it?" I jumped and without my even answering her, she went on, "Well then, you can bring us our tea." One of the more terrifying aspects of living with my mother was her uncanny ability to read my thoughts.

"Where's Tibby today?" asked Auntie Con.

"She's sleeping under my bed." I didn't tell her that Tib stayed there all the time now when Mam was home.

"Oh for goodness sake, don't encourage her to get that animal. She treats it as though it were human."

"You were never fond of cats," said Auntie Con.

"I'm as fond of them as the next one, but I believe they should he kept in their place and not allowed to crawl all over humans." Mam spoke vehemently and when Auntie Con never let on, she continued, "God says that beasts were made to face the ground but man was made to walk upright to show his dominion over them."

"That sounds more like mother than God,"

"You've always had a down on mother,"

"I know her better than you do, that's all."

"She raised me too."

"Hmmmf," said Auntie Con, "you were off and married at nineteen."

"Don't remind me," said Mam.

I handed round the tea and when Auntie Con reached for a biscuit Mam reminded her sharply that with her figure she shouldn't eat the cream filled ones. Auntie Con looked her right in the eye and helped herself to two.

Mam shrugged and leaving her tea untouched, started humming again.

Auntie Con washed down one of her biscuits with tea, and said to me, "Go in my bag." It was her way of telling me that she had something for me. I hesitated and glanced at my mother. She always said Auntie Con spoiled me and should be discouraged from doing it. I got a disgusted look. "Oh go on."

I released the catch and the bag sprang open as though its contents couldn't wait to escape. They spewed onto the hearth-rug. "Paddy's market[97]," said my mother.

Granny always said that Auntie Con's handbag was the symptom of a disordered mind but to me it was neither that nor Paddy's market. It was Aladdin's cave and Christmas rolled into one. There was the spare hankie, the initial C embroidered on the corner, that my Auntie always carried in case of emergency. She wouldn't use it for every day because I had made it

---

[97] A jumble

and she said it was too nice. Nothing untoward had happened since the last time I saw it for there was still fluff in the folds.

Careful not to dislodge it, I folded the hankie as I had found it and held it to my nose. Devon violets, growing fainter. Her comb had another tooth missing and I decided to buy her a new one for Christmas. The chemist had them with rhinestones set in and I had sixpence in the Christmas club. Her coin purse was empty enough for the contents to jingle when I shook it. I hesitated over a postcard and Auntie Con said, "Read it if you like." It was from someone called Gladys who was having a super time despite the rain. The other side was St. Andrews in the sun. Some old tram tickets, a key, safety pins on a ring, a tin of Zubes, a garter, three kirbigrips, a knitting pattern and a shopping list. Granny and Auntie Con were having a bit of fish for their tea, a quarter of pan drops and the People's Friend. At the very bottom was an envelope with a star on the front. That was me! Auntie Con sometimes called me Star because my name was Stella. I liked Star better.

I glanced at her and when she nodded, I tore open the envelope and pulled out a sheet of scraps. Little girls in pantaloons, flower filled baskets, a boy with a hoop, and several kittens.

"Look Mam," I held them up for her to see but she ignored me and my scraps.

"Have you ever wished on the moon, Con?"

Auntie Con put down her cup, lifted her knitting and started counting rows.

"Well...have you?"

"Who hasn't?" said Auntie Con, evasively.

"Come on then, tell me about it."

Auntie Con laughed doubtfully, "It's too silly."

"I can't imagine an old sober-sides like you ever being silly."

"Oh well then, if you must know... I used to wish we'd get a wealthy boarder who'd take a fancy to me. When he died in his sleep not suffering or anything - he'd leave me all his money."

Mam winked at me and I pretended not to see her. "And how would you have spent it?"

"I'd have bought my freedom. Set mother up so she could pay half a dozen people to do what I do for her single-handed."

"And what would you have done with your freedom?"

Auntie Con looked embarrassed; "I'd have married."

Mam laughed unbelievingly. "You? Marry? I can't imagine it. Who on earth would you have married?"

Auntie Con kept her eyes on her knitting and two spots appeared on her cheekbones. "Charlie Semple."

Mam laughed again. "Old jug ears? But you'd be giving up the freedom you'd just bought!"

"It would have been worth it." Auntie Con sounded fierce.

Mam looked taken aback. "I didn't think it was that serious."

My Aunt just nodded and my mother said, "Well why didn't you marry him?"

"Every time we set a date mother would have a bad turn and we'd have the devil's own job bringing her round. She said old Dr. Guthrie had told her it was her heart and she'd have to live without upset or she'd be a permanent invalid, maybe even die."

"Did you check with the doctor to see if it was true?" Auntie Con shook her head, "It seemed right enough - she'd look waxen and her lips would take on a blue tinge. By the time I realised she was having the adult equivalent of a temper tantrum it was too late. Charlie had been shifted to Leeds and we had stopped writing. Keeping it going kept the pain and frustration going too. The hurt stopped when I accepted that it was never to be. Mother would never let it. Then I heard that Charlie had married someone he met there."

"I've no patience with that attitude. You should have stuck up for your rights."

"I didn't know I had any."

You see, you're whining about your lot yet you did nothing to change it. I'd have run off with the man I wanted to marry."

Now all of Auntie Con's face was red and her neck as well. "You did!" she cried.

I missed what followed for I was trying to imagine Auntie Con in love. I wondered if she cried when Charlie Semple married someone else. I wondered if she was so upset that she forgot Granny's tea, and I wondered if Granny was glad when she heard she didn't need to have any more bad turns. Certainly, to me, my Granny always seemed healthy enough. I often heard her tell Auntie Con that she could work rings round her at that age. She said Auntie Con puffed going upstairs because she had let herself go. "I could run upstairs at your age and my heart didn't even beat faster." Auntie Con had muttered "What heart?" but Granny didn't hear. She was too busy turning this way and that way before the big mirror. Patting her tummy, she said, "Five children and still flat."

Auntie Con sniggered and Granny heard her that time all right. "What's amusing you?"

"Why mother, you did it five times!"

For a minute Granny looked blank then two big red patches appeared on her cheeks and her eyes went like slits. Between the narrowed lids, they glittered. "The wrath of the Lord will descend on you my girl. To say such a wicked thing in front of the bairn[98] and about your own mother."

Auntie Con shrugged like she didn't care but she had a feart look on her face just the same and I wondered what she had said wrong. It must have meant something bad for Granny never spoke another word to her all the rest of the time I was there. She wrote down the daily instructions and if there were changes she told me and I told my Auntie.

I was brought back to the kitchen by Mam's voice telling me that her tea was cold. "Empty it out and pour me another cup."

"In many ways you remind me of mother," said Auntie Con.

---

[98] Child

Mam shot right back with, "Knowing what you think of mother I take it you're insulting me."

The red was fading from Auntie Con's face and my mother was looking reflectively into the fire again. "Fancy all that high drama going on and I didn't even know."

"How could you know," said Auntie Con, "you were always away and too busy leading your own life to think about anyone else's."

"How can you sit there knitting socks for father when you know the drastic consequences his actions had on your life. I'd stick the knitting needles through his heart."

"She wouldn't have been any different if he had stayed home."

Mam sighed. "You can't have suffered as much as I or you wouldn't be so magnanimous."

"There's your tea Mam," I said.

"I've told you before about interrupting adults when they're talking." She said it almost absently, then: "I never believed for a minute what he wrote to mother about Salt Lake City turning out to be Babylon. There's a lot more to his coming home than that. How did he get involved with Mormons anyway?"

"Door to door missionaries. And actually it was mother who invited them in."

Mam laughed. "Trust her. She probably intended to convert them to the gospel according to Alice."

"Well she got more than she bargained for. It was father who got converted and it was to their gospel." Auntie Con shook her head. "Oh the quarrels! They used to go on half the night."

"I used to hear them," said my mother, "but I thought they had something to do with sex."

My Aunt's face got very pink and keeping her eyes on her knitting she asked me to go and get my scrapbook to show her. As I left the room she said something to my mother that I couldn't catch and Mam laughed.

When I returned with the scrapbook Auntie Con was folding up her knitting and she seemed surprised when I handed it to her. "Oh. Is this your scrapbook?"

"That one's always demanding attention," said Mam.

"Well I'd love to see it pet, but I have to get home for mother's tea."

And then, "You're too hard on her, Rachel."

"I'm doing her a good turn. If she learns discipline at home, her life will be that much easier when she's out in the world."

"I still say you're too hard on her."

"And what does an old maid know about raising children?"

Auntie Con flushed and said nothing. I started to put things back in her bag. I glanced at Mam and caught her gaze. Her face was expressionless but her eyes made me shiver and wish I could go home with Auntie Con. "Can I come home with you?" I asked Auntie Con.

"You'll have to ask your Mam."

"Can I Mam?"

"No you can't. You're not fit to live with when you come home from there."

My mind slipped into the trick. "No you can't," Mam would say, "I'd miss you too much." Then to Auntie Con, "It's a wonder she never gets spoiled, the fuss you make over her."

Auntie Con would say, "We love her so much."

Mam would reply, "Well so do I."

"Why are you looking at me like that? said Mam and I jumped. Then, to Auntie Con, "Look at the hostility in that face." I felt ashamed like they had seen right into me, like that time my Da came in my room while I was getting dressed. "Cover yourself, for God's sake. You should be ashamed. A big girl like you parading herself before her father." I was ashamed. I hadn't known he was there, but still I felt sinful for not keeping myself covered even when I was by myself.

Before Auntie Con left, she laid two shillings on the table and said, "Tell the old man I stopped by and give him this. It's not much but it will buy his tobacco. Mother keeps me short of housekeeping money."

Mam said, "Never mind, you'll get it all one day."

Auntie Con said, "I've earned it."

After Auntie Con left, Mam started in: "She's away in the huff. Well she can stay in it. I get sick of folk telling me how to raise you. You'd think I was hard on you. Well, I can take you anywhere – you're no trouble to anyone. Now, Eddie and Mary's brats, folk dread to see them coming.

No discipline. I suppose that's how she'd like me to raise you! Well I won't, I'll continue to do what I think is best."

I lowered my eyes to my plate. When Mam got on to this, it usually went on for a long, long time.

Chapter 39 : Granda Finds Work

The very next day my Granda came home with the news that he had found a job doing something called piecework. It was casual work and though he wouldn't earn much, and couldn't know from one day to the next what he'd be earning he'd be out of the house. "And that's the main thing," Mam said. I thought of all the days that Tibby and I would have been alone had it not been for my Granda. It was to free her, and her conscience, that she had taken him in. Now that my Da was coming home she didn't need him, or even want him.

"Con left this for you." She gave him a shilling.

Granda shook his head. "Take it towards my keep."

Mam pocketed it without a word. She looked at me and saw me watching. "Come here," she said, "I want to talk to you."

When we were in my bedroom she said, "Don't you breathe a word about it being two shillings your Auntie left. Remember, I'm morally entitled to it all. Do you understand me?" Her fingers were pressing painfully into my arm and I nodded my head. "Mind, then."

Granda left the house early mornings and sometimes wasn't home till nearly six. And sometimes he'd go out again after he had eaten so I didn't see much of him and I missed him. The days were long when he was gone. I tried to stay awake for his coming home but didn't always succeed. Always he'd hand over his day's money, sometimes in small change. My Mam said it was a queer way to get paid but Granda said it was mostly tips and money was money and he was glad to be earning it. Sometimes he looked awfully tired and he was always thin.

Then one night when my grandfather came home, he said he had another job. "It's only two weeks work but it will pay better." He was to do two weeks night duty at the desk in a hotel, and he'd have the chance of helping in the kitchen when there were functions to cater. "And you never know where it will lead", he said.

Granda told me stories about the people he saw in the hotel. It was one of the middle class hotels where everything was roomy and comfortable but the age of the furniture and the style of the decoration branded it as "down at heel". Some of the people there were "characters".

Even better than the stories was the "pauchle[99]" my Granda brought home. Sandwiches and once a piece of wedding cake.

"Put it under your pillow and you'll dream of the man you'll marry." I did that, but I didn't remember in the morning if I had dreamt at all. Indeed I woke up earlier in my anxiety about it. I ate it sitting up in bed and though I tried to eat every crumb, there were still bits and crumbs and the royal icing was jaggy under me.

My Da was due home any day and Mam was out a lot because, she said, there would be precious little freedom once my Da was home.

I wished that when my Da came home I could go out with my Granda. My Da annoyed my Mam and there was always trouble when he was home.

---

[99] Parcel

When Da did come home he hardly looked at my grandfather. It was almost like Granda wasn't there. Granda stayed out as much as possible. My Da didn't look at me very much, either. I was glad of that. Da's eyes followed my mother everywhere and finally Mam shouted, "For God's sake, stop watching me."

"I can't help wondering what you were up to while I was gone."

"What could I be up to with a child and an old man round my neck?"

"I know you," said Da. "You're like a bitch in heat. You'd find some way to get off on your own."

"Why don't you stay home, then?"

"I couldn't find a shore job just now and you know it."

"Then shut your damned mouth!" said Mam. "And remember that you have more chance to play dirty than I do."

Granda was out and I went in my room and put my pillow over my head. I wished my Da would go away again. I got feart and sometimes I was feart to sleep at night. Sometimes I'd go and plead with them to stop it and they'd both turn on me. The next day Mam would be singing and my Da would be patting her behind. I hated that more than when they were angry. I wished I could run away but there was nowhere to go. Maybe now that I had my Granda we could run away together.

My Granda tried to act the same. But when he tried to talk to my Da, my Da wouldn't listen and pretended that Granda wasn't there. It was like there was my Mam and Da, and here was my Granda and I. We orbited around each other in pairs. I was glad when Da went back to his ship.

Stella Maris   by   Nan O'Dell

Chapter 40 : Granda's Death

Granda was getting up later and later. Mam was fed up about it. She said he was being inconsiderate. He said she was being inconsiderate for minding. Sometimes my Mam was already gone for the day when he woke up. The house was awfully quiet with just me and Tibby up. Sometimes I opened his door quietly and tried to will him to wake up. Sometimes it worked. That day it didn't. Finally I knocked on the door as hard as I was able. He still didn't let on. This time I felt sure that Granda was dead, and I couldn't bring myself to enter his room.

With Granda here Mam didn't lock the door when she left, so I could run out and get someone, but who to get? Mam was away visiting Uncle Jim and he lived away in Bruntsfield. And I didn't have the tram fare.

Miss Vincent lived in the next close but Mam had forbidden me to ever speak to her again. Then I remembered Betty & Sheila Willis across the street. We had never been good friends, but their parents had been kind. I ran across the street and up the stair and knocked the door. Mrs Willis answered the door. She was alone.

"Please, Mrs. Willis, my mother's away out and I think my Granda is dead."

She came immediately. When we got to Granda's door I knocked again. No response. Mrs Willis said, "You wait here, Stella." and she went in alone. Two minutes later she came back out. "I'm sorry, Stella, your grandfather is dead."

It came as no surprise to me, yet I had hoped, and when she confirmed what I already knew I sobbed uncontrollably. She held me close for a long time until my sobs subsided.

Then she asked, "Where is your mother? When do you expect her back?"

"She said she was going to visit Uncle Jim. She didn't say when she'd be back."

"Where is your Uncle Jim?"

"Bruntsfield."

"Do you know your way there?"

"Yes, but I don't have the tram fare."

"Well you get your coat and hat and I'll get mine and we'll find your mother."

On the tram I told her what a wonderful man Granda was, and how happy we had been that summer.

When we got to Uncle Jim's Mam was just leaving. When I told her Granda was dead, Uncle Jim said he'd come too.

I introduced Mrs Willis; Mam had never met her. On the tram going back home, there was just polite conversation. I think my mother was embarrassed having Mrs Willis there, but when we got home she said, "That was very good of you to drop everything to take Stella out to Bruntsfield. We're very grateful for your kindness."

"It was the least I could do. Fortunately the girls were away at the zoo with their father so I was free to go."

Then Mrs Willis went home and we climbed our stair. Mam sent me to my room and when she called me out a while later, Uncle Jim was away to the undertaker with Granda and all of Granda's possessions.

I wouldn't go in my Granda's room after that. As long as I didn't see how empty it was with Granda and all his few possessions gone, I could pretend that he was still in there just sleeping late.

For all that my Mam and her brothers weren't nice to him, there had to be a funeral. I didn't know how Auntie Con felt about him.

"You can't bury him like a dog," said Uncle Eddie.

"It would be appropriate, you must admit," said Mam."

Granda's children were all at the funeral. None of them seemed very sorry that he was gone. Auntie Con said that Granny really couldn't come; she wasn't at all well. It seemed that I was the only one in the family who mourned Granda's passing. Miss Vincent was there at the cemetery – she was standing back where my mother wouldn't see her. She was crying, but she smiled and waved at me before she left. Many of Granda's old friends came to the funeral, and they had only praise for him.

One of them, Archie Glass, told me they had all played together in the temperance band before Granda went to Salt Lake City. It was Mr. Glass who told me what Granda's "piecework" was: busking. Granda went around singing with a friend who played the accordion. The coins dropped in his hat were the "tips" that he brought home and gave to Mam.

Stella Maris   by   Nan O'Dell

Archie also told me why Granda left Salt Lake City. It was the altitude. Salt Lake City is up high in the mountains and the air is thin there. Then Granda developed some kind of health problem so he couldn't breathe very well, couldn't sing or play his trumpet. So he sold his trumpet for his fare home.

Chapter 41 : Granny's Will

The glass sided hearse bearing Granny's tulip wreathed coffin was an impressive sight, but not unusual in 1935. Pulled by black plumed horses it was followed by black-handed mourners. Some of them hadn't liked, or even known, my Granny but they liked funerals and the spread afterwards.

As the sea of bowler hats bobbed by I pictured the weeping clouds parting and the cortege heading straight up to the pearly gates but the bedraggled procession continued at solemn and rain-soaked pace along Drum Terrace and through the gates of the Eastern cemetery.

When it had passed from sight I ran all the way to the Links and the house that had been Granny's. When I arrived my mother was setting out the funeral tea and grumbling because my Auntie Con wasn't there to help.

"God knows where she is. Surely if she'd seen the death notice in the papers she'd have come back," Mam muttered as she slapped slices of boiled ham onto Granny's best plates. "It's a bit much to expect me to do everything."

Despite her words, my mother had earlier spurned Auntie Olive's offer of help on the grounds that she was but a scheming in-law with an eye to Granny's wedding china. Now Mam ordered me, "Don't stand there goggling - take the plates to the table before the hypocrites get back."

The dining room was empty save for Auntie Olive taking a careful inventory of its contents. Auntie Ivy hadn't come because Hamish was wheezing again and Auntie Mary, about to bear her seventh, was barred from the proceedings lest she be an embarrassment to all.

The kettle was on the boil when the men returned from the cemetery looking hearty and rubbing their hands. A quick nip of whisky all round and the crowd thinned.

The rest of us sat down at table. Uncle George at the head with Mr. Lawrie, the minister on his right hand and Mr. Murdo, the lawyer, on his left. I was put at the foot where the tablecloth didn't quite reach. Next to me was a man with a walrus moustache and a stiff shiny collar. Forgetting that at my grandfather's funeral he had claimed to be a distant relative of Granda's and said to call him Uncle Eddie, he now told me the connection was on my Granny's side and I should call him Uncle Adam. Puzzled, I opened my mouth to ask him about this and my mother glared at me. I shut it again.

The man started tucking in[100] though everyone else was holding back till the minister said grace. Mam tutted loudly and when he looked up and saw the expression on her face his jaws were temporarily stilled.

Mr. Lawrie said his piece and everyone fell to. My mother nudged me with her elbow as she hurried by with the teapot. "The faster you eat the sooner we'll get on with the business."

I realised I had been staring at the drops of tea clinging to the end of the walrus moustache. Wondering when they would fall, I lifted my fork and pretended to eat. Auntie Olive was pretending too, her fork picking at her plate but never touching her lips. Uncle Jim ate his food very quickly and started on his fingernails. Next to him Mrs. Williams, Granny's only surviving friend from the Mothers' Meeting, was working her dentures as though something were caught under them.

Mr. Jack, a former boarder of Granny's, had seen the death notice in the "News", and come to pay his respects, and was invited to stay and partake. This was obviously regretted when he asked about Auntie Con for no one could tell him anything. My mother murmured something vague and asked if she could refill his cup. Everyone started talking at once then but I wasn't listening.

---

[100] Eating

Stella Maris   by   Nan O'Dell

I was watching the man who called himself Uncle Adam. He had been eyeing the last scone on the plate for some time but it wasn't till this diversion that his hand shot out and picked it up.

Granny's cousin from Kirkintilloch dozed off and Uncle Eddie, his plate empty but for a lettuce leaf, tilted his chair back and was whistling soundlessly at the ceiling. Uncle George fidgeted impatiently as he twirled his signet ring. The lawyer looked solemn and the minister sad.

I was sorry Archie Glass had left after the whisky but Mam wasn't. She said he had an awful cheek to come at all for Archie, my Granda's best friend from the silver band had been a thorn in Granny's flesh, she maintaining that he had helped lead my Granda astray. I hoped Archie hadn't heard my mother's loud comment that he had probably seen the cortege from the Four in Hand bar and decided to join it for a free drink. "He'd be fair pleased to learn it was your Granny in the box."

I had looked at Archie and longed to have my Granda back, and Granny too. I had wished my mother would forget the fighting and invite Archie to stay to his tea. But she didn't, and if Archie had heard her remarks he never let on. He finished his drink, shook hands politely, and left.

I looked down at my plate. My slice of ham had gone and Uncle Adam's jaws were working though he had long since finished his. I was glad he had saved me the bother of forcing it past the lump in my throat.

A warning look from my mother. "Wheesht," she said though I hadn't been speaking. Her eyes and everyone else's fixed on the lawyer as he drained his cup. This time he wasn't offered more tea. The room went so quiet that when he cleared his throat the cousin from Kirkintilloch woke with a start.

Mr. Murdo then took off his specs and wiped them with great deliberation before setting them back on his thin high—bridged nose. The tension in the room mounted as he slowly rose to his feet. A stern glance at the company and another clearing of the throat. Then a rustle of the papers he was holding. A pause. He was ready to read Granny's Last Will and Testament.

To Uncle George, as expected, the house and all but fifty pounds of what remained in Granny's bank account after funeral expenses.

To Uncle Jim, the fifty pounds and Granda's gold chiming watch.

To Uncle Eddie, the iron horse that had pawed the mantelpiece for as long as I could remember. Nothing else for fear that the priest might benefit. Uncle Eddie reached for the decanter. "The old bugger," he said.

My mother got Granny's jewellery and the wedding china.

Auntie Con was to receive Granny's bible with the proviso that my mother should deliver it personally into her hands.

"The rotten old bugger," said Uncle Eddie tossing back his third whisky since the lawyer started reading.

My mother shot him a dirty look. "Con forfeited her right to anything when she deserted mother."

"You're a pair of rotten buggers," declared Uncle Eddie.

The lawyer waited till they had finished before continuing.

To me came the jug I hated with the soldier in blood-stained bandages on one side and the words," Might in the Right shall Prevail" on the other; a sentiment much quoted by Granny.

Uncle Eddie's Catholic crew got nothing at all.

The surprise beneficiary was Mrs. Williams who inherited Granny's fur coat, moth-eaten despite its stinging smell of camphor.

The contents of the house were to be disposed of as my mother and Auntie Olive saw fit.

The lawyer sat down and Uncle George wrung him by the hand. Uncle George was sweating.

My mother and Auntie Olive started arguing right away about their joint responsibility. Auntie Olive opted to sell the lot, and split the money, on the grounds that there was nothing worth keeping. Mam lost her rag at this and shouted who did Olive think she was? My God, the Morrisons didn't need the likes of her looking down her snooty nose at their possessions. It was all very noisy, everyone joining in while Auntie Olive looked with contempt on one and all.

Uncle Eddie was the noisiest and kept wiping his eyes and saying he wouldn't have missed the fun for anything. "Wait till I tell Mary," he gasped between guffaws.

Even Uncle George joined the fray, forgetting he was working his way up to a management position. "Olive knows what she's talking about. Let her sell the stuff."

My mother shouted back, "Let her sell it? So she can feather her nest? No no, it won't wash. I'm onto her."

The cousin from Kirkintilloch was wide-awake now, her eyes going from Mam to Auntie Olive as though she were watching a match at Wimbledon.

Auntie Olive's regal voice cut across the din. "I am the eldest son's wife and as such have first say.

"You brass-necked bitch," shouted my mother, but Auntie Olive refused to be drawn.

In measured tones she went on, "With all the mouths she has to feed, Mary should have what's in the pantry."

Uncle Eddie let out a whoop. "Since all that's ever in it are stale biscuits and runny jam, Mary's getting damn all."

The minister, looking distressed rose and raised a hand for silence. Uncle Eddie stopped laughing and turned on him. "You keep out of it. Religion has caused enough trouble in this family."

At this insult to the cloth, Uncle Jim leapt to his feet and shouted in a shaky voice, "Mother must he spinning in her grave at this carry-on..."

"Spinning my arse," yelled Uncle Eddie. "The old bitch planned it!"

Suddenly I saw my Granny shut up in a coffin, unable to spin, or even breathe and as she struggled to get out, worms and slaters[101] struggling to get in. Now I was spinning, and gasping for air. From a long way off I heard Uncle Eddie's voice; felt his warm whiskey breath as he bent over me. "Come home with me out o' this rammy[102]. You get your coat while I get my horse." He was laughing again as he wrapped it in the Dispatch.

Once outside I started shivering and Uncle Eddie, fixing his cap firmly on his head, urged me, "Walk fast and you'll soon he warm."

I saw he was shivering too for his thin jacket was no protection against the cutting wind.

As I trotted along at his side, half out of breath, I asked him about the man with the walrus moustache. "God might know who he is but nobody else does. He's been coming to everybody's funerals for years but he's never turned away for it's probably the only good feed the poor soul ever gets."

"He picks his teeth with a match."

"Aye, he's not very bright. Brighter than me all the same. I don't get many free meals." He laughed. "Now if we can go a wee bit faster we might get home before the rain comes on again."

---

[101] Woodlice

[102] Free-for-all

"Uncle Eddie, will my Granny get wet?"

His calloused hand covered mine. "Not at all."

"Is she cold?"

His grip tightened. "The very opposite. Your Granny has gone to her reward and she's warm all right. Now step smartly and we'll nip into the Tallie's[103] for chips to take home..."

We swung hands as, reassured about Granny and happy about chips, I skipped along beside him.

"...but first," he went on, "we'll take a wee detour round by the docks. It should only take a minute. You know, Stella," he said reflectively, "that lot back there think Eddie Morrison's a failure and a bauchle[104] forbye[105]...too many weans[106] and too little work and here's Mary again...och well... that's the story of, that's the glory of, love..." He started whistling the tune.

As we reached Victoria docks a thin shaft of sunlight split the clouds and sparkled briefly on the black expanse of water.

"The sun shines on the righteous and also on the unrighteous," intoned Uncle Eddie as he heaved his inheritance into the water. It sank like an iron horse.

---

[103] Italian's (chip shop)

[104] An old, worn-out shoe

[105] As well

[106] Children (wee ones)

Chapter 42 : Auntie Con

When the final break came between my mother and my Auntie Con, it was over Granny's bible.

"I've told you before, I don't want the damn thing," shouted Auntie Con, transformed. Gone was the Auntie who seemed to disappear into whatever background she stood against; who sang in a whispery voice, "Less than the dust beneath your chariot wheels," as she cooked and cleaned and answered Granny's bell. This vivid creature dared to blaspheme and her voice reverberated off the walls. She wasn't beneath anyone's chariot wheels now! She was in the driver's seat and she was driving straight to hell!

Shivering in fearful anticipation, I pressed my eye closer to the crack in the door.

The look on Auntie Con's face reminded me of the look on my mother's face the day that Granny's letter came. I had overheard my Mam telling my da, "She's getting out of the hospital next week and she says she's coming to live with us because she's fed up with Con."

Then Mam had thrown open the door and she had looked then as Auntie Con was looking now. I had been feart, for I thought she would tell me off for listening at the door, but she had swept past me like I wasn't there.

Just before she had exited through the front door, she had called over her shoulder to da, "I'm away to tell Con I won't even consider it. Mother is her responsibility and it's up to Con to keep her happy and see her needs are met." The slam she had given the door was an exclamation point that went through my eardrums like an arrow.

Now here was Auntie Con with the same expression on her face, not frightened of my Mam at all, and all because Granny had left her God's words bound in soft leather; Granny's name tooled on the Cover, "Alice B. Morrison." I wouldn't have minded getting it.

Mam was shouting now as well, "I'm just doing what she asked me to do."

Auntie Con, shouting back, "When were you ever around to do anything she asked?"

My Mam shouted, "Well I was around for that. To carry out her last request. To deliver her bible into your own hands. So here it is and I'm through with it!"

"Well so - am - I." Auntie Con lifted the lid off the bucket and sent the bible sailing to join some mouldy potato peelings.

Rigid with horror, I waited for Auntie Con to be whisked away in a sulphurous cloud, or at the very least, to sprout horns and a tail. Even my Mam looked scared. Her face had gone the colour Granny's was when I saw her in her coffin, and she seemed to have trouble moving her lips. "What possessed you to do that?"

"The same thing that possessed her to write that inscription on the fly-leaf. Badness. Rotten badness."

Then something worse than horns and a tail happened to Auntie Con. She sank to the floor in a sort of slow motion like a candle melting into itself. I half expected to see a puddle of wax forming about her feet.

Water spurted from her eyes and even her nose, like it spurted from our broken rone pipe on rainy days.

Her face, and the sounds that came from it, made me think of the tortures I had heard Granny tell about from the Book of the Martyrs. Granny kept it beside her bed to read on the nights when her rheumatism was bad. She said it eased her pains to read about someone else's and got her to sleep faster than the medicine the doctor left her.

Now my Mam was trying to get Auntie Con to her feet but it was like trying to catch a fish with her bare hands. Auntie Con kept slipping away from Mam and she was moaning, "All my life I've wanted to be dead, but now I'm frightened I might see her again. Oh sweet Jesus, if she's in heaven I want to go to hell."

"That's just where you will go if you carry on like this." My Mam tried to shake her but Auntie Con flopped to the floor again.

I remembered the stuff Granny took when she said she needed heartening and I ran to her bedroom to get it. I tried not to look at the bed for fear I'd see Granny still lying there. I really had the grues. Carrying the bottle of heartener, I rushed into the kitchen where Auntie Con, limp as a rag doll, was draped over Mam's arm.

Mam's face was scarlet and she was breathing in gasps. When she saw me, she let go of Auntie Con who hit the floor a thump, but the awful noises coming from her didn't stop. My Mam yelled above them, "Get you out of here and don't come back in till I tell you to." She birled[107] me around and shoved me towards the door. She shut it firmly behind me so there was no crack to look through. I wasn't that sure I wanted to see any more anyway. I wished I couldn't hear any more either.

I was feart to go back to Granny's room, and Auntie Con's was up the dark stairs, so I went into the parlour at the front of the house. I shut the door and leaned against it till my heart slowed down. The blind, still drawn from the day of the funeral, shut out the warm sun, and the smell of rotting flowers lay thick on the cold air. I pulled the draw cord to raise the blind and it shot upwards, out of my hand, and whipped madly round the roller. My heart nearly flew clean out of my mouth that time, and I had to hurry and sit down on the Sunday sofa. Auntie Con called it that for she said the jagginess of it was the only thing that kept her awake during Granny's Sunday bible readings.

My heart jumped again when the black marble clock, that always reminded me of a tombstone, tolled four times. I stuck my fingers in my ears and shut my eyes tight. If we were home, the kettle would be sputtering on the hob and bread toasting for tea. I pictured Tibby stretched out before the fire, her ginger stripes blending with the colours in the hearthrug. Would I ever see my cat again?

I needed heartening so I took a long drink straight from Granny's bottle. It tasted terrible, but Granny was right, it was a heartener. A warm comforting wave washed over me, and the noises from the kitchen and the sick smell of the flowers didn't bother me any more. I lifted the bottle and took another drink.

---

[107] Whirled

I remember no more till I woke up, back in the kitchen and covered with a blanket in front of the fire. The only sound now was the hiss of the flames in the grate as they tried to consume a damp coal. Outside the circle of firelight in which I lay, the room was full of shadows and someone watched me from a dark corner.

I shot bolt upright and my heart was in my mouth again. "Maaam."

She was suddenly there and I grabbed her and held on. "There's someone watching me."

"Nooo," she whispered, rocking me.

"Yes there is."

She laid her cheek on the top of my head and the smell of the scent she used was soothing and familiar. "You've been dreaming."

"No. Auntie Con was shouting about wanting to go to hell and her nose was running."

The rocking stopped briefly, then went on faster than before. My stomach began rocking too, but not in time to the rest of me.

"Only dreams, bad dreams," she crooned. "Auntie Con's not even here."

I jerked away from her and looked up at her face. "But she was here, Mam and you were here with her."

Mam's face was in part shadow and I could sense rather than see that she was displeased. When she spoke her tone was the one she used when she didn't want to talk about something. "You must learn to tell the difference between dreams and reality. Now it's time we were away home, so stir yourself while I get our things together." Before she left the room she lit the gas jet above the mantel.

I lay blinking in the harsh white glare and I knew from the hurt in my chest that my heart was back where it belonged. I was always getting into trouble for seeing and hearing things that Mam said were imagined, but I had been sure about this. My stomach felt the way it had when Auntie Con took me to the shows. All jumpy like it was keeping time to the lurching of the cakewalk. I had been sick all over the front of my new jersey that day, and though Auntie Con cleaned it up, Mam found out anyway and wouldn't let me go anywhere with my Auntie again. Auntie Con was upset then, but not nearly as upset as she was now about Granny's bible.

The bible! I scrambled to my feet, falling over myself in my hurry to check the bucket before Mam came back. When I lifted the lid, I nearly shouted out loud, for there was the bible, lying right side up, and Granny's name staring me straight in the face. "Alice B. Morrison".

I hadn't been dreaming or making things up! Then I remembered Auntie Con shouting that Granny was bad because of what she had written on the flyleaf. I could hear Mam coming back along the lobby, but I had to know what Granny had said to drive Auntie Con daft. I snatched up the bible and flipped back the cover but all I could see at a glance was something about a serpent's tooth and Acts and Proverbs, with numbers after them. Mam's hand was on the door handle now so I ripped out the fly-leaf, stuffed it in my pocket, and flung the bible back into the bucket. Only then did I notice that my hand was smeared with something slimy from the bucket. My stomach gave one terrible heave and Granny's heartener went to join the Bible and the potato peelings.

On the tram going home, I sagged against Mam. I felt hollow inside. Just before we reached our stop, she said quietly, "Make no mention to your Da of anything you dreamed."

I was too tired to speak, and she asked, "Are you listening to me?" I nodded. "Well mind, if you do tell him, I'll have no choice but to send you to the home for bad girls."

My hand tightened round the wad of paper in my pocket. "I won't say anything."

And I didn't. Till my Da left to rejoin his ship two days later, I was never alone with him. Mam watched me closely and I didn't get to check the fly-leaf either. It was still crumpled up in my pocket.

The morning after Da left, Mam said she had to be away all day and I was to stay indoors for fear a bad man would take me away. To make sure I was safe, she locked the door behind her as she left. I didn't mind too much for the rain was running down the outside of the windows in little rivers. Tibby and I watched them for a long time and when we got tired of that, I took out her string. We could race up and down the lobby being as noisy as we liked when Mam was out. It was Tib's favourite game, but that day she got fed up with it before I did, and once she lost interest, there was no getting her started again. The hands of the clock didn't seem to be moving at all. It would be a long time yet before Mam was back. I sighed.

"Would you like to hear a story Tib? It's a true one, not made up, and I can prove it."

I took our bible from the shelf and the crumpled flyleaf from my pocket. While I told Tibby all that had happened, I checked what Granny had written against the books in the bible.

"Recognising the truth of Proverbs 16, verse 16," said Granny, "I wish Constance to have this bible."

I checked Proverbs 16 & 16. "How much better it is to get wisdom than gold."

But my Mam had been pleased enough to get Granny's gold locket and her rings and my Uncles hadn't said "no" to the contents of Granny's bank account. They didn't offer to exchange what they were left for Auntie Con's bible. I went on to the next reference. Proverbs 15 verse 9 lines 1 & 2. "The way of the wicked is an abomination unto the Lord."

Acts 8 verses 22 & 23. "Repent therefore of this, thy wickedness and pray God if perhaps the thought of thine heart may be forgiven thee. For I perceive that thou art in the gall of bitterness and in the bond of iniquity."

The last thing on the page was almost engraved into the paper, so hard had Granny leaned on the pen, "Sharper than a serpent's tooth is a thankless child."

Granny hadn't given the reference for that quote and I wondered why. Auntie Con sharper than a serpent's tooth? Wicked? I crushed the paper into a ball and hurled it from me as far as I could. Tibby shot after it and shredded it with her teeth.

In time I learned that the bible doesn't say anything about serpent's teeth. Granny must have lost some sleep looking for that one. I know I did. I didn't see Auntie Con for many years. Children weren't allowed to visit the big house on the hill. Not that anyone would have taken me, for when Auntie Con's usefulness to her family ended, she ceased to exist for them.

But I didn't forget her and when finally I sought her out, I was an adult and in far greater need of her than she had ever been of me. In the years between, I thought often of my supposedly teetotal grandmother and how she mixed Acts, Proverbs, and King Lear into a mind-blowing cocktail that, with my mother's assistance, she forced down Auntie Con's throat.

END